MORLEY LIBRARY

W9-AUS-247

3 0112 1042 6447 5

ANY
RESEMBLANCE
TO ACTUAL
PERSONS

KEVIN ALLARDICE

A NOVEL

COUNTERPOINT PRESS

Copyright © 2013 Kevin Allardice

All rights reserved under International and Pan-American Copyright Conventions. No part of this book may be used or reproduced in any manner whatsoever without written permission from the publisher, except in the case of brief quotations embodied in critical articles and reviews.

Library of Congress Cataloging-in-Publication Data

Allardice, Kevin.
 Any resemblance to actual persons : a novel / Kevin Allardice.
    pages cm
1. Memory—Fiction. 2. Psychological fiction. I. Title.

PS3601.L4149A36 2013
813›.6—dc23

2013014414

ISBN 978-1-61902-197-6

Cover design by Faceout Studios
Interior design by Domini Dragoone

Counterpoint Press
1919 Fifth Street
Berkeley, CA 94710
www.counterpointpress.com

Printed in the United States of America
Distributed by Publishers Group West

10 9 8 7 6 5 4 3 2 1

"Choose a suitable design and hold to it."

—Strunk & White's <u>The Elements of Style</u>

"Hold fast . . . "

—<u>Macbeth</u>, Act 4, scene 3

Paul McWeeney

344 Lawn Street

Los Angeles, CA 90028

June 3, 1996

New Wye Press

625 East 68th Street

New York, NY 10012

Dear New Wye Press, True Crime Division,

I am writing in regard to a book that you are set to publish this
fall, *The Black Dahlia Dossier: Hollywood's Most Notorious Killer Revealed*
by Edith (Edie) McWeeney. My name is Paul McWeeney. I am Edie's
brother, and I have read a galley copy of the book, sent to me by Oliver
Kelly, Edie's current (and my former) literary agent. I also have a very
early draft in manuscript form, and, although I see that only superficial
aspects of the book have been revised since then (which does not speak
well of your editors), I will be addressing the content of—and any pagi-
nation mentioned herein refers to—the galley copy. First of all, I am
not sure how much crossover there is between people in the New Wye

true crime wing and the folks in the literary wing, but if my name looks familiar, I should admit up front (in an effort to clear any and all accusations of bias from the argument I must make here) that over the years, I have corresponded, by way of Oliver, with your literary brothers down the hall. They have read, or at least used as doorstops, the manuscripts of my novels *Season of All Natures* and *Rarer Monsters*, and I, in turn, have read their dear-johns telling me, by way of Oliver, that I have a strong voice but that my work lacks narrative momentum and that it's just not right for them at this time, considering the market for literary fiction. Fair enough. I have not been all that impressed with their catalogue anyway. Since I imagine you guys in the true crime wing are of a different breed—comfortable with your low- to middle-brow output—and no doubt a little annoyed with those literary boys down the hall, just as a wayward youth is annoyed with his high-achieving older sibling, I assume you won't mind a little friendly trash-talking. It will bond us, this mutual contempt for the boys down the hall, those Eustace Tilleys all dressed in tweeds and monocles, their blood blue, their pens quivered. Anyway. I did not know until recently that New Wye Press even had a true crime imprint.

As I said, you are set to publish my sister's book this fall, a fortuitous date, I'm sure you know, as it anticipates the fiftieth anniversary of the infamous murder that Edie claims to solve, that of Elizabeth "Betty" Short, a.k.a. the Black Dahlia. The advance copy of her book, which I have here on my desk, is complete with dust jacket copy, and I see that you are not concerned with giving away the ending, since you actually name, right here on the back of the book, the person she claims is the real killer. I suppose this "spoiler" goes to show that the conceits of the true crime genre are different from those of the murder mystery, and I was foolish to assume otherwise, although it's clear to me that, structurally, my sister's book is heavily informed by Agatha Christie's Poirot books, many of which I remember her poring over one summer at Lake Tahoe. My sister, for all the chaos of her life, is someone who has always been attracted to art that offers tidiness, solutions, order, so it makes sense that she'd try to emulate the British approach to murder. Her prose, however, is entrenched entirely in the American pulp tradition, which prized the grotesque, the lurid, and offered a powerfully ominous antidote to postwar optimism. If I were teaching this book, I could spend quite a lot of time on the tension between her sentences and her narrative. But I'm not teaching this book; I'm refuting it.

I understand perfectly well that you, as the publisher, make no claim to authority here. You are not the judge, my sister not the plaintiff, and publication not the definitive verdict. I understand that in releasing this book to impressionable readers, you are not claiming it represents a fair weighing of the facts. In short, I understand that you are not responsible for the claims it makes. Only my sister is. I understand that your motives here have nothing to do with truth and justice, and everything to do with money. A sensational book that makes a wildly erroneous claim will certainly sell. So I will try to couch my appeal for rationality and justice in monetary terms. I have consulted a lawyer—or actually, a colleague of mine who wrote her doctoral dissertation on media law, a course of study that one could argue (and she has, repeatedly) is far more rigorous than law school—and she has assured me that if you go through with publishing *The Black Dahlia*

Dossier, there would be sufficient grounds for a civil suit against you for libel and defamation. I'm sure you know that while the publicity surrounding a trial like that would certainly mean increased interest in the book, the ultimate cost to you, when I win, would be far greater than revenue from the book's sales.

I do not want to begin on a note of animosity. I simply need to make clear the stakes. But make no mistake: This is a cease and desist letter.

To get straight to it, then: My sister, Edie McWeeney, claims in this book that in January of 1947, a young woman named Betty Short—who would in short time be nicknamed by the media the Black Dahlia—was murdered by none other than George McWeeney, our late father. She claims to offer an eyewitness account of the murder itself, as well as "irrefutable" evidence not only of the murder but of a cover-up by the LAPD. She claims that George McWeeney had the motive, means, and opportunity.

I will disprove all of this. Our father did no such thing.

My sister is not of sound mind, and this should disqualify her from having a book published.

Since we're dealing with questionable claims of irrefutability here, I feel we should start with some truly irrefutable facts. A quick overview of the participants is necessary. My father, George Wendell McWeeney, was born on August 20, 1914, in Canton, Ohio. He attended the Ohio State University, class of 1936. That same year, he was accepted to Yale School of Medicine and moved to New Haven to begin his medical studies. In 1938, he took a leave of absence from medical school (which would turn out to be permanent) and enrolled in Yale School of

Drama. In June 1941, a month after receiving his MFA in playwriting, he married my and Edie's mother, Iris Lowell, and moved her to Los Angeles where he'd secured a job writing for the then-radio (soon-to-be TV) show *Rampart*. Edie was born on October 29, 1941. And on March 14, 1947, I was born. Edie and I had happy childhoods.

These are facts. All of the above can be verified, proven on paper. It is important to begin here, on neutral ground. In my composition classes, I tell my students that academic debates must always begin at a place of agreement. Author A and Author B must first agree on the problem before they can disagree on the solution. But perhaps the parallel doesn't quite hold, since these facts do not present a problem. I suppose the problem, then, is this: On January 15, 1947, passersby discovered the gruesomely murdered body of twenty-two-year-old Betty Short in a vacant Los Angeles lot. The police never found her murderer, but nearly a half century later my sister found evidence she claims links our father to the victim.

But I should start elsewhere. I should explain a thing or two about Edie as I know her today, explain how this book of hers came to be, as I think it will go a long way in shedding some light on its disturbing and erroneous content.

For her entire adult life, Edie has been something of a transient. She moves somewhere, quickly develops relationships, both platonic and not, of a rather disturbing intensity. Then those relationships get destroyed for reasons she is always evasive about later, and she moves on to the next city, repeats. (I always envied her ease in forging friendships—even if they are always toxic—and when I was younger I thought that's what adulthood would be like. It isn't.) This lifestyle of hers—and as I just typed it, I realized how suspicious the word "lifestyle" now sounds, how it seems to imply, with a kind of right-wing condescension, deviant sex and depraved drug-use, and while we can safely assume her travels have included these activities, I do not mean to use the word "lifestyle" in that way, just to be clear—this lifestyle of hers will occasionally bring her back to Los Angeles, where I still live, just over the hill from the house we grew up in, and she will kick up a fuss about something; she'll stay at my place for a while, borrow money, complain about some crazy ex of hers who's trying to kill her. This whole book project of hers is simply the latest fuss she's kicked up. Up until last year, I hadn't seen her for quite some time. I would think about her on occasion but was content to assume that she was managing to take care of herself, or, to be more honest about where her true skills lie, managing to find someone to take care of her. And then our aunt Paige passed away, and Edie showed up.

I should back up again. Aunt Paige was our father's sister. She was seven years George's junior, and in 1948, after her husband died in an accident in a Coca-Cola bottling plant, she moved to L.A. for some familial support from her older brother. Their parents had both passed away by then, and Paige was adrift. (Please keep the adrift female relatives straight; there won't be too many of them.) When Aunt Paige came west, she stayed in our pool house—the same pool house where Edie sets that horrific and entirely fictitious death scene in her manuscript—but by the time I was old enough to form memories, Paige had moved into an apartment in Marina Del Rey and was teaching kindergarten. I remember her as a short, round woman in series of colorful sweaters, which she wore year-round, even when the dry, hot Santa Ana winds made every housewife contemplate murder. (That last bit there I paraphrased from a Raymond Chandler story.) I remember her coming to our place in Van Nuys to babysit, dispensing hard mint candies that reminded me of the dentist, sitting by the pool in Cadillac-fin sunglasses, watching me and Edie splash, cheerily turning bits of our profound-sounding kid-speak into songs ("the sky is low" is how I apparently described an overcast day and she quickly set it to a swinging Bobby Darin–style melody).

My favorite anecdote about Aunt Paige comes from one of those babysitting sessions. Dad worked from home, which meant that even when he was there he was busy behind the closed door of the spare room he'd converted into an office, so, whenever Mom had to dash out, Paige would volunteer to come over and keep us entertained. It was Christmastime, and my mom had hung a series of (now that I think about it) rather cubist-looking stained-glass nativity scenes on our front windows. Each one was about six inches in diameter and affixed to the window with a suction cup. Aunt Paige—whose much-vaunted "zaniness" I then found exciting and hilarious but now strikes me as masking a profound loneliness and an inability to connect with anyone other than small children—took one of these decorations off a window—*pop* went the suction cup—and stuck it to her forehead. I squealed as Aunt Paige chased me around the house with three stained-glass wise men suction-cupped to her forehead. "I'm looking for baby Jesus!" she exclaimed in an Italian accent. (She was quite fond of accents, though no matter the intended nationality, after a few sentences as a Japanese or a German—Paige never really got over the War—she always bounced into one of her Guinea schticks. [I use that term, "Guinea," not as my enlightened self of today, but as my childhood self who had been raised amid the casual anti-Axis racism. The term for this, narratologically speaking, is "focalizing," whereby language is filtered through the character whose point of view we're in, and I feel I should make this clear, lest you think I'm a bigot—I like Italians!]) Aunt Paige caught up to me in the hallway, grabbed me, and said, "Found him!" I was hyperventilating from laughter but managed to calm down a bit until, as a final punch line, she pulled the Christmas decoration off her forehead to reveal a bright red, silver-dollar-size welt above her left eyebrow. The center was a brighter red, making it look like a target. When she saw my reaction (more laughing), she went to the bathroom mirror. I could see a moment of self-kicking sadness on her face, but then she saw me watching her and started doing her funny accent again, until Edie came around the corner and scolded us, said we were making too much noise, said we were disturbing Dad.

(I just checked the Chandler story I paraphrased that Santa Ana line from on the previous page, and I got it all wrong. The original, from "Red Wind," goes like this: "There was a desert wind blowing that night. It was one of those hot dry Santa Anas that come down through the mountain passes and curl your hair and make your nerves jump and your skin itch. On nights like that every booze party ends in a fight. Meek little wives feel the edge of the carving knife and study their husbands' necks. Anything can happen." Great stuff, huh? Oliver said that my novels *Season of All Natures* and *Rarer Monsters*, which are still on the market, have a certain Chandler-esque evocation of Los Angeles and prose style.)

Anyway, when my father died in 1964, Aunt Paige moved into our house, where she preserved all of Dad's old scripts (the plays he wrote in school; the countless *Rampart* episodes, mimeographed in purple ink on tissue-like paper; the novel he'd worked on for years without ever completing) and Hollywood memorabilia (including the Emmy Award that she'd later have to write the National Academy of Television Arts and Sciences to get a replacement for after Edie, about twenty years ago, pawned it for, we can assume, drug money). Aunt Paige adored her brother, and that house became a museum, though a rather disorganized one, in his honor. She lived for those moments when some amateur Hollywood historian or grad student would contact her to ask her questions about George McWeeney's contribution to *Rampart*, and *Rampart*'s contribution to the mythology of the American cop. She'd invite them over, tell them her nostalgia-tinted memories of her Brother the Great Writer, give them a tour of the house. Then she'd call me, tell me that someone was writing a biography of my father, which would surely spark serious interest in him and his work, so I'd better come over and help her organize his papers. I'd say, "Sure, Aunt Paige, I'm a little busy now, but soon," knowing full well that this biography she was imagining would actually be a small footnote in a book or article no one would ever read.

Anyway. So Aunt Paige passed away over a year and a half ago, September 1994. And when she did, Edie came back into town. She (Edie) called me at home one Saturday morning.

"Paulie."

"Edie?"

"It's Edie."

"Hi."

"I heard about Aunt Paige."

"Yeah."

These were our first words to each other in (what she later calculated to be) over four years, and as I transcribe them from memory I find myself wishing for more to type, for a less staccato style between us, but I suppose it was pretty easy for us to slip back into the old rhythms.

"Did I miss the funeral?" she asked. "The obit didn't mention one."

"Oh. There hasn't been one. Or at least not yet. I've been trying to find friends of hers, people who'd like to come, but so far haven't found many people." This was, I admit, a lie. I'd been meaning to do this, or at least considered it, briefly, but I was simply too busy.

On the line, I heard the ionic crepitation of either static or my sister clicking her teeth, a strange habit of hers.

"Where are you?" I asked.

"Can I come over?"

"Are you in L.A.?"

"Are you still in that place off Franklin?"

"Are you in L.A.?"

"Can you come pick me up?"

"Where are you?"

"Eagle Rock. In a motel. Come pick me up."

This was not a good time for me to drive across Los Angeles. I had papers to grade. Forty of them, to be exact. I should mention here that I teach at the College of Los Angeles, better known by the acronym COLA. It used to be the City College of Los Angeles, but they dropped the "City" to make it sound less like what people used to call, back before smoking was bad for you, "high school with ashtrays." (As a former COLA student myself from the days of ashtrays, I can attest to the accuracy of that description.) Every semester I teach seven classes, a combination of English 1 (freshman composition) and English 2 (intro to literature), which means I have on average about two hundred students per semester. There is never a time when I am not mired in grading, and the only way to get through it is to give myself daily quotas (that day it was forty essays) and occasionally some Ritalin (which I'd taken that day to keep me focused on the Sisyphean task). Perhaps it was the drug that gave me a slight rush of capability— yes, of course I could go pick up my sister, come back, and finish all these papers—or maybe it was the fact that Edie needed me again, but either way I got in my car and made my start-stop way east on the 101 to Eagle Rock, a small and generally pleasant nook between Glendale and Pasadena so named because of a large rock formation that people say has an eagle-shaped jut, though every time I look at it I just see a rock-shaped jut, perfectly amorphous in the way that large rocks are and free of zoomorphic contours. As a literary artist, however, my failure to see the eagle makes me worried, every I time I visit its eponymous neighborhood, that I'm too literal minded, that my failure as a novelist has something to do with my failure to imagine some great raptor emerging from stone, my failure to recognize the similarity between disparate things, my failure to harmonize the world with a network of similes. I mean, sure, I can make an okay metaphor, but it's always such a labored, conscious act, forcing myself to see the world in a way I'm no longer sure I actually do. It's not an innate skill, and that's what worries me. Don't they give kids tests like this in those Montessori schools, along with allergy fetishism and disdain for the conventions of grammar? The kids who say the splotch of ink looks like something other than what it is—they grow up to be the artists, teaching the rest of the world how to navigate the horrors of postmodernity; while the kids who say that's just a splotch of ink—they grow up to be the unambitious number-pushers and pencil-crunchers of the world. I'm pretty sure they have tests like that.

I took the Eagle Rock exit, noticing that those clouds over there looked like cotton balls, while those other clouds looked like slightly dirty cotton balls, and that cloud there looked like an eagle, covered in cotton balls. I found my sister's motel, found her room, and knocked on the door.

"Coming, coming," she said from inside. She opened the door and said, "Come in, come in," and I wondered if she was doing that childhood thing she'd do when she wanted to be annoying, that thing of saying everything twice. "I'm just getting my stuff together." She went back into the room and I walked in.

Edie scooted around the room in slippers. There was stuff everywhere. She gathered all the stuff into a suitcase. She tried to zip up the suitcase but some of the stuff was sticking out the sides, so it wouldn't zip up. Then she opened it back up to arrange all the stuff, and a lot of stuff fell out onto the floor, and the whole stuff-gathering process began again.

She was wearing a tank top that had some sort of wolf howling on it. She was looking her age, a realization that made me consider my own age, only five years less than hers, and I snuck a glimpse of myself in the mirror beside the TV. The narrow peninsula of hair that was stubbornly holding ground on my freckled pate was matted to the side thanks to a cowlick that just exaggerated the sparser side of my head.

I finger-combed it a bit, tried to counteract the cowlick, without going full comb-over with it. A comb-over conveys vanity; vanity conveys, paradoxically, vulnerability. A man comfortable with his aging is the epitome of virility. Ralph Hockney, the dean at COLA, said that in a meeting once. He's bald as a bean. I think he waxes his dome; it's awfully shiny. I noticed, too, in the motel mirror, that my stomach was looking a little fuller than I'd like. I suppose one is more likely to notice these things in a strange new mirror, since we become so accustomed to our appearances in the mirrors we encounter on a daily basis. The mirror in my own bathroom, for example, is fairly flattering, if only because it's not very large and doesn't show a great deal of me. When I go into Chris's bedroom, however—which is not very often, as the cloistered rituals of the teenage male make me nervous (is he merely masturbating or drawing detailed pictures of slaughtered class-mates?), all the more so since he's not actually my brood and so I feel nervous even acknowledging whatever it is he does in there, like I don't have the parental right, though by this point I should have the de facto parental right—when I go into Chris's room, and catch a glimpse of myself in those floor-to-ceiling mirrored closet doors, I'm always taken aback. I am never quite the man I imagine I am.

Edie seemed concerned about the time (almost eleven), so we hustled out of the room and down to the front desk to deposit the key before checkout time (eleven).

Edie was hungry, so I drove us first to a Starbucks for some scones and coffee. I was thinking now about all those papers to grade and wor-ried that I would lose steam if this detour became too much of a detour, so I got a venti Americano. Once back on the highway, I tried to break the awkwardness with Edie by riffing on the ridiculous language of coffee sizes at Starbucks, trying to connect its rebranding of basic small, medium, and large to a bigger problem of what I will call (though it did not occur to me in the moment) the cult of esotericism: that is, the renaming of things to give the sayer of those names and user of those things (presumably the same person) the warming sensation of inclusion in a small, elite group who knows the meaning of those names, despite the fact that those new names are utter gibberish, an example of language as social marker, a corporate co-opting of the black bebop argotic methods of the postwar years. "It's a class issue," I said.

"Actually, it's Italian," Edie said. "'Venti' means twenty. That coffee is twenty ounces."

Traffic suddenly slowed, and I said, "Be careful with that scone, please. Those crumbs get everywhere."

"Didn't you take Italian in college?" she asked.

I hoped that there was an accident up ahead. While that might sound sadistic, let me explain: If the traffic was slowing because of an accident, that meant that once we passed the accident, things would speed up again—and there is really nothing as satisfying as suddenly having free rein of the open highway after being packed into a traffic jam, the pleasure almost sexual in its tense-release combo. Plus, an accident would mean that someone had suffered the appropriate consequence for making the rest of us late.

"We have to have a funeral for Aunt Paige," Edie said.

"Okay. You have to organize it, though. I'm too busy."

If, however, traffic was slowing due to the inexplicable groupthink of the commuting populace, then we'd be here awhile.

"Then I will organize it," Edie said. "It's important. Without a funeral her soul will be forever tethered to her earthly shell."

I wondered if she was serious or sarcastic, but didn't pursue it. Perhaps her howling wolf tank top was a sign that in the vision quest of her life she'd begun dabbling in some ancient Comanche religion, or at least the misapprehended and misappropriated white stoner version of it that surely thrived out in the dive bars and twelve-step groups of California's Central Valley.

"So I'm gonna need to stay with you for a bit," she said. "Until something comes through. Okay, little brother?"

I hadn't thought about this. But no, that wouldn't do. Not with my current living situation. "You could stay at the old house," I said. "Someone needs to get all of Paige's things organized, all of Dad's things organized, for that matter, prepare the place to sell, you know. I don't really have time right now."

"So busy, so busy," she said. "You're such a busy body, so many important things to do."

There was no sign of an accident up ahead.

"Are you still seeing that woman?"

"What woman?"

"What woman?" she said. "Wow, such a playboy. That woman you were seeing the last time I saw you. She kind of looked like the less attractive one from *Three's Company*. She had that dykey haircut and a son."

"Brenda," I said. "No, not since the Bush administration."

"Well, the last time I saw you, you were with her."

I exited and started making my way to Van Nuys on side streets. "I should tell you that Aunt Paige died in her bed."

"Why should you tell me that?"

"So you can sleep in one of the guest rooms. The bed she died in is still there, and, you know, it's—well, when a person dies, they . . . void themselves."

"Honey, I've slept on worse. But thank you for the heads-up."

"I just thought that was like a thing you're supposed to tell people. An ex of mine—Brenda, I mean—she was a realtor and she always had to tell potential buyers if the previous resident had died in the house. I always figured it was for the voiding issue, but I guess I never really thought about it."

She wasn't paying attention anymore. She was staring out the window at all the liquor stores with disturbingly child-oriented themes (e.g., Circus Liquor) and all the adult bookstores with their windows covered in big yellow banners advertising ninety-nine-cent videos and peep shows, and all the dollar stores that sold food with smudged-off expiration dates. I knew what she was thinking—whither be those sylvan parklands and friendly ice-creameries of our youth?—so I said, "You know this is now the porn capital of the world?" hoping it would get a laugh. It didn't.

When I finally pulled up to our old home—a ranch-style house, so low and flat, so lacking in dramatic protrusions, you could imagine it had slowly grown out of the pavement, or could just as slowly sink back into it, its genesis more tectonic than architectural—Edie said, "At least one thing hasn't changed."

And it certainly had not. Walking into the old place, it was impossible not to think of the proverbial fly trapped in amber. True, that might have been because the window shades cast the room in a distinctly amber light, and there were a few dozen flies buzzing about, but I think the metaphor is still apt. On the mantel was our father's Emmy (Outstanding Writing for a Drama Series, 1956, its like-new shine a reminder that it was a replacement), flanked by framed black-and-white photos of him tuxedoed and shaking hands with various luminaries of midcentury Hollywood, Elia Kazan, Orson Welles, *Rampart* creator and star Jack Hale. Hale was probably the only guy whom our father actually knew; the rest were just handshake photo ops at various award shows and fund-raising galas. You can tell from the pictures themselves: With Kazan and Welles, he's shaking their hands, his body "cheating out," to use stage-direction parlance, eager to show the camera his momentary acquaintance, his smile betraying excitement, theirs betraying toler- ance. What I doubt Aunt Paige ever really saw here was that these pho- tos do not reveal a Hollywood insider, but a fan, just like any of us, who beat his moth wings against someone else's light for a fleeting, annoy- ing moment. With Hale, however, he's different. They are facing each other, clearly sharing an inside joke or pride in some mutual accom- plishment. Here it is the camera that is intruding, not my father. The George McWeeney in these photos is short, a little paunchy, his cum- merbund appearing more girdle-like in the way it restrains a burgeoning belly, but his face retains the thinness of his youth, his chin pointed in a way that gives his head a crescent-moon quality. Jack Hale, that familiar face, looks in this photo as he always did on TV: small, wiry, but with features that seem drawn in charcoal, both precise and smeared.

"Oh, man," Edie said. "I remember this furniture. Oh, the days when couches were stiff and scratchy. Really made standing up seem appealing, huh?"

"Yes," I said. "It actually had a lot to do with the furniture industry combating postwar complacency. You know, 'Stand up, mobilize.' The Red Scare and all that. Domestic props have always been fascinating in how they reveal deep-seated sociopolitical anxieties."

"Jesus, Paulie, I was exaggerating. When did you become such a— whatever. It's not like you're a real professor, you know, so don't try to impress me. You wanna impress me? Loan me some walking-around money. Show me your opulence."

"Well. It was a real thing. That guy Eames, the chair-maker, he was a total Trotskyite."

"Either way," Edie said, examining the clay ashtrays on the coffee table. She was already barefoot. "I don't think real comfort was invented until the eighties. Gimme a fuckin' La-Z-Boy. Poor Paige—her life was frozen in 1964. Like the Amish. Only, you know, a century later."

I bit my tongue. She was clearly baiting me—with her subtle and knowing allusion to how Reagan's revision of American notions of comfort was in fact an ideological countering to a deeply politicized asceticism, of which the Amish were part and parcel—clearly baiting me to further my very valid point about domestic space being a theater of political conflict, baiting me only so she could accuse me of being a fraud.

"I'm a little short on lending money these days," I said.

Then I turned back to the pictures on the mantel, as I now turn back to my train of thought about Jack Hale, since this is relevant information that Edie does not cover in her book, despite the large role Hale plays in her utterly fantastical narrative.

Jack Hale's voice is probably one of the most unintentionally impersonated in America. I say "unintentionally" because his voice is so ingrained in our national psyche as what a cop is supposed to sound like that most people don't realize that the casually authoritative, detached but engaged, clipped but never agitated, slightly nasally tenor was originally Hale's. It has been said (though offhand, I can remember only Aunt Paige saying this, and I am unsure of her source) that after *Rampart* premiered on the radio, applications to police academies doubled and every new flatfoot on the beat was doing his best impression of Jack Hale (a.k.a. Det. Mike Nolan), and you can still hear that voice today—if only faintly, the influence generations removed—in every incarnation of a cop, real or fictional, just as you can still hear the influence of Orson Welles's stentorian droll in such sundry pop culture artifacts as the animated *Transformers* movie, and a little cartoon show called *Pinky and the Brain*, which Chris used to watch and for which I picked up an unashamed affection. When Hale had his first success with *Rampart* as a radio show in the late 1930s—as the star, producer, writer, and director—he quickly codified the now widely imitated three-act police procedural structure. The plot was always pretty simple. The sergeant, a gruff and cantankerous old-timer, told Det. Mike Nolan (Hale) about a murder in the Rampart District of Los Angeles. Nolan investigated. Nolan found the killer. Plot points were strung together with ironic quippery. The success of the show brought Hale to New Haven, Connecticut, in the spring of 1941 to give a talk at Yale School of Drama. Hale himself had spent a year in his late teens apprenticing at the National Theatre on Broadway, and he was eager to legitimize radio acting to the young Ivy League thespians. My father attended the talk and years later reported that it was "a rather uncomfortable display of insecurity" on Hale's part. Regardless, on that same visit, Hale attended a preview performance of the play my father had written for his MFA thesis, a tense domestic drama called *Hieroglyphs*. This was in the waning years of what we now refer to as Orientalism, but my father's interest in ancient Egypt was not trendy, fetishistic, or imperialistic. He simply wanted to mine the place for metaphors. The play is about an Egyptologist who comes home from a Cairo expedition to find that his wife and sons have changed in his yearlong absence. He sees that he is no longer a necessary part of their lives, and struggles to make himself needed again. It's a fantastic piece of work. I've read it countless times. I have a copy of it here on my desk, a Xerox of the original, since my constant thumbing over the years began to compromise the integrity of the pages. It's subtle, nuanced, and even if the main character's unnecessarily detailed monologues describing the mummification process underscore the fact that my dad was a recent med school dropout (though in my years as an actor, I would use those monologues in auditions), the play is still incredibly perceptive about the ways people ignore and hurt each other, and I'm sure these were the qualities Jack Hale saw in 1941, motivating him to offer my father a job in Hollywood. My father accepted the offer and began spinning murder mysteries for Det. Mike Nolan to solve. But when NBC brought *Rampart* from radio to television in 1948, its popularity suddenly dipped. Audiences saw that Hale's body did not match his voice. Hale was a small guy who'd learned at an early age to sound big. There was no hiding his stature on television, though they certainly tried. Hale stood on boxes, while other actors stood in dug-out sections of the floor. The prop department even made Hale a gun that was two-thirds scale to make him look bigger. But all these tricks just made him look ridiculous. If you don't believe me, check out *Rampart*'s first TV season. There's a reason why those episodes never come on Nick at Nite. My father is the one who came up with the solution. Give Det. Nolan a partner, a sidekick. The Nolan of the radio show was so outsized anyway, so superhuman, that in order to render him in the visual spectrum, he needed to be two men. Nolan was now the brains of the operation, while his new partner, Det. Rob Hawkes, was the muscle. Together they delivered on the promise of the radio show, giving audiences the perfect model of postwar mascu-linity: Nolan coolly shrugging off the ideals of brawn, ironically com-menting on them, while Hawkes reconfirmed their necessity in such a violent world. Besides, now Det. Nolan had someone to talk to. On the radio, he would just soliloquize to himself, and on TV this looked rather lunatic. So that was my father's contribution; he split the origi-nal Nolan in two, separating the brain from the brawn, and it ensured *Rampart*'s place in TV history.

In her book, Edie mentions this Nolan-Hawkes bifurcation only once, almost in passing on page 170, in order to suggest that since it occurred about a year after the Black Dahlia murder, our father, still traumatized by what he'd—allegedly—done, was in effect "splitting" his own psyche, separating the superego (Nolan) from the id (Hawkes). It's a cute theory but smacks of high school–level psychoanalytic lit crit and presumes that Dad saw the character of Nolan as an extension of himself, which is utterly ridiculous. Nolan was not a stand-in for Dad; he was obviously an expression of the conflicted role governmental authority played in the shifting postwar nexus of public and private life. A grad student who interviewed Aunt Paige a couple years ago wrote as much in his master's thesis; I have a copy of it, and it is far more incisive than Edie's reductive Freudian pronouncements.

But I'm getting ahead of myself. I'm going to get to the specifics of Edie's claims later. I will. I have three full boxes of evidence, each box labeled *evidence*, beside my desk. It's all sitting right here, waiting to be unpacked before the jury, my sturdy blockade of justice. (The one hole in the dam, of course, is the autopsy report. Still need to track that down. And I will.) But before I get to all of that, I do need to get back to that day in our Van Nuys house, before Edie met Rory and concocted this whole murder theory, back when she was just a slightly lost middle-aged woman who, like me, missed her dead dad and was now pulling her huge suitcase (it had wheels and a leash) into her childhood bedroom.

"Fuck," she said.

Her room had not gotten the preservationist treatment that the rest of the house had received. Aunt Paige had apparently used Edie's old room for storage. Boxes were stacked everywhere, each one labeled in black marker: *Taxes 1989, Taxes 1990, Taxes 1991/Camping Stuff,* and one that was labeled, simply and inexplicably, *Cats.* I counted three sewing machines and eight lamps.

"She hated me," Edie said.

I chose not to remind Edie of the reasons Paige had to hate her, most notably Edie's 1972 Emmy theft, and said, "She just needed the space is all."

Paige's old clothes covered the twin bed in the corner, and I helped clear them off.

"I bet *your* bedroom is in pristine childhood condition," Edie said. "Of course it is. You were the heir to everything George McWeeney.

Don't you think it's a little sick? Like she was trying to keep you a child? I mean, she never could acknowledge us as adults. I don't think she ever really saw me, like really saw me, you know? Even when we were kids, she showered you with attention and completely ignored me."

(On an impulse I just looked up *Transformers: The Movie* [1986, dir. Nelson Shin] in *Fleeber's Encyclopedia of Film*, which sits on a shelf near my desk, and it turns out that the voice that sounds like Orson Welles actually *is* Orson Welles. I'm a bit baffled and troubled by this. Before I took up this project, compiling the research to properly refute my sister's claims, I had been engrossed in a new three-volume biography of Welles, but I had to set it aside before I got to the end of his life. I'd read all about the tough times Welles went through, how he was forced to do projects simply for the money, but what makes this voice appearance in *Transformers* worse is that it was his final performance in a film; it came out within months of his passing. Grieving audiences were left not with the grandeur of *Kane* or his ophidian performance as Harry Lime in *The Third Man* fresh in their minds, but rather some piece of Sunday morning confection, a toy advertisement masquerading as a film. Indeed, "Angels are bright still, though the brightest fell.")

"Aunt Paige was crazy," Edie concluded. "Admit it. You have to admit it."

I admitted that Aunt Paige was a little eccentric, perhaps, but that that was probably inevitable at her age. But if she was really this devoted to our dear old dad, didn't we all deserve our own Aunt Paige, keeper of the flame, Boswell to our Johnson, Bruccoli to our Fitzgerald, Kinbote to our Shade? If the fear of death is not a fear of an end to our consciousness but rather others' consciousness of us, i.e., really just a fear that we'll be forgotten, and if here we were in a shrine to our father thirty years after his passing, then hadn't Aunt Paige effectively offered an antidote to death itself?

Edie didn't seem very satisfied with my answer, which was enormously frustrating, but it was not a point I had time to elucidate. I still had a fuck-ton of grading to do. I told Edie this (the part about the grading), and left.

As you can see, Edie probably did not come back to L.A. with ill intentions. She has always been a bit excitable and drama-prone, but she was not yet, at this point, an insane person. So where exactly did this all come from? A man named Rory Beach. You surely know the name, if not the man, as he appears in Edie's book both on the "acknowledgments" page and in the character—because this so-called nonfiction book is, as I will prove, a piece of fiction—of "Dr. Beach," the man who helps Edie "recover" "repressed" "memories." I have seen no evidence that this man actually has an advanced degree, so I will refer to him as Rory, not "Dr. Beach."

Anyway. After I dropped Edie off at our old house that day, I didn't see her again for some time. My teaching kept me busy. Plus, during that fall semester, Chris got suspended from school for fighting, and I had to home-school him for a month to ensure that he would not get left behind. (I found his math lessons not only impenetrable but frighteningly Masonic in their cryptic iconography, so I spent most of that month helping him stay up on his English, but since I've always found Steinbeck's depiction of the American West to be a bit pedantic I substituted in McCarthy's *Blood Meridian*, and the ancillary readings on the antebellum scalp-trade filled in for Chris's history lessons.)

Also, I started dating someone, a new teacher at COLA named Julia. We are still together and I think it is going quite well. (She is, no point in hiding it, the colleague I mentioned on page 7; her legal expertise has helped me enormously in preparing to write this, and will continue to aid me should this issue go to court, and the fact that we have a sexual relationship—on average, three times a week, which, I've read, is one above the national average for monogamous middle-aged couples—should in no way be seen as affecting the objectivity of her counsel.) The point is, I was busy, and I assumed Edie was getting on fine, sleeping in her old childhood bed, getting her life back together. That assumption was incorrect. It would be foolish now to spend too much time regretting not seeing more of her during that time, thinking that I could have stepped in earlier. *What-ifs* and *if-onlys* always annoy me, the way people invest so much in what could have been, like a warped belief in alternate universes in which different decisions were made. I can't change what I didn't do. I can only try to correct what has been done.

The next time I saw Edie was in August 1995. The new school year had just started and I was, once again, quite busy, but I managed to make some time for her when she called and asked to meet for lunch. She suggested Jerry's Famous Deli on Ventura Blvd., a place I've always had a mild fascination with simply because of the brilliant tautology of its name. Were it simply Jerry's Deli, after all, it would not be famous. But it is Famous, and so it is famous. This was, however, my first time inside, and I was delighted to find it a bustling place with geriatric waiters and vaguely sapphic waitresses rushing by, holding trays of sandwiches the size of my head. It reminded me a little of

Katz's Deli, which I'm sure you New Yorkers are more familiar with; I used to make Oliver take me there whenever I visited your side of the country, and I'd ask him if it was a hot spot of publishing types—was that George Plimpton noshing a pile of pastrami between two slices of rye? the ghost of Max Perkins waiting in line with his ticket for corned beef? an improvised Algonquin Round Table being cleared of mustardy plates?—No, Oliver would say. But, still, you must be familiar with the place. Although, Jerry's Famous is, in true West Coast fashion, a bit glossier than Katz's: shinier, the arrangement of celeb-signed headshots on the walls more calculated than casual.

I met Edie by the front counter, which displayed an impressive array of dessert items, everything looking lacquered with sugar, voluptuous pastries with nippley cherries.

"Thanks for meeting me," Edie said. "You're a hard one to get a hold of these days. This'll be on me, okay? A business expense."

"No problem, Edie." I noticed a framed poster of *What Ever Happened to Baby Jane?* over by the corner booths near the restrooms. I could make out a looping signature but couldn't tell if it was Bette Davis or Joan Crawford. "Do you think we can get one of those corner booths?" I asked.

She began looking very urgently to the corner booths.

"I know," I said, "I can't make out the signature either."

"Listen," she said, "I want you to meet someone, okay? I've been trying to get you two together for a while now. You'll really like him, I promise. Here he comes. Like each other, okay? Please?"

She waved to a tall man with slicked-back hair who'd just left the restroom and was walking over to us. When he approached I noticed what looked like a pet ferret resting on his shoulder, and I realized that the hair I'd taken to be slicked back was, in fact, pulled back, pony-tailed, and I adjusted my prejudices accordingly. Edie introduced us. Rory, this is Paul. Paul, this is Rory. We shook hands. Or rather, Rory shook my hand. That's the way it felt, at least. Not a mutual action to meet in the middle, but one man taking the hand of the other, moving it around as if checking the integrity of its manufacture, then giving it back. It was hard not to feel like my hand had somehow failed whatever inspection this hawkish man had just made of it.

"Paul, yes," Rory said. "I've heard so much about you. A novelist. Wow. I must say, I have so much admiration for writers." For a moment, it looked like he had eyes of two different colors, like one of those ridiculous husky dogs, or David Bowie, but then I realized it was just a trick of the light. Both eyes were, in fact, quite green, narrowly set atop a nose that was really, now that I saw it, more Romanesque than aquiline. "Tell me," he continued, "what is your latest project? I'm very interested."

I explained that I was, at the moment, between projects, but that my latest novel, *Rarer Monsters*, was still being shopped around to publishers by my agent and longtime friend Oliver Kelly. It was a coming-of-age story about a boy who blames his father when his mother abandons the family, and finds himself drawn to the more overtly masculine father of his best friend. I hesitated, worried that my summary sounded trite, and admitted that I am not very good at giving concise pitches of my work, that authors never are since we understand our creations to be incredibly complicated and nuanced things, and that a summary is, by its very nature, reductive, though necessary in this marketplace.

"I understand completely," Rory said. "It sounds marvelously interesting. The title—from *Macbeth*, yes?"

It was! As the hostess showed us to our table—a corner booth!— I explained the subtle network of Macbethian themes that interlace the novel, how the perspective of the boy is, in a way, an imagining of Fleance's perspective, who of course witnessed the murder of his father, Banquo, but eventually became, as was prophesied, the ancestor of a line of great kings. In order to fully explain this, I had to go into some detail about the events in the novel that lead up to the scene when the boy witnesses what he perceives as his father's metaphorical castration but which turns out to be a contemporary play on what literary critics refer to as "the bed trick." By the time I got to the part about our young protagonist masturbating into a catcher's mitt, our waitress was already at our table demanding orders.

I hadn't had time to consult the menu yet, so I asked to go last. The menu at Jerry's Famous advertises an impressive seven hundred items, and I was fairly overwhelmed. This very American overabundance of choice often results, paradoxically, in a subversion of choice. While I was trying to think of a pithier package of that observation to deliver to Rory, the waitress looked at me, and I panicked and simply got what Rory had ordered, a Rueben and an iced tea.

When the waitress left, I leaned over to Edie and said, "Robert Aldrich."

"What?"

"The autograph on the *Baby Jane* poster. It's not Bette Davis or Joan Crawford. It's Robert Aldrich."

"Paul," she said in that doubting way of hers.

"You don't believe me? Look."

"We need to discuss something." This was the exact thing our mother said to us before she (Mom) went to Africa. I felt a little offended by her (Edie) co-opting this phrase, along with our mother's flat cadence, but realized that it could have been unintentional. I also realized—as I had not when I was a kid—that the inclusiveness of the first person plural subject, not to mention that verb, was a lie. *We* would not be *discussing* anything. *She* would be *talking*. But I played along. I listened. Besides, I knew from experience that if you don't take Edie's crises as seriously as she wants you to, she'll only exaggerate them to absurd heights. So I listened.

"I should say that when I came back last year," she said, "I was a little out of sorts. I'd gotten into some trouble and needed a home base, needed to regroup. I won't get into what sort of trouble, just say that it is irrelevant to everything that followed and that it's all being sorted out. I want to say this up front to apologize for the way I simply arrived back in your life as I did. It was unannounced, unexpected, and I had no right to intrude like that. I say this because it's important that you know I completely understand why you couldn't make it to Paige's funeral and why you've neglected my calls since then. Relationships cannot be repaired as easily as a phone can be dialed."

What is it about aphorisms that seem to require the passive voice? People seem to think the passive voice bestows on that which is said a kind of yogic—if not Yodic—wisdom. She could just as easily have said, I cannot repair a relationship as easily as I can dial a phone. Boom—passive voice eliminated.

"But I did as you said," she continued. "I went through George's—Dad's—things, began to get everything organized. There was, as I'm sure you can imagine, a lot of it. I found—I'm not sure how I should say this. I found a number of documents."

Or perhaps it is the intrusion of the "I"—which returns agency to a previously passive construction—that makes an aphorism too person-specific to be aphoristic?

"A manuscript, for one," Edie said. "I'm sure you know, he'd been working on a novel for—some time. He kept it in a locked trunk, along with a number of other documents that I will get to. But first, I read this manuscript. Read it with great interest. I remember him locked up in his office, writing, always writing. Even when the TV show was on hiatus, he was in there writing. I wanted to know what he'd been writing all that time." She looked at Rory, who did the sort of hand-over-hers/comforting-nod thing that I—and surely he—had seen on countless daytime talk shows in which some traumatized woman must recount the details of her trauma to a salivating host. "It was not what I expected. It was—disturbing."

The waitress brought our food. This was, I see now, remarkable turnaround time. Perhaps I am omitting something in the conversation between the waitress's order-taking and food-delivering, or perhaps my sense of time had gotten compressed (I remember us already having our beverages, so perhaps this is the case), but either way, I distinctly remember my—our—food being brought at this moment, my and Rory's twin Reuben sandwiches—their melted Swiss cheese congealing with the sauerkraut above densely striated layers of pastrami, a pile of meat so high it could not actually support itself as a sandwich anymore, was pushing the very limits of its structure, the top slice of marbled rye having slid off—along with Edie's food, a salad maybe, or soup.

"But I kept reading," Edie said. "There were scenes in there that struck me as familiar in a way I couldn't place. It didn't make sense. It wasn't until I met Rory here that I did place those scenes, that I figured out why I knew them, I mean really *knew* them, like I could anticipate everything that was going to happen as I was reading . . . Oh, um, no thank you, Paulie, I try to avoid red meat these days. So—the other documents. In the trunk, I also found a scrapbook. You know, like a photo album, but it contained newspaper clippings. Do you know about the Black Dahlia murder?"

She paused. Apparently this wasn't a rhetorical question. "Yes," I said. I did know something about it, though only faintly. I knew about it for the same reason I knew about how Bob Crane from *Hogan's Heroes* had a secret porn hobby, or how Fatty Arbuckle coitally squashed some poor girl to death on a hotel room floor. It was old Hollywood legend, the sort of story that exists now more on "ghost tours" of Los Angeles than on any single page of credible journalism. What I remembered of the story was the basic outline: A young woman, nicknamed the Black Dahlia, was murdered in a rather unpleasant way, and her killer was never found. The fact that she was an aspiring actress probably validated a lot of people's fears about the dangerous allure of Hollywood—*we will blind your daughters with our dazzling spotlights, only to slaughter them in the streets!*—which is, let's face it, the only purpose those sort of legends serve.

"How is everything?" our passing-by waitress asked, and, suddenly concerned that she'd overheard the word "murder" at our table just then, I—though not at all insincerely—said that everything was great and that I was enjoying my sandwich very much. And I certainly was enjoying my sandwich. I think Rory was enjoying his too. The pastrami was moist, the ratio of meat to fixin's actually quite perfect. I really had to admit to myself a deep love for Jewish delicatessens, a deep love for, now that I thought about it, much in the Jewish culture. Having read their Torah only for how it informed canonical literature, I really knew nothing about the specifics of their doctrines, aside from the obvious bit about not being into Jesus, whom I can't really claim any affection for either, but my admiration for the Jews was really more cultural than religious. I came of age, artistically speaking, in the 1970s, at a time when the great iconoclasts were Jewish atheists, and I realized then that I'd always wished I were Jewish, wished I could make those jokes about mother-induced guilt, fuck shiksas to get back at that mother, share in the culture of exclusion and then be excluded from that culture when I shared it with the goys through novels. In fact, it was this shunning by the orthodoxy that seemed to unify those I admired. I'd read Philip Roth's novels, watched Woody Allen's films, even followed the spiritual crises of the two Bobbies, Fischer and Dylan. It wasn't really that I wanted to be Jewish; I wanted to be a—or at least an *alleged*—self-hating Jew. So, as a non-Jew, did that make me anti-Semitic? Was my semito-philia actually—how could this be?—bigotry?

"So these newspaper clippings," Edie continued, "they were all about the Black Dahlia murder. And the details of the case, along with another murder from years earlier, corresponded pretty closely to some details in Dad's novel."

"I really—genuinely—love this restaurant," I said.

"Now of course, as a writer for that TV show," Edie said, "he had to keep himself pretty well informed about crime and crime-solving. And of course he drew inspiration from actual cases for the show. And of course it would seem that he was simply doing the same thing with his novel. But reading all that, it got a lot of stuff kicked up, so to speak, in me. I couldn't sleep, and when I did I had these terrible nightmares. When I called you that time? Back in the spring sometime? When I left that really long message for you? I'm not sure you got it, but I feel I should apologize about that. I was going through some stuff then that I didn't quite understand. I knew I needed help. I started seeing Rory here. Dr. Beach, I mean." She looked at him, smiled. "Only shrink in the yellow pages who says 'sliding scale' and means it." He again covered her hand in his. "He helped me understand."

Beach. Was that a Jewish name? Sort of like an anglicized version of Bech? Of course, I only knew that Bech is a Jewish name because the terminally WASPy John Updike, in what is surely the most famous act of literary semitophilia, wrote those books in the eighties about a chronically (but hilariously) kvetching Henry Bech. Was my fretting about Rory's surname—or my earlier noting of his nose—in fact proof of my latent bigotry? Or was my current kvetching about bigotry proof of my nonbigotry?

"Paul, are you familiar with the concept of repressed memories?" Edie asked.

I began to hear, beneath the babel of the midday crowd, a hollow crashing sound, many of them, repeating at various levels of intensity.

"That's the layman's term for it," Rory said. "You might know it as psychogenic amnesia, a learned man like yourself. And it can be the root of enormous psychic pain if not properly explored."

"Do you hear that?" I asked.

"You're familiar with Freud's 'Zur Ätiologie der Hysterie,' yes?" Rory said.

"Me? Yes. I mean, it's been awhile." I looked around to see where those crashing sounds were coming from. Our waitress, who was now across the restaurant, saw me prairie-dogging my head around, thought I was trying to get her attention, and began waddling over to us.

"Then you'll know the distinction between repression and dis-association," Rory said.

"Rory," Edie said. "Let me."

"How is everything, hon?" Our waitress was at our table, and suddenly she looked remarkably familiar—a thirtysomething woman with helmet-y bangs and a pleasant pudge around the cheeks—and, as often happens, I panicked, not knowing if I recognized her because she'd been one of my students at some point, or if she'd just been in a Sprite commercial. Possibly both.

"Oh, hello!" I said, to cover my bases. She looked taken aback (probably just a Sprite commercial). "Do you hear that crashing sound?" I asked.

"Oh," she said, "I learned to tune it out long ago," and walked away.

"Paul," Edie said. "Listen to me." Rory was patting her on the back now, his patting in sync with her talking, looking as if he were the ventriloquist, the Bergen to my sister's McCarthy. "Our father—he was a man capable of—monstrous things."

Across the restaurant, a line cook was shouting, "Pick up," the hostess was saying, "Right this way," several conversations volleyed interjections like "You're kidding me!" and "Don't even go there," and as I parsed out the different sounds, identifying the individual sonic threads from which the din of the lunch rush was woven, I began to identify approximately where the crashing sounds were coming from: somewhere in the opposite corner of the restaurant, near the green exit sign and retro-painted restroom signs.

"I've been working on a book of my own," Edie said. "It's kind of about this."

"Paul?" Rory said.

Then Edie echoed, "Paul?"

"Listen," I said. "Edie. Dr. Beach. I'm sorry, I must be rude and excuse myself." Rory did that reassuring eyebrow rustle that shrinks do. "And Rory, please don't think I'm being anti-Semitic."

"I promise I won't."

"Good."

Edie was crying.

I stood up, placed my napkin on the table, and walked toward the far corner of the deli, passing busboys with tubs full of dishes, servers with trays of food, trying not to think about how much people in the service industry make me nervous—their stressed-out annoyance veiled by the imperative to be hospitable, my sincere desire for them to like me, to know that I'm not like all their other asshole customers—and managed to arrive unmolested at the crash-sounding corner with the exit and restroom signs. There was a row of pay phones; two bathroom doors with their blockish male and female avatars, those perfectly sexless Platonic Ideals; and beyond that a glass door made opaque by a patchwork of scotch-taped flyers. No, I did not want to see your band or take Spanish lessons; no, I would not take a tear-off tab with your number.

I opened the door and went through and found myself in a bustling bowling alley. The place was a neon-lit Coney Island, the sounds of winning and prize-getting pinging around everywhere. Looking at the whole scene, you could see how all the lanes reached toward the vanishing point, that invisible dot in the universe toward which the lines of every competent composition must point. I recalled, as a boy in art class, eschewing the vanishing point, perhaps getting a whiff of the religious in its *creation-ex-nihilo* logic and expressing a child's natural and healthy anti-orthodox attitude, and so I was content to let my buildings—my houses and barns and fire stations—wobble, but I now saw an incredible beauty in this geometry, as well as in the nonsensical ritual of sport, sport being something I'd always rejected as an absurd triumph of the superego over the id, an attempt to quell the primal chaos with rules and borders and scores, but this—these colorfully shod people hurling balls down a dozen veneered, oversize planks into an abyss—made perfect sense.

"Why is this here?" I asked.

"Because we've always been here." Standing next to me was a teen-age boy in a red and blue polyester jumper, *Pinz* stitched into his lapel. "Would you like to rent some shoes?"

"Yes," I said. "I would."

But the point here is that Rory was clearly the puppet master (see my earlier ventriloquist metaphor), my sister clearly suffering a loss of agency. She'd always attached herself to strong-willed and manipulative men, and Rory was simply the latest. But I didn't realize the depth of his Svengali-like hold over my sister until a day or week later when I was at home—grading papers in the overstuffed armchair I'd saved from someone's front lawn a couple of years ago, an armchair Chris refers to as The Itch because he's convinced that it confers some sort of invisible rash to every sitter—when the phone started ringing. I—calm, pharmaceutically focused on my task, between papers enjoying the view of my weed-wild backyard—wanted to let the machine take the call, but just then Chris burst through the door, back from school, and hurried to answer the phone (I wondered what sort of call he could be expecting, this taciturn and seemingly friendless teen with buckshot acne and BO like a towel left on a locker-room floor) and he said, dejected, "Oh," then shouted at me, "Hey, it's for you." By the time I stood up, the only thing in sight to prove he'd been there was the phone receiver resting on the kitchen counter.

"Hello?" I answered.

"Paulie." Edie sighed. "Where did you go yesterday? Listen, I'm sorry, okay? There was no good way to have that conversation, but we needed to have it. By the way, who was that who answered the phone?" In the background, I heard Rory say something indecipherable and Edie said, her mouth a few inches farther away from the phone, "I got it. Just—let me." Then back to me: "Listen." (This, I was starting to notice, was a rather strange verbal tic of hers, *Listen*, a fitting imperative, I suppose, from a woman who has spent her life trying to get attention.) "Listen, Paulie, we—I have a favor to ask of you. What's your agent's name? I remember you introduced us at a party a long time ago. I know I'm a jerk for not remembering because he's been your friend since Iowa, but just remind me."

"Oliver."

"Oliver, yeah. The guy with that hair. He was a charmer, that one." Then to Rory: "What?" Back to me: "Oliver what? He had a lady's last name, right?"

"Oliver Kelly," I said, stupidly.

"Right, right. Oliver Kelly. Okay. So, I'm calling to ask for your blessing in contacting him."

"My blessing? What? Why?"

"That's what I said. Why would I need your blessing? It's not like you're my father. But Rory said it would be better this way. First, he said we could have you introduce us, but when we saw how you spazzed out at lunch, we reassessed. I guess we don't really need you as an inter-mediary—is that the right word? I mean, we have his name, maybe he's on the Internet, but Rory said it would be better with your blessing." To Rory: "What? This is me talking to my brother, so just pipe down over there." There was a pause, then to me she said, "Rory wants to talk to you."

I hung up the phone. I dialed Oliver's office.

"Elkin Media," the receptionist answered.

"This is Paul McWeeney. I need to speak with Oliver Kelly."

"I'm sorry, he's unavailable at the moment. May I ask who's calling?"

"This is Paul McWeeney."

"I'm sorry, it sounded like you said "palm tree"? Is that your name? You need to speak slower."

I hung up. I dialed Oliver's home phone. A child of indeterminate sex answered, his/her voice like a shoe-squeak on linoleum. "Hello?"

"This is Paul . . . McWeeney. Is Oliver Kelly available?"

"Who?"

I hung up. I dialed his office.

"Elkin Media," the receptionist answered.

"This is palm tree. I'm trying to reach Oliver Kelly."

"He is unavailable at the moment. May I ask who's calling?"

"Did he move? Is he still at his 201 number?"

"I'm afraid I can't give out that information, sir."

I hung up. I dialed his home number. The androgynous child answered. "Hello?"

"Oliver Kelly," I said. "Does he live there?"

"What?"

I hung up. Maybe I was having a stroke. I was pretty sure I was saying the words I thought I was saying, but none of them seemed to be landing the way I intended. Maybe I was actually spouting some incomprehensible Esperanto, a salad of meaningless phonemes. I walked down the hall to Chris's room where some sort of frightening music throbbed against the walls like a headache. I knocked. "Chris," I think I said.

"What?"

"Do you mean 'what?' as in what do I want? Or 'what?' as in what did I say? It's an important distinction."

"What?"

I opened the door. Chris was huddled over his computer, the screen facing away from me but illuminating his face like one of those light boxes people treat seasonal affective disorder with, and, considering the blackout curtains he'd covered his windows with, he was probably a candidate for this treatment.

"*What?*" he said.

"Repeat what I say."

"No."

"Good enough."

I closed the door. I was running interception. I had to get to Oliver before Edie did. She'd tricked me into giving up his name and was now finding her own way to him, using me as some unwitting reference. She'd mentioned the possibility of him being on the Internet. I could try that. The only computer in the house was Chris's. (I didn't have a computer, still don't. I'm composing this on an IBM Wheelwriter 1000, a sturdy electric typewriter that hums in a soothing way. I tend not to trust computers, with all those ones and zeros that are as ephemeral as fairy farts. With my Wheelwriter, I know that what I type is there, here, in indelible ink, immediately. I am typing this now. It is here now, on the page, real. Look. Now is the time for all good men to come to the aid of their country. The quick brown fox jumps over the lazy dog. See?)

I opened Chris's door again, and he shouted, "Fucking knock, dude!"

I said I needed his technical savvy to help me get someone's contact info from the Internet, and he begrudgingly agreed.

"Don't pretend you don't know how to use this thing," he said. "I know you come in here while I'm at school and use my computer—it's all there in the browser history."

I pulled a chair up next to him, and said, "How's that acne medicine working out? Do you still have an oily T-zone?"

"Who are you looking for?"

"Just type 'Oliver Kelly' and see what comes up."

"Oliver Kelly—your friend, right?"

Looking over at his rumbling stereo, I said, "Would you call this music thrash metal or speed metal?"

Chris started typing.

"I think T-zone would be a good name for one of these bands," I said. "The 'T' evokes the Christian iconography that these bands seem so fascinated with, while the 'zone' suggests an almost marshal state of doom."

"Yeah, so you gonna tell me what this is all about?"

Chris was right to be suspicious of my Luddite claims. Truth be told, I had been sneaking into his room to use his computer. It started when I noticed that my students suddenly seemed more informed about my past than ever before. For years, I'd been teaching at COLA confident that my students saw me as Mr. McWeeney or Prof. McWeeney (which is not entirely accurate, as I am, along with every other member of the COLA faculty, not a professor but rather an adjunct instructor) or Dr. McWeeney (which is not accurate either, as I have only a master's degree, but after a few too many misunderstood jokes asking my students to call me "master," and realizing that both the "Prof." and "Dr." titles have nothing to do with me and everything to do with my students' genuine desire to be at a real four-year institution where those labels would be legion, I now respond to both), confident that my students saw me only as their wise and affable teacher, a tweed-coated man of letters, grader of papers and too-lenient forgiver of absences. I felt— and still feel—that maintaining this persona was important not just for the classroom dynamic but for shaping their understandings of how an educated person looked, behaved, carried himself. There would only occasionally be rifts, chinks in the armor, so to speak, moments when the mask fell, or, to be more precise, was pulled away. Every now and then some plucky young student would pipe up with, "Hey, Donny . . . I mean, uh, Mr. McWeeney, do you think the Ancient Mariner is a *loose cannon* in this poem?" and I would have to stay unfazed while saying, "Yes, there is a great deal of emotional volatility here," knowing that an errant episode of the short-lived sitcom *Loose Cannons* (1966–1966) had surfaced late night on some cable channel and my astute student had recognized my name in the credits playing young Donny Cannon, oldest of the Cannon brood whose patriarch was psychologist Dr. Kurt Cannon, played by Fred McMurray in an always-frazzled performance. So yes, I was an actor. In my late teens, having recently lost my father, I was adrift and drifted into the same industry that surely caused Dad's heart attack. It—that ridiculous show and my ridiculous performance— was something I thought I'd put behind me. When the show was canceled I began taking classes at COLA, finished the high school requirements I'd neglected, got my associate's degree, transferred to UCLA, got drunk on the poststructuralists, wrote essays about the evils of the American sitcom, got my bachelor's, then moved all the way to Iowa for writer school, where I thought I'd finally shake off the stigma of my youthful and all-too-public attempts at commercial artistry and claim my bona fides as a commercially unviable artist by writing avant-garde short stories about empty rooms and characters who discovered they were just math equations, but sure enough, the first thing anyone (Oliver Kelly) said to me when I arrived at Iowa—my hair long, my chin hairy, looking as un-Donny-like as I could—was, "Hey, man, fuckin' *Loose Cannons*, right?" And although I don't want to say that I'm ashamed of my brief acting career, I do feel that it has stigmatized me a bit, and I have a sneaking suspicion that when every publishing house in New York rejected first *Season of All Natures* and then *Rarer Monsters*, it had something to do with my past, publishers surely doubting they could take little Donny Cannon seriously as a novelist. Of course, you folks in the true crime department don't share those prejudices with the boys down the hall, which is why I like you and feel you will understand. But the point is that in recent years, my students had been piping up more and more about *Loose Cannons*. Someone would come up to me after class and say, "Hey, um, this might be crazy but were you on TV in like the sixties?" and I, my voice low, would say yes, it was a thing I did, and then the student would inevitably admit that he was an aspiring actor and could I hook him up with my agent? Instances like those were becoming more frequent, until one day— when a student, mid-discussion of Samuel Pepys's diaries, interrupted to ask what it was like being on TV, and the whole class said, "Yeah, Mr. M.," not a single person seeming surprised by this revelation—I realized that it was just common knowledge now. This has been quite stressful and I have struggled with different ways of maintaining my (as I've said, pedagogically vital) professorial persona (the word "professorial"—adj., relating or *similar to* a professor—being the closest I can come, it seems, to an actual professorship, since I am not, technically, a professor), and during this first instance, I'm afraid to admit, I snapped at the student, telling him to stop trying to derail the class, and I then spent the rest of the period reading aloud Pepys's description of the 1666 London Fire in a monotone, defiantly un-actorly voice, though I have now become more skilled at deflecting the issue without appearing so insanely insecure. After that Pepys class, however, I rushed back to the English Department office, paranoid and panicked, wondering aloud to anyone who would listen how it was that everyone suddenly knew everything, and Hazel, a pathologically cheery colleague who competes in a women's arm-wrestling league under the name Harriet Clubman, said, "It's the Internet, silly. They look you up. It's all there. Things are different now. You can't compartmentalize. I have eighteen-year-old girls coming up to me wanting to arm-wrestle for better grades. You should be flattered, though. If they're taking the time to type your name into a search engine, it means they like you." And that was when I started sneaking into Chris's room to search for myself. It was all there online, my life unfurling on the screen. I had a profile on something called the Internet Movie Database featuring a picture of a very young me from a *Loose Cannons* publicity still, my hair full, floppy, and feathered, my stomach effortlessly flat. And people (who? devoted fans? archivists? felons?) had uploaded all thirteen terrible episodes for the whole world to see. But as horrible as that moment was, it's not what turned me into a chronic violator of Chris's *stay out of my room* policy (a policy explicitly stated and posted on his door). Peter Matthiessen's self-searching book *The Snow Leopard* had meant so much to me when I first read it in the late seventies, and I'd always imagined that I too would disappear into the mountains one day to look for myself. But instead of braving the Himalayas of Tibet, I'd snuck into a teenage boy's room, and found myself on a dim pixilated screen to the deafening screeches and pops of a dial-up modem—accessing the Internet sounding like such a violent, industrial act—and what I'd found, after all the *Loose Cannons* stuff, was a website called Grade-a-Prof, where students, as you might imagine, grade their profs. And there I was. No picture in this profile, just my name, my school, and my averaged grade. *Paul McWeeney. College of Los Angeles.* And my grade? It would be incorrect and lazily cliché to write here that my heart sank when I saw C-. Rather, my heart did a sort of writhing thing and I experienced a little acid reflux—the latter was probably due to my vending machine diet but it was still emotionally appropriate. I told myself not to scroll down the page—just as an author shouldn't read his reviews—but I found myself doing it anyway. Sixty-three reviews dating back only one year, apparently since the website's launch, proclaiming in all caps and strange phonetic spelling things like *this guy SUXXX* and *I HATED this class mor then life itself* and, simply, *STOOPID!* I kept scrolling. I couldn't stop myself. I read through all sixty-three of those reviews, which ranged from the psychotically angry to the completely indifferent. Most of them veered toward the latter, which made me wonder why so many people would log on to this website simply to say *this man made no impression on me.* At least those who hated me felt something. I heard someone somewhere say something along the lines of: A good teacher will make five percent of his class absolutely hate him, and five percent absolutely love him. So I went hunting for that other five percent. After an hour of scrolling and reading, I found one review that said, *hes nice i liked the class.* I stared at that comment until the rods and cones in the back of my eyeballs had its every pixel memorized. I deduced that the person who wrote it was a female: prefacing the "like" with "nice" revealed as much. She was shy: The lack of capital letters suggested a fear of self-assertion, which probably meant she'd been surrounded by dominating male figures who'd been telling her to keep her mouth shut her whole life. In my experience, women like that are almost always physically attractive (aesthetically unappealing women tend to be loud, thinking that personality can make up the difference). This beneficent commenter was surely small, mousy, not the kind of beauty who'd make every head turn, but undeniably beautiful once you took notice of her. A brunette, probably, with glasses. And she said I was nice, which probably meant I'd helped her with some assignment she was having trouble with. The comment was dated February 1994, so she probably took one of my classes in the fall of 1993. As I've said, I have on average about two hundred students every semester, so I couldn't immediately bring to mind everyone in my roster who fit that description. But that's not the point. The point is that I had developed a small habit of sneaking into Chris's room every day and checking Grade-a-Prof to see if there were any more—positive—comments posted. In an effort to boost that C-, I started telling jokes in my classes, funny ones, but had to stop when I accidentally made the same Wordsworth pun three times in one class, each time feigning spontaneity, until one student said, "Dude, you're stuck on repeat," which got the biggest laugh of my teaching career. With seven classes each semester, it's inevitable that you forget which class you said what to, and no one seems to care when it's some note of pedantry, but at the first hint that humor might be calculated—that a quip comes from anything other than a flash of pure inspiration—people get angry.

"There you go," Chris said. "Oliver's email." We were looking at the Elkin Media website, a handsome display, sleek presentation, much nicer than Grade-a-Prof, which, graphically, was like a junior high AV club production; Elkinmedia.com, however, was a Simpson-Bruckheimer production, each bit of text, it seemed, a link, a wormhole to something else.

"The way you talk about this guy, I thought he was like your best friend," Chris said.

"How many best friends you got?" I said. "Scoot." I shooed him out of the way, sat down, and drafted a quick email to Oliver from my new COLA email account: *Oliver, buddy. It's me. Call me ASAP.* I hit send. Then I wrote a second email: *By "me" I mean Paul McWeeney,* and I included my phone number.

Then I went back to the phone.

I see the first page of this letter is dated June 3, which means I've been writing for over a week now. I didn't anticipate it taking this long. I thought I would belly up to the IBM Wheelwriter 1000, set down what I needed to set down, make my case clear, refute the points Edie makes in her book, send it off to you, and that would be it. I'd be able to get on with my life. Or at least that was Julia's theory—just sit down, get it out, and walk away. Setting aside the fact that her almost scatological description of the writing process probably reveals her true feelings about writers, I knew it wouldn't be that simple. I did not, however, realize the depth and breadth this refutation would necessarily have to take. I have been at this every night for over a week now and have not yet come to the most damning counterevidence, the irrefutable proof that Edie's claim about our father is entirely without merit. To be fair, though, I have been quite busy, not just writing this but trying to figure how exactly to get my hands on that specific piece of counter-evidence, which is proving more elusive that I anticipated. I'm speaking, of course, of the autopsy report. As a matter of policy, autopsy reports are public record, but the LAPD never released Betty Short's. Their official stance was that they wanted certain information to be kept secret, information that could be used to identify the killer and weed out the nut-jobs eager to file false confessions. Still, fifty years later, it has not been made public. I have now read countless tales of reporters trying to uncover this document and they have all failed. The very notion that Edie, an amateur investigator, and one clearly driven by dubious motives, would actually be able to recover this autopsy report—which is, let us not forget, the only real, tangible evidence she uses to validate her version of things—is ludicrous. Whatever report she claims to have is clearly an act of forgery, forgery being something Edie has experience with—not just being gullible and eager to believe the work of frauds (that time she bought a plastic Rolex for me), but on the flip side of naïveté, actually forging documents herself (fake IDs, fake report cards, even fake letters of recommendation). The only thing she writes about the origins of this mysterious document is that it is "a copy made by a former L.A. County Sheriff's Department employee" (245). If I can get my hands on this document, and prove it a fake, then my sister's case will crumble—I'm tempted to say "like a house of cards" but the image that pops into my head is of a gingerbread house, spe-cifically the one Edie brought home from school one hot Los Angeles December, and which I, an excitable and sugar-starved seven-year-old, accidentally crushed when I pounced on its edible everything. So: Her case will crumble like a gingerbread house. But in good time. I'll get to all that, I will. It's just that the more I write, the more I realize there's more to write, since I know what I need to offer here is not simply a dry wrangling of facts: I am also a character witness, after all, someone who can attest to the honorable character of George McWeeney and the mendacious, attention-seeking character of Edie McWeeney. But I'm running out of time. I'm trying to cram this into the two-week break between spring and summer classes. Next week, I'm back in the classroom, teaching four classes during the compressed and intensive summer session, and I won't have time for anything else. And yet why am I taking the time to write that fact instead of plowing on with my case? It's one in the morning. I should call it a night, go to bed. Tomorrow, I'll have a clearer mind for this. But I can't sleep. I took another Ritalin an hour ago and it's still ticking away in my blood. Julia is in my bed, surely asleep by now. She said she'd wait up for me so we could have sex, but she always conks out early. She's been staying over a lot lately. She says it's because her place has a mold problem but I think she's trying move in. We've been dating long enough, I suppose it's a natural next step, but it's strange that she's going about it in such an oblique way. I'm perfectly fine with the idea of living with her. I'm not doing the typical intimacy-avoidance guy thing. I *like* intimacy; after all, women I date are often impressed by the fact that I enjoy providing oral sex. If I seem hesitant to let Julia move in, it's out of concern for Chris. The last thing he needs is to become attached to another mother figure who will abandon him. He's already been through that. It's been three years since his mother died, and he's still vulnerable. It was a sudden thing, so the grieving process takes longer and is more jagged and chaotic. Had Brenda died of some terrible illness, after months in a hospital bed with tubes stuck in her vital parts, Chris would have had all that time to come to terms with death. But it was a simple car accident that did it, Brenda's little Honda cruising obliviously in the blind spot of an eighteen-wheeler that wanted to change lanes. So, just like that, she was gone, and Chris, whom I'd gotten to know only a little during the seven or eight months Brenda and I dated, had nowhere to go. Brenda had no family to speak of, so when it looked like Chris was headed for foster care, I stepped in. At first things were great. Women nearly fell over themselves when I told them this story, their genitals swelling up to the size of catcher-mitts, like baboons in estrus. But when I would bring one home, Chris's acting out—especially his refusal to respect the standard necktie-on-the-doorknob code—would drive my date away. Chris was both the biggest lady-bait and cock-blocker a middle-age bachelor could have. Of course, I knew his behavior was simply coming from grief, from his reluctance to get hurt by any of these women. Which is why it bothers me so much—why I feel a pang of fear for Chris—when I see Julia trying to ingratiate herself with him, buying him those concert tickets for his birthday a couple weeks ago, a suspiciously excessive gesture. Sure, he was happy at the time, but, as I tried to explain to Julia later, he doesn't have any friends and when he realizes that he has no one to give the second ticket to he'll resent her. Plus, he still feels abandoned by his mother, I said, so if he attaches himself to you, he'll only get hurt, which is why for his birthday I bought him the far more appropriate (and Pulitzer Prize–winning) *The Denial of Death* by Dr. Ernest Becker. Tomorrow, Julia's taking him to see the new *Mission Impossible* movie and then dinner at Planet Hollywood, and I really need to sit him down and explain how he's only going to get hurt here, how he should really be keeping her at arm's length. It's all there in the book, I'll explain, how he's vulnerable and too eager to latch on to another mother figure.

Oddly enough, Edie also references *The Denial of Death* when she writes about Mom dying. The book was published some thirteen years after the fact, but she claims it helped her "make sense of our orphaning" (230). I'd like to point out, however, that the sense she makes is more self-aggrandizement than self-awareness. For instance, she uses me—me!—as an example of what Becker identifies as the "anal" personality, trying to distance himself against the reality of death. Of course, she hurls this diagnosis at me only in order to make herself seem like the picture of mental health by comparison, and it's a completely ludicrous accusation. All she has as proof that I refused to acknowledge Mom's death is just one small incident in which I asked Aunt Paige to pose as my mother for a few years whenever friends came around. But I was a teenager then. And besides, Mom's death is not the issue here.

I'm getting off track. I need to stay focused. I thought the Ritalin would help, but I think I made a mistake in crushing it up and snorting it. The guy who sold it to me—a former student of mine whose name I should probably keep out of this, seeing as how it's a legal document of sorts—said it was time-release, which I frankly did not have the patience for, and I thought sending it up my nose would make it work faster—you know, giving it a more direct path. But now I'm not sure it's working faster. It's always hard to tell. Either way, I'm now experiencing what is called the drip, when the snorted substance works its way through your sinuses and can be tasted in the back of your throat, something I haven't felt in many years. Even though it makes you feel mucusy, it's not an altogether unpleasant sensation, if only for the sense-memory it evokes. It's my own personal madeleine.

Since we cannot understate Oliver's culpability in the defamation of my father, what I have to say here will certainly be important background info. You surely know Oliver Kelly as the guy who sold you Edie's book, but the folks in the literary wing down the hall from you probably have had more experience with him, as he is the guy who dutifully submitted my novels *Season of All Natures* and *Rarer Monsters* to publishers, tried valiantly to sell them in a world that is no longer receptive to literature, an upside-down world that thinks "nonfiction" denotes truth and "fiction" untruth, despite the fact that my sister's book of lies will be shelved as nonfiction while my fiction walked the razor's edge of existence and shone the hard light of truth on the world.

I first met Oliver when I arrived in Iowa in 1974, having fled L.A., the place where everyone knew my résumé, now ready to remake myself as a bona fide man of letters. It was my first time in the Midwest and as I drove along I-80, my car packed with my every belonging, I found the resolute flatness existentially daunting, the silos phallic in a strangely druidic way, the general corn-centric culture (the maize-mazes advertised on the side of the interstate, the corn-on-the-cob-shaped flashlights displayed for impulse buys at gas stations) quasi-religious, but when I got to Iowa City, I was relieved to see that it was a city beset by writers from across the country. You could spot them everywhere, looking as bewildered as I felt. Through my windshield, which was splattered with a sampling of the entire insectoid biosphere that existed between California and Iowa, I saw a man in a leather jacket holding a portable typewriter like a lunchbox; he appeared to be window-shopping for antiques. I figured this must be the place. But the first time I got to see a dense concentration of these displaced persons (there were twenty-five of us in the incoming fiction class) was at an orientation hosted by Henry Winters, our esteemed teacher and prophet of the short story, and despite the domestic setting, it felt like a singles mixer. People had name tags. Everyone, independently, thought it would be funny to write obscure literary pseudonyms on their name tags, and then all felt slightly stupid when they realized everyone else had done the same thing. I was chatting up a young woman who'd also written *Vivian Darkbloom* on her nametag, when a guy with no visible nametag but with an impressive molding of dark hair came up to me and shouted, "Hey, man, fuckin' *Loose Cannons*, right? I fuckin' love that show!" (I suddenly remembered—perhaps not consciously but emotionally, somewhere in the monkey part of my brain—when I was a kid at summer camp leaving the showers one crisp foggy morn when my thick-necked bunkmate came up behind me and ripped off my towel and pointed at my hairless cluster just as a group of girls walked by, the air redolent of kiwi shampoo, while I just withered in shame.) I looked at the other Vivian Darkbloom, then at all the other literary hopefuls milling about the famous author's living room. Everyone's collective attention turned from the various bric-a-brac that signified all their high-brow aspirations, and in their collective gaze I saw—or at least imagined I saw—the ambivalence of the literati toward everything pop culture: the class-infused loathing mixed with genuine envy of recognition, no matter how egregious and vacuous that recognition might be. But then the other Vivian Darkbloom laughed, and everyone went back to sneaking glances at our host's bookshelf. I'd learn later that no one in that room aside from Oliver had any idea what *Loose Cannons* was, and they were reacting more to Oliver's loud and sudden outburst, but at the time all I could do was stand there and try to cover my suddenly exposed, chill-shriveled genitals. "I'm gonna buy this man a beer," Oliver said directly to me. There was no beer in the house, just plenty of free wine, and Oliver was suddenly intent on not just getting a beer for me but actually *buying* it for me, so he announced to the room that we were going to a bar and that anyone interested in the history of television could follow. Our cohort was presented with an option: stay here to meet-and-greet in the living room of a Pulitzer winner, or follow Oliver and me to a nearby watering hole where he would ply me with beers and questions about life in L.A., obscure TV stardom, etc. No one came with us. Oliver in effect befriended me and alienated me from everyone else before the first day of classes had even started, and I'd come to suspect that this was just his MO, that when he decided someone would be his friend he must also assure that no one else could befriend them with the same level of intensity, a freaky way of saying, You're mine and no one else's. At the bar, I was at first put off by him, confused by his aggressive friendliness and questioning, wondering if he was simply fucking with me, but at the same time I couldn't help feeling flattered. This was, after all, attention, approval, even if it was approval for something I no longer approved of. One of the less touristy questions Oliver asked me that day was about my family: Did I have any siblings? Yes, I said, an older sister. He said he had a younger sister; she was in high school. An odd and seemingly pointless point, but looking back on our friendship I think it's an important one. That's when I realized that just about everyone who'd befriended me in my twenty-seven years had been an older sibling. As a younger sibling myself, I'd always sought the friendship and approval of people who had that older-brother mien, just as I'm sure Oliver, despite being my junior (he was twenty-two, had graduated from Princeton at twenty-one, a fact that made me rabidly insecure about my own academic achievements), always sought younger brothers to take under his wing. And that's exactly what he did. He taught me to appreciate fine scotch and obscure punk, often at the same time, sitting on his couch at three in the morning after the bars had closed and he'd whip out a bottle of Lagavulin sixteen-year ("Smells like a campfire, right?") and LPs by the Dictators and Double-Sided Dildo ("You can actually hear the feedback from the singer's mike picking up the guitar amp"). At twenty-seven, I suppose it was a little late in life for me to suddenly start appreciating punk, but I latched on to the stuff, missing all the angst and anger I'd had to set aside during my late teen years, which I'd spent on a studio set, seeking the approval of adults rather than rebelling against them. By four in the morning, Oliver would usually start teaching me to appreciate not just refined booze and intentionally unrefined music but fine cocaine as well. Enjoying the irony that I had to leave showbiz before anyone even offered me the stuff, I indulged as a mere dilettante, thrilled just as much by the novelty of it as by the dopamine. In a not-so-subtle nod to Hunter S. Thompson, Oliver kept a couple grams in a saltshaker.

Iowa City in the seventies felt like summer camp, people from all over the map converging into one diverse but insular mob. Rumor spread that John Cheever was visiting and so we'd stare at every foppish drunk in every bar and wonder if this was him, the suburban surrealist, lyricist of the middle class, until the man would get paranoid and shout things that were decidedly unlyrical, and we'd move on. Poets had the most sex. There was one married couple, both poets, who had an open marriage, wrote villanelles about their dalliances, workshopped them. I heard about this from a poet friend who snuck me copies of the wife's work, which I pored over, hoping for some oblique allusion to our own drunken dry-hump—just one alliterative description of my boner-taut denim, please?—but found not a one. By second year, they were workshopping divorce-themed blank verse. Everyone seemed to know the names of obscure flora and fauna, and filled their work with them the same way class-climbing urbanites casually name-drop expensive brands. Knowing the names of things, I thought, that was what real writing was about, and I still have the copies of National Geographic's *Guide to North American Birds* and *Guide to North American Trees* that I bought at a yard sale in Dubuque. In my fiction workshops, I sat across the seminar table from grizzled guys in olive-green army jackets who wrote stories that contained hauntingly precise descriptions of what a Vietcong's blood felt like splattered on your face after you'd bayoneted them in their dark viscera, and I worried I didn't have enough real-world experience to be a writer. Or at least I didn't have the right kind of experience. My own descriptions of blood-splattered faces smacked of hackery and cheap imitation. Which is why if you asked me back then what I wrote about, I'd say, "The crisis of simulacra." My fear that I didn't have the right kind of experience to write the gritty realism I was surrounded with was also what made me appreciate my late-night jaw sessions with Oliver, the Schedule-Two stimulant mixing with a genuine giddiness that I was actually experiencing something real and illicit and fun and that Oliver was laughing at my jokes and intensely interested in everything I had to say about L.A., even though when I ran out of my own (relatively few) interesting stories about showbiz, I began to appropriate stories I'd read elsewhere, stories from Milton Berle's memoir or Hedda Hopper's tell-all. "Dude," he said, "you're like the most interesting person I know." Or at least he said something to that effect. Point being, he seemed pretty primed on California in general and Hollywood in particular, and I figured after the MFA we'd move westward together, be the vanguard of a new literary Los Angeles. But at a party the night of our graduation, Oliver said he didn't want to write anymore; instead he was "going to New York to see how the sausage is made." At the time, I hadn't actually heard that expression before, so I initially thought it was some sort of gay thing, that, in addition to walking away from the literary ambition that enslaved the rest of us, Oliver was walking away from heterosexual pretenses as well. (People often said he was very handsome, and the way he maintained rapt eye contact in conversation always sparked pangs of homophobia in some men, made uncomfortable with his particular brand of homosocial friendship, which a mutual acquaintance once called "armingly disarming.") But as we kept talking into the night and next day, the expression's real meaning began to emerge. "You angry at me?" he asked. No, I said, I just had to figure out a different roommate situation in L.A., was all.

It wasn't until years later that I began to suspect his reasons for getting disillusioned with Hollywood, or at least the Hollywood I'd presented to him. He had just begun agenting and tried to get me a job ghostwriting the memoir of Ken Aurora, that insufferable talk-show host with the veneer smile, called *Don't Spit on Superman's Cape, Don't Tug on the Wind: Lessons Learned on the Big Red Couch.* "This is right up your alley," he said, rather flatly. "*Hollywood Babylon*-type stuff. Doesn't have to be true." At the time, however (this must have been around '84 since for reasons I don't understand I associate this period with watching Reagan/Mondale debates on TV), I was seven or eight hundred pages into a first draft of *Season of All Natures*, which I thought would be my magnum opus, and I said I didn't want to be distracted from my real writing. I also told him that if word of my involvement in Aurora's egregious bit of pop pulp leaked once *Season of All Natures* was published, the Pulitzer committee would refuse to take me seriously. "Okay, then," he said. Of course, *Season of All Natures* was not published, and I often mourn the money I could have made penning Aurora's book of showbiz sycophancy, those countless-told (and surely apocryphal) tales of drinking with Peter O'Toole, of bedding Liz Taylor, of giving Johnny Carson the idea for the Carnac bit. But when I see that paperback available in airport bookstores, along with its follow-ups *Talking Heads, Taking Beds: More Lessons from the Big Red Couch* and *Couch Surfing: Even More Lessons from the Big Red Couch*, I still feel a pang of fear that Oliver's offering me that job was his way of saying he knew how much of my showbiz tales—which he'd always responded to with rich laughter—I'd stolen from cheap Hollywood memoirs, how much of my life had effectively been ghostwritten. "Doesn't have to be true."

Well, the talk with Chris did not go well. He and Julia are currently at the movie. But that just means I have more time to myself to get some writing done. The house is empty, free of distractions. My mind is clear and I'm ready to proceed with the task at hand. I am sitting here in the spare room, constellations of dust motes drifting through a shaft of early afternoon sunlight, the only sound the rubbery *vroom* of each passing car's Doppler effect. (I suddenly feel obligated to admit that those last two clauses I've written before. They appeared in chapter 86 of *Season of All Natures* when the character of Gavin is wandering through his old childhood home, but they are still applicable here. Is it wrong that I'm now poaching descriptions from my decade-old unpublished novel? Is my guilt based in a fear that I cannot come up with something original, that my best writing is behind me, or that in stripping *Season of All Natures* for parts I'm finally admitting that it is officially—as Oliver told me it was—dead in the water? Or is my guilt based in my increasing awareness that this legal document is beginning to take on a novelistic form? Do I hope that you at New Wye True Crime are impressed enough with my wordsmithing that you will tell the literary guys down the hall to reconsider *Rarer Monsters*? Sure, it's only natural for that to be floating somewhere in the back of my mind, although I am fully aware that true crime editors are drawn to a, shall we say, *louder* style than are higher-brow editors [I've seen the kind of pulps you print—all those *italics*, all that emotive punctuation!—you must be a very demonstrative bunch], but that is good because it allows me to loosen up the narrative voice that your literary brothers so praised in their gentle rejections: I am no longer hiding behind the terse telegraphese that I picked up in writer school: I am angry. But does all that suggest that selfish ulterior motives are eclipsing the real objective of this letter—i.e., to thoroughly debunk my sister's claim that our father was responsible for the death of Betty Short before her book goes to press, while there is still time for you to pull it from publication? I don't think so. I believe my fundamental intentions here are pure, but I must admit biases where they crop up—even at the sentence level—in order to let the case for my father's good name stay untainted. But I must move on, as I see that I have already wasted fifteen minutes and one page on this issue, which I probably should have relegated to a footnote so it wouldn't stand in the way of the case for my father.) (In theory, I prefer footnotes to parentheticals. Philosophically, I agree with footnotes, the way they allow thoughts to branch off in their own direction, without the terminus that a paren-thesis necessitates. Thoughts should not be terminal—they are not *matryoshka* dolls, neatly fitting into each other, nooked cozily into the larger narrative. Thoughts, ideas, revelations, are endlessly subdividing tributaries that should be given enough water to allow them to rival the river from whence they came. But it's just not practical. Composing footnotes on a typewriter, paradoxically, requires a kind of forethought that goes against the very anti-terminus, free-branching ethos of foot-notes, simply because you have to plan ahead, know exactly how long a given footnote will be, so you can format your page accordingly. I really should get a computer. But, as it is, I'm trapped in a terminus.)

On with my case.

Oliver finally got back to me. I was at home, in the garage, going through the box of final research papers marked *Fall 1993*, trying to jog my memory for a small, shy, bespectacled brunette, when I heard the phone ring. I went into the kitchen and answered.

"Paul," Oliver said. "What's up? Hey, I'm going to be out there in L.A. this weekend. We'll have lunch on Sunday, okay? Better yet, you want to come do the Universal Studios tour with me? I'm bringing my niece. Do you know her? She's eight. She really wants to do the *Back to the Future* ride, and the birthday gift I'm giving my sister this year is taking the little ankle-biter off her hands for a week. My sister named this girl Yuna. You believe that? I hate my sister sometimes. I'll be honest, Yuna creeps me out a little. It's like she has no affect, just that blank stare you see in movies about kids who'll kill you in your sleep. Anyway, I'll be out there with her, and I'm taking her on the Universal tour because she wants to do the *Back to the Future* ride, so maybe you can meet us there, tell her neat things about Hollywood or something. Great, it's settled then. Sunday it is. I look forward to it."

I'm pretty sure I must have said something in all of this, but all I remember now is Oliver's block of monologue. We didn't actually end up meeting at Universal Studios. He called me the morning of and said Yuna had woken up early and so they were already there, about to hop on the tour bus, so I spent the afternoon at Pinz, playing a few guttery frames, and then met up with them at Mel's Diner on Sunset after they'd finished with Universal. When I walked in, I saw Oliver waiting beside the hostess stand, an oversize T-shirt, *Hollywood* emblazoned across the front, awkwardly fit over a blue button-up. He was holding a Universal Studios tote in one hand and a novelty plastic Academy Award in the other. I approached and was going to do a handshake-hug combo, but all the souvenirs got in the way and I just patted him on the shoulder. After some standard platitudes, I said, "Are we just waiting for a table?"

"No," Oliver said, his eyes scanning the restaurant under thick eyebrows that were starting to go gray. "Yuna's in the bathroom. She's a bit tuckered out from the day, I guess. I have to get her back to the hotel."

"Okay, she can take a nap and we can grab a drink or something. I'll take you to this place that has over a hundred scotches on the menu."

He put the plastic award in his tote bag and ran his fingers through his hair (which, to my annoyance, was showing no signs of thinning, until I reminded myself that anti-balding medications often cause impotence, so perhaps he was paying the price for that mane), then he pulled out a thick manila envelope. "I'm meeting up with Edie later. I just wanted to give this to you. I asked her if you'd seen it and she said no."

Suddenly there was a small girl standing beside Oliver, her frizzy hair looking electroshocked, wiping her wet hands on his khakis. "Honey, darling," he said, "what are you doing?"

"They didn't have paper towels," Yuna said.

"Okay," Oliver said, grabbing her hand. "Oh, God. Your hands are slimy. You have to rinse the soap off, sunshine." Then to me, he said, "I know it's been a while, but I do want to bring you in on this. I want you and Edie to work together on it."

I was holding the manila envelope, thick as a manuscript. "Any news on *Rarer Monsters*?"

He looked at me the same way he'd been looking at Yuna. "That was four years ago, Paul. I'm sorry."

"I'm tired!" the girl shouted.

"Highland Grounds," I said.

"What?" Oliver said.

"The scotch bar, that's what it's called."

And then Oliver and his weekend charge were gone. I'd like to report that I ran after him, grabbed him by the lapels, told him not to buy this story, that Edie was mentally unstable, that she was raping our family's memory, but I just stood there between the hostess stand and a row of arcade games, holding the manila envelope. I looked it over but didn't open it, wondered if manila envelopes actually came from Manila. Everything I knew about Manila and the Philippines

I'd learned from an episode of *20/20* about sex tourism, so as far as I knew it was quite possible that Manilans had an unusual amount of documents that needed enveloping.

I can see myself standing there in some autistic trance as the hostess approached me, and I'd like to shout at myself to wake the fuck up and do something, but instead, when the pretty young hostess holding the large menu and an impossibly white smile said, "One, sir?" I just said yes and allowed her to seat me at the counter with all the other parties of one, guys sipping coffee and staring straight ahead like they were at a bank of urinals. I just ordered a coffee and slice of apple pie, and left the envelope sitting beside me for the next four cups of dreggy joe. When my nerves felt like piano wires, I finally opened the envelope. There was no title yet, just *My Book* by Edith McWeeney. The formatting on the table of contents was a little funny, everything centered like a submission for a junior high poetry class. I flipped through the manuscript until I came to one page that read, *Part Two: The Case of the Black Dahlia.*

I let the hefty manuscript sit there while I sipped cup number five. My dad had always said to drink coffee black (which seemed strong, manly) so you don't get fat (which seemed weak, effete) so when I made the decision to become caffeine-dependent in high school, I poured in the cream and sugar, a habit I've never been able to shake. And now I'm getting fat.

"That for the Cooley adaptation?" It was the guy sitting next to me. He was wearing a tropically patterned shirt and a hat with *Jumanji* stitched onto it.

"Excuse me?"

He made a head-butting gesture toward the manuscript. "I heard Paramount scored the rights to Cooley's Black Dahlia book. You working on that? Buddy a mine said they got Elmore Leonard to do the screenplay. That'd be a lineup, huh? Leonard adapting a Cooley novel, it'd be like Chandler adapting Cain's *Double Indemnity*, right?" He flagged down the waitress, said, "S'cuse me, can this Rob Roy get a little more grenadine, please?" and as the girl poured a three-count of cherry syrup into his Coke, he turned back to me and said, "So is it true Cooley lives in the Sharon Tate house? Name's Burnet," wiping his hand on his cargo shorts then extending it to me for a shake.

I took some bills from my wallet, threw them on the counter, gathered my sister's manuscript, and left. As I drove to our old Van Nuys house, the sun was starting to go down, its orange rays shooting straight down Ventura Blvd., illuminating every speck of dirt on the inside of my windshield, turning it opaque. When I got to our old house, the sun was down, no longer a nuisance. Lights were on and a car was in the driveway, so I parked a few houses down, turned off my headlights. I sat there for quite a while, turned on the radio, found Garrison Keillor spinning some folksy yarn. With one eye on my childhood home, I rooted through the glove box, found a pack of cigarettes that must have been Chris's. Perhaps feeling a little insecure, like *A Prairie Home Companion* was not a proper stakeout soundtrack, I pushed the cigarette lighter down, let its coil get red-hot, and lit myself a smoke. I coughed for a good long while, opened the car door to throw up a little on the side of the road, but by the second cigarette I had it down cold. I cracked the car window, Garrison Keillor's avuncular voice suddenly seeming wraith-like as it crept out into the night with my smoky exhalations. The lights in my old house finally went out and Edie came out, followed by Rory. They got into what must have been Rory's car—a sensible Dodge station wagon, which disappointed me, as I imagined him driving an old VW van, some Merry Prankstersish doodles graffitied onto the sides—and they drove off, with me following at a safe, unnoticeable distance. They went to a small Greek restaurant in North Hollywood, which, like an alarming number of local establishments, seemed secretively cloaked in tropical flora, as if all the restaurateurs in the San Fernando Valley hoped for low-rent Mafioso clientele. Because of this, I had to park my car and walk around to the side of the restaurant where the Dumpsters sat, and peer in a window through a bush with large, Jurassic leaves, just in order to see anything.

Oliver had been waiting for them, and all three were now shaking hands, smiling. It seemed as though this were their first face-to-face meeting, but there was a familiarity surely bred from multiple phone conversations. The restaurant was not very busy and the servers lounged in the background like extras uninterested in playing their parts. It was a Sunday night, and I wondered if orthodox Greeks had any special rules about Sundays. (That Anthony Quinn movie didn't mention anything about Sundays, as far as I could remember, but perhaps it was sacrosanct and the proprietors of this restaurant had to break from tradition in order to accommodate hungry Americans whose appetites were indifferent to the Sabbath. I imagined passionate intergenerational arguments between swarthy men in aprons.) Oliver, Edie, and Rory sat at a table in front of a large mural depicting a Mediterranean paradise: Corinthian columns flanking a sylvan landscape, winged cherubs hovering over plump grapevines; there was also a goat. Oliver seemed very excited as he (I can assume) told Edie and Rory about all the wonderful things that he could do for her (their?) book, how she would become the darling of the publishing world.

"You've really got something here," he'd said to me, ten years ago, upon reading my first novel. We were sitting in his Hoboken loft, drinking bourbon, and he hefted the twelve-hundred-page manuscript and made a herniating face. "A whole *lot* of something." We laughed and got drunk and he did his Tom Snyder impression, interviewing me about my big debut novel. I slept on his couch that night and in the morning woke up to his girlfriend standing over me. She looked insomniac, or maybe Eastern European, and she told me to follow her. I did, to the bedroom closet, where she threw me a T-shirt and told me to put it on. Oliver was just waking up in the bed next to us, his hair a tsunami pompadour, his eyes looking swollen shut like a newborn puppy's. I put on the T-shirt. It was very old and very soft and had the Clash's *London Calling* cover screenprinted on it. "You are small like a girl," she said. "I bought it but it doesn't fit me, so it is yours." I wore that shirt on the flight back home that day and imagined I'd wear it when the real Tom Snyder interviewed me about my big debut. I don't know what happened to that girl, but I saw someone who looks like her on a recent episode of *Law & Order*, so maybe things are working out for her. Regardless, the shirt doesn't fit me anymore.

When Oliver and Edie and Rory were done with their meal, they all shook hands again and smiled some more. Oliver's client-greasing had gotten much more professional, I suppose, less personal. At their dinner, I saw a lot of spanakopita, saw a lot of baklava, but I didn't see any bourbon, didn't see any vintage T-shirts. I followed Oliver's rental car back to his hotel, a La Quinta Inn near the freeway. The Oliver of ten years ago, the Oliver who would never have given Edie's egregious tripe a second glance, would have been staying on the other side of the hill at the Chateau Marmont, or at least a nice Radisson. But here he was, in the copper light of an empty parking lot. Of course it wasn't just Oliver's professional fortunes that seemed to be waning. I wasn't blind. I knew that our relationship had been waning for some time as well. If it hadn't, I wouldn't have been so hesitant to get out of my car, walk up and talk some sense into him right there in the parking lot. But most of our friendship, in fact, had consisted of me trying to save it, keeping those memories of grad school alive. Even that night in Hoboken had been my initiative. We'd talked on the phone about my book and when I said I was coming into town, he said to meet at his office. I then said I needed a place to crash and suggested his couch. I had to make a plea for the old days, hoping he was finding post-MFA life as lonesome as I was. Although I like to remember leaving New York that day with that T-shirt and Oliver's approval for the novel I'd spent years writing, I often forget that I also left with the knowledge that real friendship was a luxury of maudlin youth, that grad school had simply been a desperate attempt to prolong that longer than was societally responsible, so we could have a few more years of late-night drunk talk, our attentions coke-piqued, about Things That Mattered, like the state of American fiction, how we'd be friends forever, how this blow tastes like sweetener. We had now graduated, moved on into grown-up solitude, finally understood that comradeship was a matter of convenience and proximity. But if I am to be honest with myself here, I'd have to admit that our friendship had started to wane even before graduation.

In our final semester at Iowa, Oliver asked me to go with him to Chicago to buy some blow. He said his regular guy was gone, so he'd found a new guy, but he needed a spotter, since this was a new guy. I was happy to be his spotter. It was February, still gray and cold, and the heater in my car was busted. A resolute easterner, Oliver still didn't have a car of his own. As a Californian, I was baffled—and inexplicably offended—that anyone could get by without a car, like someone saying they just didn't bother to grow feet. So we drove the five hours to Chicago with our breath visible in front of us like empty voice bubbles in a rather dull comic strip. The gray sky matched the gray ground, the horizon just a blurry line drawn across a slab of cement. When we got to Chicago, I was amazed to be in what seemed to be a real American city for the first time, amazed to realize that this was the farthest east I'd ever been before. It was so dense and so tall, and I wanted everyone to be walking around with fedoras and briefcases, hurrying to get to whatever it was people did in cities like this—meetings, rendezvous with mistresses, more meetings. Instead I just saw people bundled in parkas looking like they had no particular place to go.

We stopped at a gas station where Oliver hopped out and called the guy from a pay phone.

"He gave me directions," Oliver said, getting back in the car.

"To his place?" I asked.

"To another pay phone."

We followed the directions to the other pay phone, which was outside an OTB place so there was a short line of trenchcoated gamblers waiting for the phone. Oliver waited patiently in line, while I waited nervously in the car, my emergency lights on while I idled in front of a hydrant. I tried to catch his eye a few times—conversation had been as sparse as the flora on the drive and I probably just wanted some sort of reassurance, though of what I'm not exactly sure—but he was intently focused on his line-waiting, on fitting in with these degenerate gamblers so as not to arouse suspicion. He finally made it to the pay phone and made the call.

"He gave me directions," Oliver said, getting back in the car.

"To another pay phone?" I asked.

"To his place. Find a place to park. It's on the next block."

The only spot I could find was outside a convenience store where half a dozen guys of indeterminate ethnicity huddled. As we wandered around looking for the address, bundled up in our peacoats, I said, "I feel like that scene in *Some Like It Hot*," following behind him, "you know when Tony Curtis and Jack Lemmon are wandering around Chicago, when it's all blizzardy, after they lose their winter coats on a horse race. Greased Lightning! You remember that part?"

"What?" he said, trying to find the address on the awning of a building. "No."

"Yeah, you remember. *Some Like It Hot*, right before they witness the St. Valentine's Day Massacre."

"Never saw it."

"What? Sure you did. Tony Curtis, Jack Lemmon, Marilyn Monroe."

"Okay, shut up," he said. "This is it."

We were at an unassuming door on the side of a brick building, the dozen tiny mailboxes on the wall beside it the only way you'd know it was a place of residence. Oliver rang the buzzer and we heard a static-y voice say, "What."

"Mongoose," Oliver said.

I was quietly thrilled by the clichéd theatricality of it all—there was a password!—and wanted to comment on this to Oliver but he seemed too in-character to be receptive at the moment.

The guy rang us in and we trudged up four flights of stairs so steep I was eye-level with Oliver's oxfords.

"This is like that scene in *Vertigo*," I said.

The chamber acoustics of the stairwell amplified my voice.

"Just play this cool, okay?" Oliver said.

When we got to the door, Oliver knocked. We heard heavy foot-steps approach the door and, assuming that the guy was looking at us through the peephole, we—or at least I—tried to look as uncoplike as possible while not looking so naïve as to be easily conned. Sometimes I think part of me has forever lived in the moment when you suspect someone is looking at you through a peephole, trying to look respectable, all the while knowing my face is distorted into absurdity by the fish-eye lens.

The guy opened the door. He looked like a linebacker. (Days later, as Oliver and I told a heavily censored version of this story to some classmates, having already agreed on which parts we'd omit, Oliver would gloss my description: "By 'linebacker,' of course Paul means he was a big black guy. Don't be coy with your racism.") He was wearing a baby blue terry cloth robe, and there were little geometric bits of shaving cream on his otherwise freshly shorn head, which glowed in a faint halo, a bright light coming from inside the apartment.

"You Olly?" he said.

"Yeah. This is Paul."

"You didn't say the password," I said.

"He already said it," the guy said, "at the intercom. Don't need to say it twice."

"Oh, right."

He let us into the living room, locking the door behind us. The windows were covered in sheets. At first, I thought it was for aesthetic reasons, as they gave the room a nice harem feel, but then I saw the sixteen-millimeter film projector set up behind the couch, projecting a blank square of light onto the screen pulled down on the other side of the room. It was the only light on in the place.

"Sit yo asses down," the guy said. We did, and he disappeared into the next room.

Oliver and I stared at the blank movie screen, and listened to distant shouting that might have actually been a dog barking.

"You must have seen *Some Like It Hot*. There's no way you haven't seen it."

Oliver placed his hand in his hip pocket where I knew he had the money. It looked like he was preparing to draw a weapon, which was probably not the smartest pose to strike, but I didn't say anything.

The guy came back into the room with a desk drawer in his hands. He set the drawer on the coffee table and then sat down between us. "Five dollars a line," he said. "I chop."

From the drawer he removed a mirror, a gold straw, and a very full plastic bag.

Oliver—I could only hear his voice on the far side of this guy—said, "We were thinking of getting a gram. Like, to go."

"No to-go orders," the guy said. "It's by the line. Dine-in only.

New policy. I chop. You put down the five spot, do what you do. It only leaves this apartment in your brain, not in your pocket. Po-po crackdowns. New policy. I chop."

I could see only Oliver's knees and his thin fingers shuffling over his knees. I could hear the guy's deviated septum as he breathed. Oliver's hand emerged from the other side of the guy and dropped a ten on the coffee table.

"All right, then," the guy said, then leaned down and started chopping. As he did, Oliver and I looked at each other over his back. Oliver shrugged, mouthed the word *Stay?*

We did. Oliver and I were usually pretty chatty on blow—logorrhea and compulsive oversharing being one of the drug's oddly pleasurable, though occasionally problematic, effects, just like the always-frustrating tumescence it gives me—but even after a few lines we were still too intimidated by this guy to say much of anything. Perhaps it was the aura of sweaty awkwardness—the three of us just sitting side by side on the couch, Oliver periodically laying down another ten—or maybe this was the plan all along, but the guy eventually said, "Got just the thing for you two," then stood up, walked behind the couch—my heart flapping wildly against my ribcage—and started tinkering with something metallic. Too scared and high to look behind me, I just stared straight ahead and imagined the various medieval torture devices the guy was piecing together. Then I heard that familiar baseball-card-in-the-spokes sound that reminded me of old home movies, and suddenly the screen in front of us was alive with action. It took a moment in my brain for the shapes to go from abstract to familiar and then congeal into coherent action. With today's proliferation of pornography, via cable, VCRs, and the

Internet, it's easy to forget what life was like when those images weren't so ubiquitous, and how surprising it could be in 1976 to see two adults in the midst of sexual congress. I probably hadn't really observed two people fucking since that screening of *I Am Curious (Yellow)* I'd gone to in Santa Monica two years earlier. Suffice it to say, my experience with smut had been severely limited to the subtitled variety shot in blurry chiaroscuro. By the time the guy sat back down between Oliver and me, the shocking focus and overlit Kodachrome palate of this feature alerted me to the fact that this was not the work of a French auteur; this was genuine filth. And it wasn't until I got over this excitement that I realized there was no lady in this mix. Though nearly hairless, the smaller of the two on-screen principals was, in fact, male.

Oliver laid down another ten.

My mind focused by the alarming amount of cocaine we were doing (I was beginning to realize that Oliver was intent on spending all the money we'd brought when we thought take-out was an option), I studied the movie, fascinated by the strange geometry of the action. I was ready to burst inside. I needed to talk. The blow was grinding my molars down to nubs, my palate and nose were numb, and I had all sorts of ideas and questions about the semiotics of gay porn, but I was following Oliver's lead and Oliver wasn't saying anything, so I did my best to remain silent; you would have needed pliers to unclench my teeth. Ron laid down another ten. I heard the barking again. It seemed closer. I desperately wanted to ask the guy if homosexual couplings always consist of a typically masculine male—hairy, brutish—with a more feminine partner—thin, smoother skin, finer features—as we saw in this particular film, or was this simply a conceit of the genre that suggested a heterosexual standard was being projected onto homo-sexual relations? I'd write a paper about this! Ron started hiccupping, something he often did on blow. The guy crossed his arms and I caught a wicked whiff of what I figured to be Cool Water. I gave a sympathy hiccup. I noticed that I'd been picking at a loose thread in my sleeve, which was now about an inch shorter. A third gentleman now joined the two on screen. Ron laid another ten on the table, and the guy kept scratching his crotch.

(I must stop here. I see that I've made a rather embarrassing blun-der. All those *Rons* in the above paragraph should really be *Olivers*. In the space between that paragraph and this paragraph was about five minutes of anxious fretting, seeing if I could simply use some liquid paper to cover up the *Rons* and replace them with *Olivers*, but of course that wouldn't work. *Ron* is only three letters. *Oliver* is six. If I were to Wite-Out every *Ron* and try to type it over with *Oliver*, the *er* of *Oliver* would inevitably overlap with each successive word. And that whole paragraph would then just be a jumble of nonsense. Once I realized this, I was moments away from tearing that whole sheet of paper from my IBM Wheelwriter 1000, crumpling it up, tossing it into the waste-basket, and starting with a clean, *Ron*-less leaf of white, 20 lb, 92 bright paper. But then I realized this was a perfect opportunity to come clean, to admit that I've been transcribing much of the above scene from a short story I wrote in 1979 called, simply, "Chicago." I have it here next to me on my desk. I brought it out because it is a largely autobiographi-cal tale, and so I figured if I were to recount the real incident here, twenty years later, I should have some assistance from the me who was, in 1979, at a better proximity to remember it with more precision.

Of course the short story version has a few fictionalized details. The narrator's brother died in Vietnam. The narrator has a girlfriend back in Iowa who is really beautiful. The narrator is six foot two. And the character based on Oliver is named Ron. But the rest is pretty spot-on. After writing the story, I mailed it to Oliver, who was at the time an intern at Doubleday and reading submissions for *The Paris Review*. I then waited eagerly for his phone call, the one in which he'd pass the phone off to George Plimpton, who would congratulate me on "such a fine piece of literary craft"—he'd communicate only in blurb-speak, of course, in his New England drawl—but after calling Oliver a couple times, he finally read it and simply mailed the manuscript back to me, its margins flourished with his Arabic-like scrawl.)

The following morning, when Oliver shouted, apropos of nothing, "We have to go! We have to go now!" (Oliver's 1979 marginalia: *"Apropos of nothing"? Is the reader supposed to take that seriously, or is it an indication of this narrator's* [the note bending up the page] *myopia, and if so, how does that inform the rest of the story?*), the profusely sweating guy just looked at us, his eyes almost albino-pink, and said, "Ya'll don't have to go. You should stay." (Oliver: *It's probably more realistic that he did not, in fact, say this, probably more likely that the narrator was, in fact, the one who wanted to stay.*) The guy just sat there, however, as Oliver and I headed for the door without turning our backs on him. "Thanks," I said. Then Oliver tried to open the door, realized we were locked in. I panicked, tried to help him manage the absurd number of bolts on the metal door. There was even one of those steel rods, one end of which sits in a metal-sheathed divot in the floor, the other end against the door. I removed the rod, and since it took some muscle and maneuvering on my part, when it finally came unwedged it swung backward in my hands and clanked cacophonously (Oliver: *"clanked cacophonously"–seriously?*) against what appeared to be a moped engine— or perhaps a motorcycle engine with pedals glued to it–sitting on the countertop behind us. "Sorry," I said, realizing that I was shouting, then began whispering, "Sorry, sorry," like an incantation as we continued to try to unlock the door, which was beginning to feel like some biblical test, the final crucible in the escape from the lion's den, the unlocking of the three dozen deadbolts of Judea. Just when I thought an aneurism was inevitable, the guy, suddenly behind us, reached over our heads, undid the small trinket of a lock at the very top of the door, opened it for us, and said, "Drive safe now."

I certainly tried to drive safe, but with my heart trying to crawl up my sinuses it wasn't easy. Oliver—both the 1976 passenger in my car and the 1979 editor in the margins of the story—remained entirely silent for the five-hour drive back home. Here follows two pages of florid descriptions of the flora-less landscape between Chicago and Iowa City, which I employed to convey the long stretched-out silence and coke-induced awareness of everything. But I'll skip all that and get to final line of the story: "That was the last time Ron and I did drugs together. I miss our conversations."

Oliver did offer one small note, after two pages of silence, tucked away at the bottom of the last page: *A bit sentimental, don't you think?*

Oliver was always excoriating me to be subtler, which at the time I took to mean he didn't want to hear what I had to say, preferred it hidden beneath artifice. But I must have feared that he was right, which was why, a year later, when I finally did get that story published,

I neglected to tell him about it. Of course, at the time I told myself that I was embarrassed not by the story but by the venue (it appeared in *COLAtitude Review*, a two-staple lit rag run by the COLA poetry club and distributed for free in the commons on a rack next to the vending machines). But I suspect now that there was something in that story that I didn't want to show Oliver again, like something I'd blurted out in a drunken moment and wished I could take back. Maybe he was right. Maybe I was sentimental. But so what? Isn't that the point? Boats against the current and all that? Not for the ever-cool Oliver, who seemed to have nothing pulling him back, had no affinity for a shared past, was wired to look only forward. Even as he stood there in the La Quinta Inn parking lot, leaning his head down to the open window of my car, he told me, "You're not very subtle, are you?"

"I wasn't trying to hide."

"What were you trying to do?"

"I just wanted to talk to you."

"There are less psychotic ways, you know."

Oliver's features looked a little more finely etched now than they had that afternoon, the seams in his face a little deeper, the lines more spidery. Perhaps it was the strange light or the contrast of my nostalgia, but I could see the gray at his temples, a single hair wiring out of his nostril. I got out of the car. He backed away a little. "Oliver," I said, "you can't seriously be taking Edie seriously. She's seriously unstable. She's seriously insane. She's just looking for attention."

"Paul. Just read the manuscript. I'm serious when I say—I mean, I mean it when I say I think there's a way you can be involved with this. Just—talk to me when you've read it, okay?"

A platoon of cleaning women was unloading from a van on the opposite side of the parking lot with military order and precision, like the A-Team disguised in dark-bunned wigs and gingham skirts.

A bouncy digital chime went off and Oliver pulled a cell phone from his pocket, one of those ones that folds clamshell-like in half. "Yeah," he said into the phone, "I'm on my way up. Don't touch that stuff, just watch some TV." He hung up, turned ten degrees toward La Quinta, looked at me.

"Hey," I said. "You remember that story about Chicago?"

"Chicago? You mean that time we saw them in concert?"

"No," I said. We'd never seen Chicago in concert; he must have been thinking of someone else. "You remember. That story I wrote. There was that guy, and we drove there."

"I'm sorry, Paul. I need to get back to the room. I need to give Yuna her nighttime pills. I'm really sorry I can't talk right now." He approached me and gave me a quick half-hug thing, and a very conclusive backslap, then before I could figure out how exactly to reciprocate, he was walking across the parking lot, looking back at me and saying, "Read your sister's book, okay? And call me."

I did what he said. Unfortunately, not in that order. First, from a pay phone a block away, its receiver redolent of vinegary piss, I called his cell phone, the number of which I had on his business card. I was going to tell him about getting "Chicago" published, though I'd probably omit the part about it being fifteen years ago in a Xeroxed zine; I'd tell him it was forthcoming in *Ploughshares*, *VQR*, or *The Quarterly*, all three maybe. His phone rang for a while, then went to voicemail. I hesitated for a moment, listened to my breath being fed back to me in the earpiece—how exactly does one address an answering machine, especially one like this that wasn't even an answering machine, this thing that was no longer a physical box to hold my message but rather something ephemeral, floating out there in the ether: *Where was my voice going?*—so I hung up, and called again. This time it went directly to his voicemail. I hung up and went home where I took forty milligrams of time-release Ritalin, sat down with my sister's manuscript, and read it straight through.

By the time I finished, it was morning. The light was orange and thick through the windows, like that old vaudeville trick of holding a bottle of rye in front of the spotlight. Chris was up and pouring himself some cereal before heading off to school. He saw me in the living room, three hundred pages stacked on my lap, and said, "Just give 'em all Bs." It took me a moment to register what he said, to realize that he thought I'd been grading papers all night again, and then I realized that I too had school to get to. It was Monday and I had four classes today, two sections of comp, two sections of lit. I stood up off the couch only to realize that my legs had lost all feeling, were now just two leg-shaped sandbags. They folded beneath me and I collapsed to the floor. Chris burst out laughing, a sound I hadn't heard in quite a while, though it was muddled and warbly from the milk and cereal in his mouth. I tried to shake my hips a little to urge some blood flow to my legs, but it wasn't working, so I just kept shaking some more. In response to all my twitching and writhing, still a pile of useless limbs on the floor, Chris said, "Oh, wait. Shit, are you having a seizure or something? Are you being real or just trying to be funny?" That "trying" rather annoyed me, since if this were an attempt at humor I'd say it damn well succeeded, since he had, after all, laughed. Despite the fact that humor was not actually my goal here, and that slapstick is not my preferred mode even when humor is my goal (I'm more Noël Coward than Three Stooges, if I can say so myself), Chris never gives me enough credit as a wit. Anyway. There I was, twitching on the floor, calmly cursing Chris for not helping me, curses that I instantly regretted since he just walked away, leaving me to help my own damn self off the floor.

I managed to shake some blood back into my legs, walk around a bit, banging my feet on the floor until I stopped feeling like someone with cerebral palsy, just in time to brew some coffee and hit the road for my morning classes, my mind the whole time trying to process what I'd spent the entire night reading. It had been surreal, reading a narrative featuring people I knew, my father, my mother, my sister, myself even, being puppetted into characters, familiar people acting in unfamiliar ways. The George McWeeney in Edie's book both was and was not my father. I recognized the man: Her descriptions of him were eerily accurate, reminding me of details I'd long since forgotten—the patchy stubble that told us he'd been working too much, the smell of the cracked Naugahyde chair in his office, the way he just said "hmmm" in a warm way instead of laughing and how you knew that was somehow more genuine than a laugh. In one scene, while Mom was pregnant with me and visiting her parents in New York, Edie describes our father trying to water the potted flowers in our backyard: He's wearing slacks, wingtips, a tie, holding our mother's handwritten "while I'm away" instructions in one hand, the hose in the other; so focused on rereading the instructions to make sure he's doing it right, he doesn't even notice that he's flooding the poor geraniums. That seems about right. But there are other scenes, other recovered memories, the crux of her case against him, of that same man doing horrific things—he was at once human and marionette to Edie's demented puppeteer.

"Yo, Mr. Weeney. Wake up."

It happens sometimes, coming to in the middle of a class. It's a bit like arriving home and not remembering the drive; when the action is something you've done a million times, your brain just doesn't bother to record the particular glitches and record-scratches that distinguish it. Same with this class. I'd been teaching it for fifteen years, saying the same thing. I'd been on autopilot, a trance, a blackout, giving the same rote lecture I'd been giving since the eighties. Or at least that's what I assumed. "Oh, yes," I said to the class. "Where was I?"

"Nowhere," a young man in a Lakers jersey said. "You've just been standing there for like ten minutes."

The young man was surely exaggerating to get a laugh from his classmates (which they enthusiastically gave). I shrugged it off and turned to the chalkboard. It was blank. I turned back to the class and—figuring it was the beginning of the semester and time to dive into some fundamentals—said, "The five elements of an argument," instantly finding the groove, those words I'd said a million times suddenly cueing me back into the scene. "The five essential building blocks of academic rhetoric. With these five tools you will join in learned and erudite conversations with your fellow student-scholars. What are they? Pens and pencils at the ready. One, thesis. Two, reasons. Three, evidence. Four, warrants. Five, counterarguments."

And so I got through the day, the whole time fragmented scenes and errant imagery from Edie's insane narrative flashing through my head. The sound of George McWeeney washing his old medical tools in the pool house sink, "the sonar ping of the stainless steel." The way Edie described our father with "a smile tucked into the side of his mouth like a toothpick." The way these little snatches popped into my head throughout the day, it was not unlike her descriptions of what recovering memories had been like, how after her first sessions with Dr. Beach, she'd be going about her business, at the grocery store, waiting for the bus, cleaning the bathroom, and there'd be a little flash of something familiar but unplaceable, "like a butterfly darting in front of a movie projector, for one brief and unrecognizable moment the light shining through its diaphanous wings, projecting a new and strange color onto the screen, but the moment the audience notices it—it's gone."

I realize that this is the second something-in-front-of-a-projecting-light metaphor in the span of four pages, the first one mine (the one about the light like someone was holding a bottle of rye in front of a spotlight), the second one my sister's (above), and sure, perhaps my sister's (admittedly) nice butterfly imagery could have been in my head when I'd been sitting there on the couch thinking that thing about the morning light, and perhaps part of my preoccupation that day was out of simple jealousy, that it was the sentences I wish I'd written that were bugging me, not the ideas they denoted, but we cannot be distracted by pretty sentences. A cute metaphor does not a truth make. We must address ourselves to the lie these sentences deliver. And I will, in short time, address the specifics of the case my sister makes against our father, thoroughly refute all of the so-called evidence she produces to tie him to the Black Dahlia murder. But first, as Det. Mike Nolan says, "Let's start with the facts."

When I was done with my classes that day, I drove over to UCLA's Research Library, where I spent the rest of the day hunched over a backlit screen reading microfiches of newspapers from 1947. I'm writing this from my notes, but the following are facts, without any of my sister's novelistic flourishes. I am laying these facts out in order to clearly distinguish what is known from what (in Edie's book) is imagined. Here goes:

Around 10:30 AM, on January 15, 1947, a passerby was pushing her three-year-old daughter by some vacant lots in the Leimert Park neighborhood of Los Angeles when she noticed the dead body of a young woman. The body was nude, and cut in half at the waist. The passerby called the police. A few blocks away, *Los Angeles Examiner* reporter Will Fowler and photographer Felix Paegel were in their car, heading back to the *Examiner* office, when they heard on their short-wave radio, which they kept tuned to the LAPD's frequency, a report of a "390 W 415" at a vacant lot in Leimert Park. "390 W 415" is cop-code for an intoxicated woman who is indecently exposing herself. Fowler and Paegel found only the second part of that. They were the first ones on the scene. If I can editorialize for a moment, I can't help but wonder if this fact, that the media were the first on the scene, was not prescient in that it prefigured how this would very quickly and forevermore be the media's case, far more than the LAPD's case. I'm not just talking about a simple harmony, a pat little anecdote; I mean to imply that there was some actual causation here. To wit: Two years ago, I took Chris on a vacation up to the Redwood National Park in

Northern California. I had gone camping there once as a kid (not with Dad; he was not an outdoorsy man; Mom took us; it was the year before she left for Africa and she was starting to get restless; I'd find out later that she'd been reading Paul Goodman; nonetheless it was fun; I went fishing), and, wanting Chris to have all the normal family vacation-type things that I'd had, I drove him up there. He was sullen the whole drive up, but as soon as we got into the redwoods, he perked up, became excited. Turns out they filmed *Return of the Jedi* there, and Chris, who used to harbor sci-fi-ish tendencies (I'm not entirely sure if he still does), was scanning the dense woods for Ewoks. Anyway, the point here is that when we got to the two-bed cabin I'd reserved (having no wish to have Chris watch me attempt any sort of tent building; those things have always seemed like some atavistic brainteaser, designed less to provide shelter than humility, the springy ribs of the construction always whipping back up at you and smacking you in the face like an errant tree branch), Chris was the first in the door, and he said in an alarmingly loud voice, "I call this bed!" jumping on what was clearly the better berth. Now, I know I was the adult in this situation, and it should have been written into my parental DNA to sacrifice myself for my child, but Darwinian evolution does not extend to bed selection, especially when one bed is near a lovely window and the other has to share a wall with the bathroom so its sleeper is forced to hear whatever nocturnal pissings the other has to make. Besides, Chris is not technically my child, so I'm exempt from parental selflessness and am allowed to desire the better bed. But of course, Chris had called it. He'd been the first in the door. He'd called it, so it was his. Those are the rules, which are surely even more primal in their logic than are any of Darwin's, and so I had to let Chris have the better bed. So too, the police—though not consciously—ceded control of the Black Dahlia case to the media. The media were there first; they called it. The police, however, for their part, did figure out a few things. Det. Sgt. Harry Hansen saw that the body had been drained of blood, almost preserved, but there was very little blood on the ground, save for some red footprints. She had been murdered elsewhere, and dumped here—or rather, displayed. Hansen had police interview people who lived in the area. Mr. R. Meyer reported seeing a black, late-thirties Ford sedan parked near the crime scene for a few minutes around 6:30 AM. Bobby Jones, a thirteen-year-old paperboy, said he saw a black Ford sedan when he began his route at about 4:00 AM. While this was originally taken as an incongruity, according to Fowler's account, Harry Hansen considered that both could be correct when a man's wristwatch was found at the scene. The watch did not seem to be affected by the elements, so it was possible that the murderer had dumped the body around 4:00 AM, then, realizing he'd left his watch, come back at 6:30 to look for it. The watch was, according to the *Hollywood Citizen News*, a "17-jewel Croton with a leather bound, steel snap band." Just like the watch, the victim's body seemed unaffected by the elements, which confirmed that she'd been dumped there in the early hours of dawn. Her killer had not just cut her in half; he had brutally slashed her breasts and cut her cheeks in what I believe is called a Glasgow smile. She was so disfigured that she remained unrecognized and unidentified for two days. During that time, she was given a full autopsy—the real results of which Edie claims to have, even though it is still officially classified.

I've been trying to track down the real report in order to prove Edie's is a fake, and while I haven't actually done that yet, I have made some excellent strides in that direction.

The past week or so I've been trying to get someone at the coroner's office to talk to me, hoping to find someone who can thoroughly invalidate Edie's supposed autopsy report. It's been harder that you might think. Calling on the phone is no good. The coroner's office is so used to fielding calls from the media, cranks, and necrophiliacs that they've set up a directory so labyrinthine, so full of *push one for this and two for that*, that by the time it connects you to an actual person, it's just some intern—"This is Tommy, how can I help you?"—reading from a script— "I'm sorry, sir, we cannot give out that information." Then, this morning, after a week of this same rote reply, when Tommy started getting snippy with me, I finally decided to head down to the morgue myself and find some answers. The county morgue is in the middle of downtown L.A., surrounded by courthouses and parking garages patrolled by tire-chalking attendants. It's the kind of square cement building that in another context you might mistake for a modern art gallery; you might think its austere anti-aesthetic was intentional. I walked in the only entrance that seemed exclusively for the living and found a lobby half filled with people studiously scratching at paperwork. I went up to the receptionist-like lady and, through the asterisk of holes in the Plexiglas window, said, "Hi, listen, I'm here on a little fact-checking mission. You see, I'm trying to find out if a document someone purports to be a copy of an official autopsy report is in fact authentic. I know it's a fake, but I need to be thorough. To whom should I speak about this? And please don't say Tommy. I've already spoken with him and found him to be quite unhelpful." Underneath the window, the receptionist pushed a clipboard with a ballpoint pen strung to it, along with a small plastic bag filled with what looked to be gauzy underwear. That's when I noticed she had earphones on, a Walkman sitting beside her elbow. I took the materials just as a door to my left swung open. A middle-aged guy with sweaty short sleeves and an oily comb-over said, "All right, everyone, get your gear on and let's get going. Follow me." Everyone in the lobby had already opened his or her plastic bag and they were all now outfitting themselves with the contents: fitting sheer cotton booties over their shoes, latex gloves over their hands, and surgical masks over their faces. These masks were not the surgical masks I'd seen before, but rather made from two cotton flaps that came together in a horizontal seam across the mouth, making the whole thing look like the bill of a giant duck. I figured this might be a good chance to get behind closed doors and find what I was looking for, so I suited up and followed the pack into a small screening room. It wasn't until the main feature started playing—*The Dangers of Drinking and Driving*, a cartoon featuring an off-brand Donald Duck named Daniel—that I realized I'd snuck in with the wrong crowd. Though a cartoon, the video featured real-life photos of people killed in drunk-driving accidents. There was one body that had been caught in a car fire, and he or she was completely charred, black and crisp, intestines literally cooked and bursting out of the belly. Beside me, a teenage girl with a fishhook brow piercing said, "Mmmm, looks like giant pasta." After the video, I tried to explain to our tour guide—whose name I'd later find out is Charles—that I was in the wrong place, to which he said, "That's what everyone says. Now follow me." And so I did follow him, along with the rest of the offenders, through two sets of swinging doors, into the morgue. "I almost forgot," Charles said, "breathe through your mouth!" But it was too late; the smell hit me like pepper spray. When my eyes cleared, I didn't see any dead bodies, just the whole awkward bunch of us making our way through a bare, fluorescent-lit hall. Charles was leading the way, saying, "Now, everyone, I'm about to take you into the main holding area. Along the sides of the hall, you will see what your active little imaginations are haunted with right now—the potential consequences of your boneheaded actions: dead folks, lined up patiently like they're here for Aerosmith tickets. Don't touch them, and they won't touch you." After months of poring over those crime-scene photos, I was expecting, without realizing it, the bodies to be black-and-white, two-dimensional, safely limited to the small rectangle of someone else's viewfinder. So when we turned the corner—"Have a good look, my little buzzards," Charles said—and actually saw them—real dead bodies, on gurneys, no sheets covering them, naked, bloated, their skin looking moldy-fruit soft—I began to get sick. "Uh-oh," Charles said, "we got a live one!" I thought for a moment he meant one of the bodies, like they'd accidentally interned a very sound sleeper who was just now waking to find himself toe-tagged in a morgue, but when Charles quickly ushered me to the restroom, I realized he was talking about me. After tearing off my duck-mask and retching in the surprisingly clean facilities, I walked out of the stall and Charles handed me a scrap of paper towel. "Thanks," I said.

"Happens to the best of us," he said.

"I only came here for some information, some help on a—a thing I'm working on."

"Well," he said, "only help I can offer you is this: Get a bigger ball."

Assuming this was some sort of testicle reference, an imperative to man-up at the specter of death, I said, "I had some bad tuna tartare for lunch. That was probably it."

"No," he said, "this," pointing to my right thumb, which had become a little swollen around the joint. "I can spot bowler's thumb a mile away. You need a ball that fits."

"I just use whatever they have at the lanes."

"There's your problem. Put 'em up," he said, holding up his hand as if to pledge allegiance. He made me put my hand, still clammy, against his own, which was cold and dry, and inspected our mirrored fingers. "You're about my size," he said.

Then one of the drunk drivers opened the restroom door, saw these two middle-aged men, shod like babies, doing what surely looked like some sort of intergalactic gesture of peace, and said, "Uh, we're still waitin' out there."

I'm still feeling a little queasy from today's adventure and wasn't able to eat much of Julia's potato skin salad tonight (it's truly disconcerting how concerned that woman is with dietary fiber), but before I left the morgue, Charles gave me his phone number, telling me to give him a call about a good bowling ball he might be able to sell me: So I now have a potential inside source, someone who might be able to help settle this whole issue of the autopsy report.

But I'm getting ahead of myself. Back to 1947: In the days after the murder, the newspapers reported what gruesome details they had, but without the identity of the victim they were quick to fly off into flights of terrifying fancy. Aggie Underwood—a reporter for *The Herald-Express* who, by all reports, was one of the few who managed to keep her lunch down at the crime scene—suspected the work of a werewolf. *The Express* was Hearst's evening paper, which flirted with bald sensationalism more than his morning paper, *The Examiner*, where Will Fowler broke the story about the victim's identity. Fingerprints, Fowler reported on January 16, identified her as Elizabeth "Betty" Short. According to FBI files, she'd been born in Hyde Park, MA, July 29, 1924, making her twenty-two at the time of her death. The reason this was on record was that she'd been arrested on September 23, 1943, after causing a drunken disturbance with a few soldiers near an army base a couple hours north of Los Angeles. Already, a real person was starting to come into focus. Here on the front page was her old mug shot—her dark hair looking wild, her mouth slightly agape, her irises appearing too light to be focused on anything you or I could see, almost spectral—and here in the three-column article was the hint of a backstory: She'd come from the East, probably with dreams of stardom, a young woman seeking attention from men in rebellious ways. But as the real person was starting to emerge in Fowler's morning paper, by day's end Aggie Underwood was recrafting it into myth. Underwood followed Betty Short's tracks to a Long Beach drugstore where regulars had given Short the nickname "Black Dahlia," a reference to her jet-black hair and clothing, but also to the popular film noir that had come out that year, *The Blue Dahlia*. In that film—written by Raymond Chandler, his only original screenplay, which got him his second Oscar nomination—the name refers not to the leading lady but to a nightclub, and yet when I found it at the video store during my research (as a devoted Chandler fan I'd already seen it countless times, just to be clear, but needed to refresh my memory), the box featured a soft-focus photo of Veronica Lake above the title, suggesting that *she* was the Blue Dahlia, which underscores how the case of the Black Dahlia has eclipsed the film, even though, aside from this one thing, they really have little to do with each other—one no more than a footnote for the other— and you cannot find any clues to the real-life crime in the film itself. Repackaging *The Blue Dahlia* to capitalize on this unfortunate associa- tion would be like putting John Hinckley Jr.'s face on the poster for *Taxi Driver*. The video store clerk didn't seem to understand what I was talking about, and since there was a line forming behind me, I paid for the video, along with a healthy late fee for some video games Chris had taken out, and left. But whatever injustices the media machine did to Chandler's film, it's nothing compared to what they did to Ms. Short. Now that Aggie Underwood had a hook—the woman in black who haunted L.A.'s seedy underbelly—she didn't let go. It's fascinating seeing these two sets of articles side by side, those by Will Fowler in the *Examiner* and those by Aggie Underwood in the *Express*. Fowler focuses on specifics, on facts, clearly trying to understand, while Underwood focuses on abstractions, on sensational hypotheticals, clearly trying to sell papers. It's like a strange sibling rivalry playing out in two differ- ent newspapers both owned by Papa Hearst, and they're both fighting over the legacy of this woman. Fowler is clearly the better writer, while Underwood is mildly insane. But of course Underwood wasn't the only one who didn't let sanity stand in the way of a good story. Fowler's editor at the *Examiner*, James Richardson, "shared William Randolph Hearst's penchant for sensational news and . . . could be inhuman" in his pursuit. That quote is from Fowler's 1991 book *Reporters: Memoirs of a Young Newspaperman*, in which I discovered that he too was the son of a screenwriter, so writing is really in the blood for both of us. Anyway, Fowler describes Richardson being so determined to get a scoop that hours before they ran the story revealing the victim's identity, he forced a young copy editor to call Betty Short's mother, who didn't yet know about her daughter. Richardson instructed the copy editor to tell the mother that her daughter had won a beauty contest, and then try to get as much information about her as he could. The mother was delighted and began chatting all about her wonderful daughter, and after Richardson—who was listening in—got what he needed, he gave the copy editor the signal to drop the façade. The copy editor then said, "Actually, ma'am, your daughter is dead. She was brutally murdered two nights ago." Of course I don't know the exact words he used, but it doesn't matter. Blunt is the only way to break news of that sort. And it is just as well. Even when the messenger tries his or her best to pad it, to ease you into an understanding of what has happened, the news itself is so unimaginably blunt that it barrels over the actual words. I really can't recall the exact words Aunt Paige used when she sat me down and told me about my mother, but in my mind it's just Aunt Paige, that cheery, giddy woman, saying, "Your mom is dead. She was brutally murdered two nights ago." Of course in my mind, for some reason, she's also wearing a *Save the Whales* T-shirt, which would have been anachronistic, since the Save the Whales campaign didn't get started until the late seventies, and my mother died in 1961, but that is probably a subconscious expression of my cetaphobia, which itself goes back to a terrifying trip to Sunday school where the teacher told us about a whale devouring poor Jonah, all of which has nothing to do with my mom's death or the veracity of my memory. Who knows what Aunt Paige was wearing—it doesn't matter. I'm not Joan Didion, after all; I'm not trying to establish verisimilitude with meaningless sartorial details. What does matter is that Aunt Paige was the messenger because my father was locked in his office, leaving it to his sister to intercept me when I came home from school. The reason this matters is because Edie makes a ridiculously big deal about it in her book, seems to use it as proof that our father was uncaring and distant, when, if anything, it should be proof of the opposite (he was distraught!). This is fairly representative of Edie's rather confused use of evidence.

For another example, just take a look at this excerpt when she's describing the events that first led our mother to leave the country, almost a year before her death:

Then my mom's old childhood friend came to dinner, having come into town for a conference at USC. Looking like Rock Hudson, he was an anthropologist who'd been studying in Africa, and he spent that night telling us about the social structure of western lowland gorillas and what happened to the structure when the alpha male died. As soon as we were done with our food, my dad went back to his office at the far end of the house to continue work on some script, and Paulie plopped himself down in front of the TV. I stayed at the table with my mom and her friend. I remember the way the little Olympic ringlets of condensation from their water glasses linked their way across the table, and how my mom watched this guy with her chin in her hands and her pinky on her lip.

> Three months later, my mom announced that she would be
> going on a missionary trip to Africa. "A little philanthropic vaca-
> tion from my life," she said. (62)

Look at the way Edie follows that "when the alpha male died" with
our father leaving the table. In this context, she makes our father's
writing seem like a self-castrating act, but what about our mother?
Doesn't she have any culpability here? It was her decision, and her
decision alone, to go to Africa. And while I admit that the water rings
forming "little Olympic ringlets" is a nice image, describing Mom's
friend as looking like Rock Hudson is just plain lazy and, considering
what we now know about Rock Hudson, undermines Edie's attempt
to prop this guy up as the alpha male whom our mother is replacing our father with. Besides, he didn't look like Rock Hudson at all.
He looked like Vincent Price. But I can't blame Edie too much for
blaming Dad for Mom first going to Africa, then getting macheted by
Eritrean separatists when she was caught in what would become the
Eritrean War of Independence, as I too was eager to blame our father.
The difference being that I blamed Dad when I was an immature four-
teen-year-old who was eager to blame anyone. Edie is a fifty-four-year-
old woman and should know that things are far more complicated
than that. That's what a great deal of *Rarer Monsters* is actually about, a
fictionalized exploration of how I spent those years after Mom's death
practically disowning my own father for what I perceived as his weakness. Consider this passage from an early chapter in that novel, which
is still available for publication (the Peter character is the one loosely
based on me):

Peter began spending more time at his friend Wyatt's house. He generally avoided hanging out at his own house for fear that Wyatt would notice just how empty it was becoming. But one day they decided to buzz their heads and, since Peter's dad had been a navy barber during the War [the backstory of Peter's father and my father are a little different, but the gist is the same], they went to Peter's house to use his dad's electric clippers.

In his dad's bathroom Peter opened the drawer to get the scissors and electric razor. Something else caught his eye: There, in the corner of the drawer, was a zigzagging link of condoms. White and blue packaging that said spermicidal lubricant. There was something toxic about that word, spermicidal, like spraying your johnson with ammonia.

Peter held up the link of condoms to show Wyatt.

"Wow," Wyatt said. "I didn't think your dad still had it in him. I guess he really was in the navy. You should take one." (23)

I should clarify that this part takes place before Peter's mom actually dies; at this point, she's just a missionary in Ethiopia. (She was not particularly religious, none of us were, so her becoming a missionary was just as shocking, and disconcerting, as her decision to go to Africa; but I've come to realize that in the days before secular plane tickets like the Peace Corps were a viable option, the church was simply a way for her to get to Africa, not to Jesus.) (And by "she" there, I meant my mother, not Peter's mother, just to be clear; in the novel I never really got into the spiritual leanings of Peter's mother.) (Or, who knows, now that I think if it, maybe Mom was finding

God. How am I to know?) The character of Wyatt here, I should also note, is generally a composite of different friends I had during that period, but his father is based entirely on the father of this guy Bobby. Bobby's mom was also absent, though I can't remember why.

The next day at school, the only thing that tempered their pride in their matching buzz cuts was the fact that the electric razor had turned the skin on the sides of their heads a patchy and painful red. It looked like they both suffered from some skin disease.

"My scalp burns like gonorrhea," Wyatt said, meeting Peter at his locker.

Not that either of them would have known what that felt like. Neither of them had actually had the opportunity to catch anything from a girl. The buzz cuts—which they imagined would make them look more adult—were supposed to change all that. But the only attention they got from girls were sad looks followed by "That looks bad."

After school, they walked back to Wyatt's house where they rooted through his bathroom, found some aloe and gooped it onto their razor burns. It looked like they'd tried to apply hair gel where they no longer had hair.

Wyatt sighed. "God, that feels good."

Peter heard some banging coming from the garage. "What's your dad up to?" he asked.

Wyatt's dad Lenny worked security at Roth's Jewelry Store and often let his consonants slip to refer to it as Roth's Jewy Store. Lenny was not a security guard, Peter knew. Lenny made a point of saying he was Head of Security: He didn't wear a rent-a-cop uniform and carry a flashlight as if it were a gun—Lenny wore a suit and a carried a real gun, which he was legally allowed to carry on his person, concealed, in a shoulder holster. Peter suspected that Lenny wore a blazer a size too small in order to emphasize that gun, the bulge of its handle noticeable under his arm.

Peter went out to the garage where Lenny was always busy restoring his antique guns. There they were, hanging from hooks in various stages of completion. And there was Lenny, a man who wore his body the way Ironman in Peter's comics wore his metal suit. (25–26)

I'm particularly proud of that Ironman simile, as I feel it really captures Peter's attraction to this new father figure, although I see now that that awkward "in Peter's comics" insert could have been eliminated if there'd been an earlier reference to Peter reading Ironman comics. Either way, the simile is much more powerful in the context of the novel, because there's a whole network of weak-man metaphors that surround Peter's father that lead up to this moment. Regardless, the point here is that I can understand Edie's need to blame our father, but I—and Peter—overcame it. The entire last act of *Rarer Monsters*, in fact, is about Peter seeing his father succumb to cancer and, understanding that he'd been wrong that whole time to blame him for the loss of his mother, reconnecting with the man. Of course, that's not exactly how it happened to me. In real life, our father died suddenly of a heart attack four years after our mom's death, and all those realizations that Peter has while playing catch with his father, I didn't have until after my father was actually gone. But I prefer the version as it is in the novel, dramatically speaking. Peter doesn't have a sister in the novel. There just wasn't room. But, in real life, Edie was still around at this time. She was twenty and living at home. After high school, she'd gone off to Bryn Mawr but halfway into her second year dropped out. We didn't call it dropping out back then, just "taking a break" after "an excess of stress." She was now living at home again, taking classes here and there at Valley College. In her book, Edie doesn't mention her Bryn Mawr breakdown—if that's indeed what it was—and I never did figure out what her retreat back home was all about. In fact, that period is so absent from her book that in order to figure out where exactly she applied her willed amnesia, I've been trying to correlate her memories to some of my own, matching up the timelines to see what's missing. The strongest point of correlation I've found—the one I can use as a fulcrum of sorts in leveraging other points of dis/agreement—is a little scene that must take place in the fall of 1961, about a year after Edie's return from Bryn Mawr. Our mother had taken her first missionary trip to Africa that summer and was back relaxing at home, spending afternoons sitting on the front lawn with some iced tea and enjoying the neighbors' scandal-ized expressions as they walked past and snuck glimpses at this wayward woman. On page 87 of Edie's manuscript, she writes,

> Mom was doing some ironing one afternoon, singing to herself, as she often did, that French ditty "Alouette." Our mom's rendi-tion of the song was not the jaunty kids' tune; it was slurred and jazzy, slipping out, as if unconsciously, like a dream she only vaguely remembered.

When I passed by on my way to the kitchen, she stopped singing, grabbed my arm and pulled me into the laundry room, a strange smile on her face. She said she wanted to show me something and she pulled up her sundress to reveal what at first I thought was some dirt, but what I soon realized was a small tattoo on her hip. Just six months before, she'd been an L.A. housewife and now here she was, tattooed like a sailor! "What do you think?" she said. I didn't know what to think. My mother had never shown me her body like this, like it was something you could show another person. Up until this point, my mom's hips were just desexed padding that she was always slapping with frustration. ("Iris," she'd say to herself, "you're a fat fatty.") But now she was showing me a hip that had been slimmed by missionary rations, tanned by the equatorial sun, and inked with a voluptuous African design. The design was called a sankofa, she told me. Looking like an overflourished heart, it was a symbol of learning from the past. All I could think to say was, "Dad's gonna kill you."

"Oh," she said, scrunching up her nose, "like he'll ever see it."

The reason I keep coming back to this scene is that I'm fairly certain I remember this exact moment. I remember Mom singing while doing the ironing, but there was nothing unusual about that—"Alouette" was a favorite refrain of hers. But I specifically remember seeing Mom pull Edie into the laundry room with a strange and excited urgency. Unless I've collapsed time in my head, which people often do when remembering things for the same reasons that I tinkered with the timeline in

Rarer Monsters—to create a tighter narrative, to have a more reassuring pattern of causality, which sometimes stands at odds with the chaotic, meaningless reality—unless I've done that, which I don't think I have since it would mean that Edie has made the same mistake, since our memories coincide with what would happen at dinner that evening, then, seeing that our mom had left the iron on and unattended, I pulled out the condom I'd stolen from my dad's bathroom. For a more detailed scene, I'll just turn to how I rewrote it for *Rarer Monsters*:

> Peter pulled out the condom he'd stolen. He slid it into his wallet. He then laid the pleather wallet down flat on the ironing board, and cautiously hovered his hand over the iron to feel for heat. He couldn't tell. He lifted it up and spit on it like he'd seen his mom do, the spittle hissing and sparking against the hot metal. Then he gently put the iron down onto the wallet and ran it back and forth over the cheap material. In less than a minute, the impression of the condom began to show through the wallet. He put the iron aside and checked out his work: It looked like it had aged this way naturally after years of carrying around countless condoms that had all settled themselves into this groove. (54)

At that point, my mom and sister came out of the laundry room and I made like I hadn't been doing anything. But they didn't seem to notice me. What makes me absolutely sure that Edie and I are referring to the same moment in our manuscripts is that we both agree that it was that night, just hours later, over dinner, that our mom announced she would be returning to Africa. She said she felt needed there, that "[h]er training as a nurse gave her skills she could put to use administering much-needed vaccines, when her church teamed with the Red Cross to combat a yellow fever outbreak in the Didessa River Valley" (E. McWeeney 89). (Re: "training as a nurse": in 1944, in what I can only assume was a fit of panicked patriotism, our mom had volunteered for the Cadet Nurse Corps, though for reasons I'm unsure of—and Edie doesn't mention—she never finished the program.) Since she had been sticking the African villagers with needles, they called her the Bee Woman with the Sharp Stinger. The moniker was, she assured us, a more fluid three syllables in their Amharic language, and she was clearly proud of it.

And then she was gone again, reduced to a voice on a phone, coming through thin and granular like a radio station lost somewhere in the stratosphere. And then in October, I came home one day from school and there was Aunt Paige wearing—though I know she wasn't—her *Save the Whales* T-shirt, telling me to sit down, that she had some news for me.

I just noticed something about that last paragraph there that I should confess. The first sentence—the one beginning "And then she was gone . . . " and ending with " . . . somewhere in the stratosphere"—is actually from Edie's manuscript. I'm pretty embarrassed that it snuck in there uncited, but I have Edie's manuscript right here on my desk, so I suppose I can forgive myself. I saw Charles today and he insisted on having a few beers, which I'm unaccustomed to in the middle of the afternoon (a depressant is the last thing I need these days), so perhaps that's the reason for my momentary slip just then. I met with Charles—Chuck—at Lucky Strike in downtown L.A., which he referred to as a bowling lounge rather than a bowling alley, and it's definitely loungy but in a wonderfully Sinatra way. We sat at the bar and drank heady Budweiser and he told me about his divorce and the daughter who hates him. He laughed at my tales of Chris's teenage antics and gave me what seemed to be a really good deal on a gently used bowling ball. It's black and I like its simplicity, its anonymity out there on the boards. Chuck and I played a few frames and then said goodbye.

Anyway, I see that I've gotten a little ahead of myself and left poor Betty Short back in 1947. The content of my sister's manuscript is of course important, but I must finish establishing the facts before I move on to Edie's fiction.

In the months after Betty Short's murder, as the newspapers filled out the legend of the Black Dahlia, countless people came forward to confess. There was Daniel Voorhees who turned himself in to the LAPD and gave a detailed account of how he had tortured and killed Ms. Short, but the police rejected his claims when he couldn't answer the "control question," which had to do with a key detail of the murder supposedly revealed in the classified autopsy report. Then there was Joseph Dumais, an army corporal who handed his commanding officer a fifty-page handwritten confession. He made the front pages of the newspapers, but the police dismissed him too for failing the control question. These guys were just coming out of the woodwork, so eager to be the guy everyone was looking for, all of them with richly imagined scenes of what they'd done to this young woman. You hear about false-confessors a lot in these high-profile murders, but I've never understood why they do that. Sure, they're nuts, but beyond that there seems to be a pathological impulse to validate one's existence by writing yourself into a nationally recognized narrative, which I just don't understand.

While the police were sorting through these false-confessors, James Richardson over at the *Examiner* was gathering together famous mystery writers. His idea was that crime writers know the criminal mind, so he would assign a few of them to profile the murderer based on the evidence at hand. For this task, he assembled screenwriter Ben Hecht, novelist David Goodis, and *Rampart* scribe George McWeeney. There it is, my father's name, casually in print. My source for this is James Richardson's 1954 memoir *For the Life of Me*, in which he admits that he'd originally tried to get Jack Hale but that Jack Hale had sent George McWeeney in his stead. There's an air of apology in this little parenthetical of Richardson's, an acknowledgment—or rather insistence—that George McWeeney was not a worthy name. This embarrassment at having been sent what Richardson saw as a lesser writer perhaps explains why in both the front-page article Richardson ran and in his memoir, he focused mostly on what the far more famous Goodis and Hecht had to say about the murderer. My father's contribution to this little brainstorming session has been lost to history, and I'd really love to see Dad's murderer-profile that Edie claims to have uncovered in his files, love to have a team of experts carbon-date the thing, because it's surely a fake. In fact, based on what she excerpts in her book, I can tell it's a fake. I may not be an expert carbon-dater, but I am an expert on my dad's prose style and he would never resort to such purple phrases as "the murderer's mendacious mien," so Edie's claim that reading that profile is like seeing a man look into a mirror is nothing but a contrivance. Anyway, Ben Hecht was the most famous of these three writers, and so Richardson gave him center stage in the final article. Hecht was a veteran not just of Hollywood (having written the screenplays for *Scarface*, *Notorious*, and a million others) but of journalism as well (having broken the case of the "Ragged Stranger Murder" at the *Chicago Daily News* before coming to Hollywood), so he surely saw the absurdity of the assignment and so it is perhaps with tongue planted in cheek that he wrote that the evidence clearly pointed to a killer who was "a dyke lesbian with a hyper-thyroid problem." I thought I might be able to find some more information on these brainstorming sessions in Ben Hecht's journals—perhaps a different view of my father—but his papers are now the property of Newberry Library in Chicago. Fortunately, around the time I was at this stage in my research (this was in February of this year), Julia was planning a trip to Chicago for a conference. She's always jetting off to conferences, delivering papers, always hopeful that this networking and paper-giving will lead to a tenure-track position at a four-year institution whose acronym does not denote a sugary carbonated beverage. Just yesterday, in fact, she came back from a conference in Baltimore. I picked her up from the airport and she told me all about the man who sat next to her on the plane, said he was a real charmer. She often describes people as charming and I'm never entirely sure what she means by this. I imagine Rudolph Valentino driving women to suicide with one arch of his eyebrow, but I know I'm wrong, that the qualities she's identifying are more mysterious, subtler than that. She always befriends the men she sits next to on planes. I've never befriended a woman sitting next to me. Of course, before takeoff, when I'm sitting in my aisle seat (I always request aisle, not window, hating to disrupt people when too many ginger ales send me to the restroom), reading my copy of Flaubert's *A Sentimental Journey* or Melville's *The Confidence-Man* (aware that a lesser known work by a canonical author is the best public reading material since the author's name immediately commands respect for the reader but the unfamiliar title proves that I'm not just some unlettered man in an adult education class, that I'm already familiar with the Great Books list and have now branched out), I always hope that some Rita Hayworth-type will walk down the aisle with her sleek black carry-on, ask me to heft it up to the overhead bin (for some reason I'm always at least six feet tall in this fantasy, very capable of hefting things into high places), then sit down next to me and ask me about the novel I'm working on, and although it's never happened quite like this, on the few instances that a nice-looking lady has sat down next me, I've never been able to take advantage of the situation. Something about air travel (the processed foods? the recycled air? the change in air pressure?) makes me gassy, and I often spend flights sitting in quiet shame, not to mention a periodic warm cushion of air, too embarrassed to strike up a flirtation. I always want to turn to my seatmate, apologize, tell her she smells of roses and I smell of rotten eggs and I'm sorry; I want to tell her that she is beautiful and I am not and I'm sorry; I want to curl up around her feet, cry onto her calves. But I do none of these things. Anyway, this man Julia sat next to yesterday, apparently he'd been to the conference too—a conference on something called Word Studies, which she's been getting into lately, having heard it's the next boom industry in academia—and he regaled her with his Wordian insights, with charm. I want to tell her that as a feminist she should be suspicious of charming men, and I will—I just need to figure out exactly how to phrase it.

Anyway, back to February, she was headed to Chicago and I needed to convince her to help me with my research while there. Problem was, I hadn't fully explained what all had been going on, why I'd been holing up at various libraries lately. It's not that I'd been lying to her; it's just that I didn't yet have a good reason to go into it all. But I had to come clean, explain the whole situation—the time was now. "Julia," I said.

"Did I lock my door?" she said from the passenger seat of my car, her mouth full of Pop-Tart. "Do you remember me locking my door?"

"Would it be too much trouble to ask you to drop by the Newberry Library while you're in Chicago?"

"Take La Cienega. The 405 is going to be shit."

"I just need you to do a quick search through some of Ben Hecht's papers."

"Wait, what?"

"Ben Hecht. He was a screenwriter. He did *His Girl Friday*, a bunch of other things. You like *His Girl Friday*, right?"

"Never saw it."

"Of course you have. Cary Grant, Rosalind Russell? Fucking Howard Hawks!"

"Jesus, Paul, I told you not to take the 405. Look at this mess. My flight is in forty minutes!"

"Didn't we rent *His Girl Friday* that night you made Greek salad? Because when I think about that line of Cary Grant's, something like, 'Put Hitler on the funny pages,' it has this very strong association with feta and sun-dried tomatoes, so it had to have been that night. You should make Greek salad more often."

"We watched *Bringing Up Baby* that night."

"Are you sure? I'm pretty sure you're extremely wrong about that."

"Take this exit here. We can take Sepulveda down."

"As a media scholar, you really should know *His Girl Friday*. I mean, it's a movie about a newspaper. Media!"

"If I miss this flight, I'm going to slap the shit out of you."

She did not miss the flight and so did not slap the shit out of me. The traffic on Sepulveda moved much faster—so fast, in fact, that I didn't have sufficient time to fully explain the situation I was in. By the time I was driving into the departures loop at LAX, she still hadn't admitted to seeing *His Girl Friday*, and so I still had not had a chance to explain things properly. I pulled up to a free patch of curb, got out, and helped her get her suitcase from the trunk. The wind was doing nice underwatery things to the strands of hair that had freed themselves from her bun, and she had a crumb stuck to her upper lip like a beauty mark.

"Okay, I'll see you in a couple days," she said.

And I blurted out: "My sister wrote a book accusing our father of being the Black Dahlia murderer and now I have to set the record straight."

She squinted at me, brushed some hair from her face, and the crumb fell away. Her mouth started to form a word, but then stopped. She must have thought of another word to say instead, because her mouth changed shape again, but then stopped again. Finally she looked at her watch. "I have to . . . um." She pulled the telescoping handle of her rolly suitcase. "I'll call you when I get in?"

And she did. I, however, was in the attic, thumbing through old term papers, still trying to find the young bespectacled brunette student who wrote the nice review of me on the Internet, and I did not hear the phone ring. I later saw that there was a message on the machine and hit play: "Paul. It's Julia. I'm in Chicago, in my hotel. The flight was nice. Sat next to this lovely man from Oregon who is a viticulturist. I'm just sitting on my bed now, going over my paper. I'm a little nervous about it, but I'm not sure if it's wise to make too many last-minute changes. Ummmmmm. I know you've been distant lately. I haven't really known what to do, if you're pulling away or what. I totally understand that it can be hard to let people in. I mean we've both been hurt. God, that's trite. Sorry. I'm just not sure I entirely understand what it was you were trying to say to me at the airport, but I just want to say that I appreciate your attempt to let me in. I know there's been some stuff going on with your sister, and I really want to know about it. And I want you to know that you can talk to me about it. Anyway. This message is getting long. Would you mind going by my place and just checking that I locked the front door?"

She was right, of course. I had to communicate with her about this. After all, as an expert in media law, she was a valuable resource if I were to make a case for libel and defamation against my sister and, well, *you.*

So when she got back into town, we sat down at my kitchen table and I laid it all down on the Formica: my sister's manuscript beside the pages of notes I'd taken at the library. Edie's pile of papers was taller than mine: I still had a lot of work to do. I explained the basic outline of my sister's argument, keeping my eyes on the table as I did so, the patterns that look like one of Chris's Magic Eye posters that he claims contain images I'm certain are not there. In my periphery Julia sorted through all that paper, and suddenly I felt like one of my students, coming to office hours, asking for help with a term paper, nervously talking and watching the teacher's face and seeing a pitying look, a look that says, You have a lot more work to do.

"Well," she said, setting down Xeroxes I'd made of some Underwood and Fowler articles. I looked up, and she looked away, thoughtfully interrogated the earthquake cracks in the drywall. She sighed, touched her lips. "Well."

Then she looked at me, pushed a smile to the surface. "I'm glad you could share this with me. I've—" She stood up, walked over to the stove. "I've been worried about you. This definitely . . . well."

Chris walked into the kitchen—with the speed of a water snake but the gait of a water buffalo—went straight to the fridge and started rooting around.

Julia filled the teakettle and put it over heat. "When was the last time you saw Edie? I mean, have you spoken with her about this?"

"I've been busy," I said. "And she's been—well, this doctor of hers seems to be keeping her under close watch."

Chris, poking his head, Whac-a-Mole-style, over the fridge door, said, "Eddie?"

"Edie," Julia said to him, as if to thwack him back down. "Your aunt. Or stepaunt, foster aunt—whatever."

"Eddie," I corrected her. "Chris calls her Eddie." I'd forgotten about Chris's little date with Edie. Apparently sometime last year, not long after she'd come back to L.A. but before she'd recovered her memories, she came to my house. I was teaching an evening class at COLA, but Chris answered the door. She smelled the cookie dough he'd been making—which he never bakes into actual cookies, just mixes and snacks on raw—and talked her way inside. By the time I got home, she was gone, but Chris told me that they'd spent the evening watching his Black Sabbath concert video and that she'd told him all about seeing them live in the seventies. God knows what else she told him, about our family, about me, but somewhere in their conversation he started calling her Eddie, and she apparently approved, even though when I'd called her that as kids she'd shown her approval with a fierce purple nurple.

Chris now closed the fridge with enough force to rustle the glass-bottled condiments and salad dressings in the door-shelves. "What's going on with her? She's been leaving messages on the machine."

"She has?" Julia asked me. Her teakettle was starting to whistle.

"Mostly nonsense," I said.

"Bullshit," Chris said, then charged out of the room.

Julia's teakettle was now screaming. She took it off the heat and said, "Sorry. A little too apt."

"I should go talk to him," I said. I'd meant it to be a question, but I guess it didn't come out that way.

"I'll be here," Julia said.

I went to Chris's room, tapped lightly on his door. From the other side, he said, "What," which I took as permission to enter.

He was at his computer. When I sat down on his unmade bed, he angled the monitor away from me and kept his eyes on it while I thought about what to say. Here's what I finally came up with: "You know, your mother and I saw Ozzy Osbourne live once."

Chris suddenly sat at attention, his posture straighter than I knew possible, as I was beginning to think he'd slouched himself into scoliosis.

"True," I said. "He was great, too. The man's still got it."

Chris crossed his arms, planted his elbows on his desk and leaned forward. "Mom hated metal."

"I know," I said. "We saw him at the airport."

Chris clenched his jaw, but I could see a smile fighting its way through.

"I was hoping I wouldn't have to admit that part," I said.

He laughed, a strange sound he was not used to making, half grunt.

When I got back to the kitchen, Julia was sitting at the table.

"That was quick," she said. "Did you explain things to him?"

I sat down across from her. "Uh-huh."

"Good," she said. "Let's get down to business. You have a lot of work to do."

She tucked some loose strands of hair back into her ponytail. I crossed my arms.

"Now. Since her claims have not been reviewed in court, you need to focus on the issue of defamation—not on disproving her case."

"I don't understand—why?"

"Because you want this to be about procedure. She's making these claims without going through the proper legal channels. So it's—at least potentially—libel. If you turn this into an issue of evidence, you run the considerable risk that at least some of her accusations are correct."

She sipped her tea—one of those therapeutic teas she keeps at my place that claims to relax you with herbal and fruity infusions. I don't have the patience for those things. This one was called Peach Passion, should have been called Peach Placebo. Whenever she steeps herself a cup of that stuff, I can't help but think of the Weird Sisters from *Macbeth*, brewing eye of newt and toe of frog to bring about the Thane of Cawdor's doom, when in fact it was their suggestion of his fate that paradoxically sealed his fate. Those who argue that Macbeth's fate is ordained by magic misunderstand the play's basic epistemology and fail to understand the psychological complexity therein, something I inevitably have to explain to my English 2 students every semester. Julia offered me some tea and I politely declined. Unlike Julia, I prefer my substances to work unequivocally. When I need to relax I take a hundred milligrams of Trazodone and fall the fuck asleep. I suppose I shouldn't have been annoyed by Julia's use of all these New Agey products, chamomile and valerian—hey, you can put in your body whatever you like—but as a woman trained to work from evidence, she should have at least taken notice of that little footnote on the side of the box of tea: *These statements have not been evaluated by the Food and Drug Administration*, and realized that she was just fooling herself into relaxation, and since she was my new council in all things legal and evidence-based, I was suddenly concerned that her tea choice revealed her preference for superstition over science.

"Which is why," she was saying, "you should be couching your own argument in monetary terms."

"Right," I said.

"And," sipping wool of bat and tongue of dog from her chipped mug, "it's great that you're doing some research here, but you really need to approach it in a more organized fashion. I mean, look at this. You have a page-long quote here, handwritten, but no indication of where it's from. A newspaper article? Which newspaper? What byline? What date? You need to be keeping track of things like this."

I grabbed the piece of paper and read it over. It appeared to be an excerpt from Will Fowler's memoir describing his editor James Richardson. I'd had to copy the passage by hand because I'd been able to find the book only in the Pepperdine library. COLA doesn't have an interlibrary loan deal worked out with them, so I couldn't check the book out, and the photocopier in the library required a pass-code I didn't have (since Pepperdine is a religious school, I tried guesstimating some Christian numerology and chapter numbers of famous Bible passages, but the machine was having none of it), so when I found Fowler's book in the stacks I had to settle into a grad student carrel and glean everything I could. (Judging from the other books piled in that carrel, I figured it had been reserved by either a lepidopterist—*Butterflies and Moths of the Jurassic Period*—or an engineering student specializing in modern weaponry—*Infrared Homing in Ballistic Artillery*—or perhaps some kind of interdisciplinary mash-up artist; images of battle-trained pterodactyls, lasers affixed to black leathery wings, fluttered through my mind.) So that particular scrap was, I admit, a bit disorganized, but that was not representative of the rest of my research.

"Here are some more," Julia said. "Just uncited scraps. I mean, shit, Paulie. How many years have you been teaching students how to write research papers? You should know better. You need a clearer plan of attack."

"I've been—intuiting my way, I suppose."

"Ohhh," she said, smiling, "you're such an MFA."

This is pretty typical of her, the proud academic condescending to the creative writer. She is always finding ways to remind me that she has the real degree and I have a fine arts degree, that she wears the intellectual pants in this relationship. It is, naturally, her own insecurities that motivate these little jibes: Having spent ten years getting her PhD, she feels humiliated that the only job she can get is as an adjunct at COLA, a place, she once said, where dreams go to die (apparently, for all she learned in PhD school, she didn't learn to avoid clichés), and so she must find ways to remind me that she's just slumming it here until something more suiting her pedigree comes along. But what really bothers me is that I take her cue and just follow along. For example, when we first met, she asked me what I had done my master's work in, and I said, "Uh, myself, I suppose. I just have an MFA." She chuckled and that set the tone for all degree-talk in our relationship. We had been standing in the faculty copy room at COLA and I had caught her admiring one of my (admittedly) passive-aggressive stunts. In the faculty copy room, there is a bulletin board where teachers had begun posting effusive notes they had received from students, notes like *Dear Mr. Hewlitt, Thank you for a wonderful semester. I learned sooo much in your class and loved it! Your the best teacher evar!* followed by a name with a heart dotting an *i*. The bulletin board had begun filling up with these ridiculous things. I hadn't yet discovered Grade-a-Prof.com, and this was the first time I realized that everyone else's classes were filled with adoring children, while all the angry contrarians were shuffled into my sections. I had been fretting about the fact that I did not have any illiterate displays of obsequiousness to post on the board, worried that Dean Hockney would notice the conspicuous absence of any *Dear Mr. McWeeney* notes and not give me any classes for the next semester (as an adjunct, this is a constant fear), so I'd gone home and spent hours attempting some fawning forgeries. It was harder than I expected, how-ever. Not the content of the notes—I am a writer, after all, and can easily imagine my way into the mind of a student who would write such a note (probably someone with an absent parent, grasping around for the first father figure she can find, in this case her teacher)—but rather the handwriting: I could not make my hand form letters in a way that looked anything other than my own, so I knocked on Chris's door. "What?" he groaned from inside. I poked my head in, saw him hunched golem-like over his precious computer, and said, "I need you to write something for me. I need to borrow your handwriting." He said, simply, infuriatingly, "No," and "Close the door." That sent me into a pacing and impotent rage in the hallway for a few minutes, but I then returned to my desk with a new approach, replacing sincerity with snark. I wrote a note that said, *Dear Mr. McWeeney: You are my one true son. Sincerely, God,* and I posted that on that bulletin board the next day. A few hours later, I was between classes and photocopying a chapter from Kant's *Kritik der reinen Vernunft* for my English 1 class when I saw a woman wearing a cardigan like a straightjacket, bent slightly at the hips, squinting through horn-rimmed glasses, to read my contribution to the faculty circle-jerk, and she laughed in a way that can only be described as hooting. She hooted. (She would turn out to be the only person to see the humor in my note. All my other colleagues misunderstood it to be a rather maniacal proclamation of faith and began treating me with the conversational kid gloves one wears when talking to the delusionally devout.) "Man," Julia said that day in the copy room, "didn't know we had the lamb of fucking God in our midst." I extended my hand for a shake. "Hi," I said. "I'm the son of God." We were the only ones in the copy room and enjoyed a few bantering minutes making fun of our colleagues' pretensions, their

desperate displays of approval. "Hey," she said, "if you're seeking validation from students at *this* school, then your compass is broken. Look
at me. My students hate me and I'm a wonderful teacher." I nodded
and laughed and agreed and made a mental note not to mention that
I myself had been a student here nearly two decades earlier, an omission that remains a year later, which is now less about embarrassment
at having attended COLA than it is about having been so embarrassed
about it that I felt the need to conceal it, and now if I admit that the
version of my life that I gave her is slightly inaccurate she will—I know
from experience—completely miss the point of the admission (honesty)
and focus entirely on what she will surely think this ultimately reveals
(dishonesty), the classic female tactic of reframing an issue to focus
on what is in the past (the lie) rather than what is in the hypothetical present (the truth), forgetting that honesty about dishonesty is still
honesty, which is why I cannot now come clean to her about my errant
youth and why I cannot show her this very document—despite the fact
that she has been eager to help me with it and, in her condescendingly
MFAish words, "workshop it," before I send it off in the mail—as I
now realize that it contains the sort of honesty about my life that she
would surely be jealous of, and isn't it strange how significant others
get so jealous of the projects we writers embark on. It happened to
Brenda when I was working on *Rarer Monsters*—she was always wondering what the hell I was doing here in my office, pecking away on my
IBM Wheelwriter 1000 when I could have been paying attention to
her. Julia should be different, as she is not just fully knowledgeable of
my project here but understands its importance and supports it, but
even she has been giving little hints lately that she's starting to see this

stack of pages as the *other woman*: "You're still working on that?" she'll say, looking at the bags under my eyes, checking their heft and hue, the same way she might investigate my shirt collar for traces of lipstick.

Just a few minutes ago, actually, after I finished that last paragraph, I had to take a pee-break and walked through the living room to get to the bathroom. Julia was (still is) sitting on my couch, watching her favorite TV show—or "text"—a sitcom called *Pass/Fail* featuring a Hispanic actor playing a young black student passing for white at the University of Mississippi in the 1950s. It's filmed before a live studio audience that laughs maniacally at punch lines Julia insists are mocking racist attitudes but are really just good old-fashion racist. A false veneer of irony was postmodernism's gift to bigotry. I said that to her—though I admit it was a line I'd read in the *Times*—and she threw a *National Geographic* at my head, the canary-yellow cover flapping at me like I'm Tippi Hedren. "Jesus," I said, "I was joking."

"So was I." And as I headed back in here, she said, "Still working on that, huh?"

Impulsively, I said, "Nope. All finished, mailed it off this morning."

She looked at me, did that lip-tightening smile thing people do to display pride in another's emotional leaps, and said, "Good. It's time to move on."

"Uh-huh."

"So sit down with me," patting the cushion next to her. "Watch some TV. You deserve a break."

"I can't," I said. "I've some work to do. Some—other work. New work."

She surely presumed I meant a new novel and smiled in her scholarly way.

But now that I think about it, that comment of hers, that it's time for me to move on, definitely suggests that she's thought this project has been about me "working through" something, rather than correcting an injustice. It's all quite ironic, since that's a very MFA perspective, while I consider this project very PhD, as it is more in line with the sort of projects she attaches value to: works based on evidence and reason that set out to right wrongs. After all, that day back in February, when she was sipping her placebo tea and contemplating my case on the kitchen table, she even said, "Looks like you finally have a real project on your hands."

I already knew that she didn't think writing fiction was a real project. Back when we started dating, she asked to see something I'd written. This is always a serious moment in a relationship, a vulnerable revelation that acts as a statement of trust in the other, like opening up about childhood traumas, discussing professional disappointments, or admitting you have genital warts. It was a big moment, and I did it, I handed her a clean manuscript of *Rarer Monsters*. She took it, eyed it over with an eager smile, and said she couldn't wait. A few days later, I said, "So you enjoying my book?" Looking up at me over one of the (to quote her) "fluffy" novels she reads compulsively—occasionally justifying it by saying she's going to write something about the tropes of female-marketed fiction—she said, "I can't wait to start reading it." A week later we made hummus and were sitting down to grade some papers when I said, "How do you like my book?"

"Oh, I've just been so busy," she said, brushing bits of minced garlic from her sweater. "I want to be able to read it when my head is clear and clutter-free."

But then one evening, as we were driving to COLA (we both had a couple of evening classes that semester), she looked up and said, "Oh," as if just remembering something, "I read your book." My heart did a pitter-pat thing that at my age very well could have been dangerous, but I managed to remain cool and detached. Oh, yeah? "It was good." That's all she said. *Good:* a precious morsel, secreted away in lean times, its single pinging syllable a blip on an otherwise empty radar screen. There was, however, a follow-up a few nights later. Lying in bed, she looked at me and asked, "Why do you write?" Wonderful, I thought. She really did think the book was good, if not great, and this was my chance to wax philosophical about the ontology of Writer and Novel. "Well," I said, "I write because art is how we as human beings access any sense of what is true." "I just mean," she interrupted, "post-Barthes, post-Derrida, poststructuralism I guess you could say—or rather, post-poststructuralism—and especially post-Bourdieu, we all know that aesthetics don't reveal any big-*T* truth, so then the question becomes: Why write?"

I'm starting to see a pattern: The first time I came home from grade school with a story I'd written—some crayon-scrawled pastiche about a dragon named Lewis—I went to show it to my dad but he was in his office and we were not to disturb him while he was in his office, so I ran to show it to my mom who said, "You did what? Why? Oh, not another writer. That's your father's business." But she obligingly read it over and gave me a pat on the head. And years later when I had to explain to Aunt Paige that I was quitting acting to focus on school, she asked why and I said I wanted to be a writer and she said, "Why? Your father was the writer. You're the actor." And sure enough when I sent

Aunt Paige my completed manuscript of *Season of All Natures* (there was a character in there based lovingly on her), it remained unread on her shelf, about which she said, "Oh, it's so hard to read when it's not a real book. I can't hold it properly." With Julia, as with my mother, as with Aunt Paige, I was unable to answer the why question.

Julia's show is over now. I heard her turn off the TV a minute ago and can now hear her in the bathroom, putting the seat down, the trill of her pee hitting the water. Next she'll floss, then brush her teeth; she always paces when she does this. She's practically moved in now. There have been some landlord issues at her place that she seems to be using to expedite this phase of the relationship. It's a little claustrophobic, to be sure, but I am looking forward to crawling into the already-warm bed tonight, after the rest of that Ritalin I took at the start of my writing session has run its course, curling up next to her, smelling her vanilla-scented hair. I really need to find better times to work. These late-night sessions are killing me. I'm always haggard in my morning classes, a little shaky from lack of sleep, my mind feeling like Silly Putty stretched too far.

The only time I manage to relax is at my regular Sunday night bowling game with Chuck. He has what he calls a coroner's sense of humor and a good supply of behind-the-scenes stories about life at the morgue (the thing about the puppet show is something I won't soon forget). For some reason I've been hesitant to do it, but just the other day I finally asked him about the autopsy report. In an effort to keep the mood light, I was very selective about how much of this whole story I told him, just said my sister claims to have a copy of a very old autopsy report and I need to see if it's real or not. He looked away and held his bowling ball under his chin, then after a moment lowered it and said, "Well, if the original report is still classified, I don't think I could get a hold of it. But if I saw this copy you're talking about, I could probably tell if it's a fake. I could compare it with others of the same era." I thanked him and tried to continue bowling, but in an effort to convince him that I wasn't simply taking advantage of his friendship—especially since I'd told him it's going to be harder for me to find time to bowl now that the summer term has started—I attacked the ensuing small talk with perhaps a bit too much gusto, and when we were leaving he said, "Just relax, Paul."

So yes, classes (obviously) have started. I was trying my best to get this finished in the two-week break between the spring and summer terms, but I didn't anticipate the scope this project would take on. Since the summer term is at an accelerated pace, I'm actually busier now than I am during the normal fall and spring semesters, and in having to balance the demands of this project with teaching I end up resorting to these late-night binge work sessions. And considering how much more work I have to do here, I don't see my schedule changing anytime soon. I have a stack of over a hundred pages and still haven't gotten down to the specifics of my sister's claim.

Since I was doing all my research this past spring around the same time that I was going over evidence-based arguments in my English 1 classes, I hit on a rather brilliant idea. I would give the case to my students. What better way for them to learn about constructing persuasive claims from evidence and identifying logical fallacies than by showing them real evidence, real fallacies? Plus, in looking at my sister's manuscript and analyzing how she misinterprets evidence, they would learn textual analysis as well, which normally doesn't come until English 2. Of course, this required a great deal of prep work on my part, wrangling this whole, wild case into a lesson plan, but I managed, and it forced me to get organized in my approach.

I admit now that Julia had been right when she said I was a mite disorganized, but once I took her advice and started tightening up my ship, so to speak, I really took to it. Just seeing everything laid out on a simple timeline, being able to look over a whole temporal scene, helped my brain relax a bit, feel less panicky about where I was going and what I was doing. One day, when I was in my home office typing up a bibliography to help guide my lesson plan, Julia strolled in with a pint glass of frothy fruit juice (she'd just bought me a juicer and was on a rampage, reducing everything in sight to pulp and water, and now when I misplaced something, the TV remote or my car keys, my first fear was she'd juiced them for extra roughage), placed it on my desk, and said, "Mango-lychee-fish oil, lots of vitamin D." She'd curiously been advocating a lot of vitamin D lately, and I was about to ask her if she was concerned I was getting rickets but stopped myself when I realized she probably had every right to, considering how much time I'd been spending in my sunless office. But I was making clear progress, and as she looked over my work—charts! timelines! proper citations!—I saw her smile approvingly. I got back to my bibliography, took a few cautious sips of her concoction, and she said, "How is it?"

"Wonderful," I said. "The fish oil gives it a real—kick."

"No," she said. "Your father's book."

I looked up. Julia was now at my bookshelf, looking at my copy of Edie's manuscript, which I'd covered in so many multicolored Post-it notes the whole thing looked feathered like a tropical bird. I'd left it open to one of the many passages in which Edie discusses our father's unpublished and unfinished novel, the one she'd found in a trunk when she'd moved back into our Van Nuys house. Julia ran her fingers over the page and said, "Have you read it?"

"Yes," I said. "Of course. It's—remarkable."

"I'll bet," she said. "What was he like?" She sat down on the floor, crossed her legs. "You don't talk much about him."

"I don't? Sure I do."

"Nope."

"Well." I made a show of stopping my work and turning to her. "My favorite memory of him—Mom was out of town. She'd left him instructions to water the garden. I remember watching him standing in our backyard, in a full suit, watering the geraniums while reading Mom's instructions so intently that he didn't even notice he was flooding the flower pots."

"That's funny," she said.

"Pretty much sums him up, I've always thought." I could see her getting cozy there on the carpet, so I began looking at the shelf just behind her. I got up and leaned over her to grab a random book. "Sorry, excuse me. Just need to grab this."

"Oh, sure," she said, getting up. "I'll leave you to your work."

She left, and I looked at the book I'd grabbed: National Geographic's *Guide to North American Trees*.

Perhaps I'd been too eager to scoot her out of my office, but I'd been nervous that she'd ask me more questions about my father's book. You see, I hadn't been entirely honest with her. No, I had not actually read it. And for some reason, this was the first time it had occurred to me. My omission stunned me, not just because Edie culled so much of her "evidence" from my father's novel and it would be necessary for my research and for my class to have the original—in order to place it side by side with my sister's book and see how she grossly misinterprets it—but also because I prided myself on having read everything my father had written, not only his TV and radio scripts but his early plays as well, and this was a crucial, if not definitive, part of his oeuvre. It was, after all, what he spent his final years working on after *Rampart* went off the air. (In fact, as a kid, I hardly would have guessed that my dad was suddenly out of work since he was still pecking away at his typewriter behind his closed office door for eight hours a day.) But I knew why I'd been unconsciously avoiding my father's novel this whole time. My sister had the manuscript, and in order to retrieve it, I'd have to confront her. I hadn't seen or spoken to her since the night I'd seen her dining with Oliver at the Greek restaurant, and I really had no idea how our interaction would go. Would I shout at her? Level her with invective? Clarify the myriad ways in which she'd misinterpreted our childhood to support her delusional theory? No. I couldn't. I did not want this to turn ugly. I had to do what Julia had suggested, get organized. I had to approach her claim with reason and tact, and I would have to do that in writing. She was, is, after all, an insane person, and as with a sleepwalker, it's safest not to startle a lunatic out of her lunacy all at once. I had to be the sane one here. So I called our old house and left a message on the answering machine, which still had Aunt Paige's voice—warbled by age or deteriorating tape, I couldn't tell. The following day, Edie called me back.

"Paul," she said. "I'm so glad to hear from you. I was afraid you were never going to return my calls."

"Yes," I said, "well, I just need to request something from you." It suddenly occurred to me that I shouldn't reveal my hand, that if she knew I were mounting Dad's defense, she might try to impede my research. "I'm wondering if I could get a copy of Dad's novel. I had one, but I guess I misplaced it. Anyway, it's just for—summer reading."

"That's why you called?"

"Yes, that is why I called."

There was a ruffle on her end, what sounded like a sigh or the receiver sliding against her shirt, then she said, with alarming force, "Sure, Paulie. I'll make a copy for you."

"Wonderful. I'll be by tomorrow. I should be in Van Nuys around two or three."

"I'm not at that house anymore. I told you that in one of my messages. There's just—too much there, too much horror, too much everything. I'm staying at Rory's now."

I was proud of myself for not responding to her "horror" comment, just letting it slide for now. I had to be the calm one, the sane one. The next day, when I pulled up to Rory's Canoga Park apartment building (somehow I imagined Rory living in Venice Beach and was thoroughly disappointed), I kept repeating it to myself: Be calm, be sane.

I knocked on apartment 103 and Rory answered in flip-flops and toenail fungus. "Paulie, man, come in, come in." He stepped sideways in the doorway to let me into the dark apartment. Considering how much people praise L.A.'s sunshine, it's strange how dim they keep their homes. This was one of those apartments that everyone in the

San Fernando Valley seemed to have, which sprung up during the second-wave suburb boom of the early sixties. The layouts are all the same, the walls all shiny and a little gummy from too many layers of cheap paint applied over decades of high tenant turnover. The only variable in these apartments is the refrigerator, renters usually having to supply their own, since landlords have grown weary of people skipping out on rent, people willing to sacrifice their security deposit in exchange for a cumbersome appliance. Rory had a nice one, decorated with what looked to be finger paintings; perhaps he also specialized in art therapy. Rory walked over to the kitchen table, which was covered with red plastic filing boxes, the tops tabbed and labeled (perhaps they'd gotten Julia's organizing lecture too). He grabbed a Kinko's box, handed it to me. "Here you go." He seemed reticent, no longer the personable man I'd met at Jerry's Famous. I wanted him to ask me about my novel again, be interested in me.

"Is Edie here?" I asked.

He looked around, scratched his chin. Then in a low voice he said, "She was afraid to see you." Behind Rory, the bedroom door was open a crack. I couldn't tell if there was a person in that crack or just a shadow. It suddenly closed. "She wanted to. But at the last minute, she panicked." He sighed, crossed his arms over a billowy white T-shirt that said *Drop Pants Not Bombs*. "I hate to be the conduit here, but she's not sure what you think of her. I mean, you haven't returned any of her calls, or her letters. She had trouble reading you when you finally spoke on the phone yesterday. She's scared that you're angry. She's, well, she's scared of you."

Be calm, be sane.

"She's going through a hard time right now and really needs your support. And the way you've been denying that support is really troubling to her, and me."

Be calm, be sane.

"What?" he said. "Did you say Saddam Hussein?"

"No." Be calm, be sane.

Just then the bedroom door swung open and Edie rushed into the living room. She was wearing one of her scarfy, Stevie Nicks shirts. Waving her arms around as she spoke she began to resemble one of those betta fish flaring at the sight of its mirror image. "No," she was saying (to Rory or me it was unclear), "that's not true! Paulie"—she was looking, most definitely, at me now—"I wanted to speak to you, but he said I shouldn't."

"Edie," Rory said. "Breathe."

"Why haven't you talked to me, Paulie? You finally come here and it's just to pick up that horrible book?" She was crying. "I've been trying—"

Rory was now in front of her, his hands on her shoulders, muttering calming things I couldn't quite make out.

"I've been trying—" Edie stopped and covered her face with her hands, inhaled slowly and steadily, seemingly beyond normal lung capacity. Rory and I watched her, wondering if she would start to inflate, float above us like a balloon at the Easter Day Parade. When she finally stopped inhaling, she held her breath for a suspenseful moment, then let it out in one big, barking exhale. She took her hands away from her face.

"I think what we need here," Rory said, "is the talking stick." He walked into the bedroom. Edie looked at me like she was taking aim.

I looked away, examined the crown molding. Rory came out of the bedroom holding two halves of a wooden staff. Judging from the fresh splinters, it looked like someone had recently cracked it over her knee. Rory held the sticks up to Edie, the splintery ends in her face. "Did you do this?"

"I figure with two sticks," she said, "we can both talk."

Rory was barely keeping his anger locked between clenched teeth. He stormed back into the bedroom, and I heard the sound of two short talking sticks thrown against the wall, then some frantic drawer openings and closings. He came back out, this time brandishing a large green flashlight. "This will have to suffice," he said.

"Oh, for Christ's sake," Edie said, crossing her arms and looking away.

"Fine," Rory said. "You don't get the talking stick. Paul gets it first." He shoved the flashlight at me.

With my father's book in one hand, I looked at the flashlight in the other, its ribbed, rubbery grip and convex lens.

"Come on," Rory said. "Use it."

Maybe this was my chance, after all, to tell Edie how wrong she was, to ask her why she'd do this to our father. But I couldn't come up with the words. Holding the flashlight, I remembered how Aunt Paige would tell us ghost stories, shining a flashlight under her face for a ghoulish effect. I turned it on.

"That's not what I meant by using it," Rory said.

Aunt's Paige's ghost stories were always improvised and never very good. She always began with "It was a dark and stormy night" but would get derailed with the characters' genealogies and grooming habits, and behind her back Edie would laugh mercilessly making fun of Paige's meandering brain.

I held the flashlight under my chin and said, "Remember, Edie? It was a dark and stormy night." With the light shining obliquely into my eyes I couldn't see her reaction, but I didn't hear anything. I finally turned the light off and saw the two of them just staring at me.

"Paul," Edie said, "what on earth are you doing?"

She'd clearly forgotten Aunt Paige's ghost stories, which baffled me. It was as if we'd taken so many of our collective memories and divided them up like assets we couldn't possibly have mutual claim to, as if our childhood had gone through probate.

I turned around and left.

I spent that night reading my father's novel straight through, ignoring the phone (Rory on the answering machine: "Hey, buddy. Listen, we're going to need that flashlight back. It's from our earthquake preparedness kit"), locked in the spare room that I'd converted into my home office just as my father had written the novel, over thirty years ago, locked in his home office. Here it was, another manuscript, unpublished just like mine, the imperfections visible on the page like scratches on film: The A's and E's on his typewriter had been worn down from use; you could tell because they occasionally looked double exposed, an effect you only get when you go over the same letter twice, which he probably did because the first time they looked hazy. I longed to feel the imprint of the letters on the page, as I had with his scripts, but the manuscript Rory had given me was not the original; it was a photocopy, which made for an almost prophylactic reading experience. Nonetheless, it was—and is—a powerful novel, and it only confirmed for me my father's status as a great American writer. The prose style is effortless and transcendent—staccato in a way that I first took to be the influence of scriptwriting but I soon realized was an evocation of Hemingway—and I could feel the weight of the protagonist on the page, smell his whiskey-infused exhalations, hear his cracked voice. The title page just said *Untitled, a novel by George McWeeney, 8th draft, 1/30/1965.* It is still a little unclear to me whether the novel was actually *sans* title, or if this was some postmodern turn on my father's part. There is, after all, something profound and even chilling about titling this bildungs-/künstlerroman *Untitled* since the unnamed protagonist himself is in search of a meaningful existence, an identity—in search of a title, if you will. As much as I want to praise my father on this point, I must be careful, as I know how easy it can be for an eager reader to read too much into nothing. In college (the second half at UCLA, not the first half at COLA), I took a modern poetry class and had a powerful reading experience with T. S. Eliot's *The Waste Land.* At first, I found it all a bit confusing and felt overwhelmed and nervous that I wasn't smart enough to be at a real university, but I kept reading and had one of those *aha* moments teachers often talk about. The poem is broken into roman-numeraled sections, and I noticed that the fourth and shortest section, titled "Death by Water," was, like the preceding section, labeled *III* rather than *IV.* It was an unsettling moment for me, sitting there on the sunny quad, realizing that in the moment Death appears in the poem, time effectively stops. Like a record skipping, time could not move forward, and section four was section three. I looked up at a midair Frisbee, saw the horrifying suspension of gravity, of time, and realized that Eliot had been right; we're all stuck in time.

I attacked that midterm paper with more energy than I had any before, because for the first time I'd experienced a poem as a wormhole connecting poet and reader, the fabric of space-time folding around for us to meet. Certainly Prof. Newton would read this and see my passion, my intelligence, my dedication to scholarly and literary pursuits, and he'd stop referring to me as "The Actor" for a few cheap laughs in class. But when he handed the paper back, I was devastated to see only one curt comment: *The numbering is a typo in the Penguin edition. That's why the syllabus says to get the Viking edition. C-.* And although I had to drop that class out of sheer humiliation, I perked up when I realized that even though my reading had been technically incorrect, my *experience* of reading had still been entirely genuine and therefore still—if not more—valid. Whether or not my father intended to title his novel *Untitled*, we will never know, but for the sake of clarity, I will refer to it here as *Untitled*.

After a few weeks of work, I had the new curriculum mapped out and ready to present to my classes. I knew which passages I would need to excerpt from Edie's manuscript, which passages I would need to excerpt from my father's, along with all of my independent research, articles, and book excerpts. I hauled a huge box of documents down to COLA's copy room in the dead of night. The copy room's eponymous machine is a wonder of modern technology. Sleek and large, with a computer screen and keypad, the Xerox IR5000S has half a dozen drawers for different kinds and sizes of paper, countless trays for the spitting-out of those papers after they've been appropriately plied with toner, and it collates and staples with a Teutonic efficiency that is truly terrifying. The size of a Yugoslavian automobile, it also projects an air of authority that one rarely comes across at a school where even the most senior faculty members hunch timidly through the halls, always afraid that there will be no sections for them to teach next semester. I felt it necessary to do all my (admittedly) excessive photocopying under the cover of night because although we technically don't have a limit on how many photocopies we're allowed to make, some might have considered the number of reams I had to feed through it to be taking advantage, and as an adjunct I always have to be cognizant of how I appear around here. Plus, I felt the material here was of a sensitive nature, and did not want some colleague thumbing through a description of a bisected corpse and question my choice of curriculum. As I stood there, feeding pages and pages into the Xerox IR5000S, I felt like I was testing the machine's endurance, seeing if it had a breaking point. I was John Henry racing the steam engine. But the thing never jammed, never overheated. I was forced to admit my defeat. If I were reading a passage like this in a novel, I would scribble "Man v. Technology" in the margin and write a fucking fantastic term paper on it. Truth is, a lot of us at COLA have conflicted feelings about this machine. Ever since Reagan tried to shake down California education for money when he was governor, many community college districts—COLA's included—have been limiting tenure, relying more and more on part-time instructors. Over the years it got so bad that while they haven't technically abolished tenure, they don't grant it anymore, and now COLA is one of many community colleges in the state whose faculty is one hundred percent adjunct, all of us teaching without benefits, trying to make up for low pay by teaching so many sections we can't keep our students straight. The last tenured faculty member at COLA retired a couple years ago. I remember seeing him walk around campus, his wavy white hair catching the sun, his tweed elbow-patches proudly earned. People would point him out the same way you'd point out a snow leopard in the wild. And yet, after decades of the district saying they can't afford to grant any of us full-time status, they somehow can afford to buy this beast of a machine and tell us we can make as many copies as we like. I tried to kill the machine that night, but I could not. I left with three boxes of paper, all perfectly collated and stapled, the pages hot like cookies straight from the oven, smelling like ionized ink.

The day I presented this new unit to my English 1 classes, I was more nervous and excited to walk into a classroom than I'd been in years. I realized that I'd been using the same curriculum since the eighties, now dusty, clotted with cobwebs. I'd been teaching Mailer's "The White Negro" for so many years that I no longer even bothered to reread it and had only a nebulous memory of it; what I did remember and reread, and what I taught semester after semester, was not Mailer's "The White Negro" but rather my notes on Mailer's "The White Negro." I was in effect teaching my teaching of it. Despite the fact that my syllabus's schedule of readings contains the bold and italicized caveat *I reserve the right to change anything and everything*, I hadn't actually changed anything in so long that I now felt like I was walking into my very first class, and my students were quick to notice.

"Hey, Mr. M.," said one student whose beanie made him look hydrocephalic, "you're looking kinda jittery this morning. And, like, more than usual."

"I'm fine, Kyle."

"I'm Robert."

Like small children, my younger students seem most astute when pointing out someone's flaws. (My neighbors, for example, are chronic, frantic breeders—probably Mormon or Catholic—and not long ago one of their ankle-biting issues sprung forth from a bush as I was walking to my car and said, "You're losing your hair," with the innocent bluntness some find endearing in children but which, I was quick to tell this child, would not help it win any friends.) As young Robert set his childlike eye on my pre-class nerves, I tried to remind myself that a little investigative truth-telling could actually translate well to our task.

"Attention, class," I began. "Today begins a new unit."

"Does that mean we're getting the papers from the last unit back?" an androgynous girl in the front asked.

"Not quite yet. Still grading. While last unit focused on arguments based on personal experience, this unit will focus on making arguments based on empirical evidence."

"What's 'empirical'?" someone in the back said. I couldn't make out who, but I saw a red hat.

"It's having to do with an empire," Robert said. "Like evidence in the Inland Empire. Field trip to some crime scenes in Riverside!"

Most of the class laughed, and a few booed invective for Riverside. "The I.E. is like Satan's asshole," a guy named (I think) Hector said, to a mixture of laughter and groans.

"After Mexican food," added Robert.

"No, no," Hector said, "that'd be too humid."

"Okay, okay," I said. "No field trips to Riverside, I'm afraid. 'Empirical' simply means that it is based on verifiable information. It has nothing to do with the word 'empire.'"

"Dude," Robert said, "I was just making a joke. I'm not an idiot."

"But Robert was right when he mentioned crime scenes," I said. "Building an argument from evidence is just like solving a crime. Which is why we're going to be looking at actual evidence from an actual crime, and try to see if we can come to some conclusions." I waited for a gasp, some applause. When it didn't come, I said, "A murder." Still no response, so I continued: "The conclusions we reach will be our thesis, and as I've said before, a good thesis should destabilize a status quo opinion. In this case, that status quo will be a false accusation someone else has made. It will be up to us to look at the evidence, and figure out where that claim went wrong."

They still didn't seem to be responding with the kind of enthusiasm I'd hoped for. Perhaps they were all contemplating better anatomical metaphors for the Inland Empire (it's always had an armpitty feel to me, personally). In order to get them fired up about *solving a real crime—* or at least exonerating someone falsely accused—I jumped ahead a little and fired up the overhead projector. I'd been saving this for later, but I figured my students needed something a little more sensational, a little less mired in comp-rhet jargon, so I shone a couple crime scene photos up onto the screen. These were the two most iconic Black Dahlia images: Betty Short's body in the grassy lot surrounded by police and reporters, and a close-up of her face, her cheeks slashed.

"This," I said, "is the crime scene we'll be investigating. Los Angeles, 1947. A young woman's body is discovered . . . "

But by then people were already groaning and shouting at me to take the photos down. The class fell apart from there. A couple girls excused themselves with their hands over their mouths, and when I failed to get the rest of them back on track, I threw in the towel and excused them for the day. Fortunately, I had another class an hour later, so I was able to change my approach a little and avoid some of the pitfalls I'd found in my 9:00 AM class. Instead of showing crime scene photos, I passed out the first week's readings, excerpts from Edie's manuscripts detailing George ——'s pre-Hollywood life. (I blacked out the name *McWeeney* so they wouldn't suspect my connection to the case.)

Edie begins George's backstory with the basics—born in Ohio, dropped out of Yale Med for Yale Drama—but fills in this outline with details pulled from *Untitled*, since its protagonist shares with his author these basic biographical facts, the assumption being that if the basic outline is autobiographical, then it's all true, right down to the description of what the gravel felt like underfoot on Hillhouse Avenue in New Haven. Edie also correlates these details with a few culled from our mother's diary from the time. And although we must eventually dismantle Edie's blurring of fact and fiction, for this section the portrait of our father that she presents does seem somewhat reliable. I recognize this George, or at least I can see the seeds of the man and father he would become. I can see his devotion to his work, his perfectionism, certain tics like the nervous underbite, the pacing, all of which you see in Edie's collage reconstruction of the early months of 1941 when George was finishing work on his thesis play at Yale. He was spending every night at rehearsals, watching the director—a fellow MFA student—wrangle the actors together, guide them through the blocking like Anne Sullivan guiding Helen Keller. The actors were still on book, holding their scripts like security blankets, which killed timing, even confused meaning. And it drove George crazy: "Imperfection on the page could be dealt with, scrutinized under the light, corrected. Imperfection in others, on the other hand, had to be endured" (G. McWeeney 15; E. McWeeney 121). (This bit reminded me of him trying to water Mom's flowers years later, so focused on the controlled world of the written instructions that he fails to notice the less controllable reality.) So after every rehearsal, he went back to his tiny room in a boarding house on Orange Street and pounded out revisions until the "thick gelatinous sunshine seeped through those famous Gothic spires" (G. McWeeney 16; E. McWeeney 122, misquoted as "sunshine *shone* through"), and then he forced these revisions on the production, making enemies with all. But it wasn't just the pressure of the play that was getting to him. For a little over a year now, he'd been seeing Iris Lowell, a senior at Radcliffe. Both would be graduating in the spring, and marriage seemed inevitable. They had met two falls before at the 1939 Harvard/Yale football game. Or rather, they'd met at a diner, just across the Charles, to which they'd both independently escaped after finding the whole "spheroid-hurling divertissement a bit too tribalistic" (according to Iris Lowell's—i.e., my mother's—diary). After this meeting they began exchanging letters and it wasn't long before George was taking the train up to Cambridge. George's letters were "so candid, so open and loquacious," that it was sometimes difficult for Iris "to reconcile them with the reserved, taciturn man" she met in person (Lowell; E. McWeeney 130). But despite the openness Iris saw in these letters, the one thing George did not seem to divulge—or at least the protagonist of *Untitled* didn't divulge to his girlfriend, and Iris never mentions it in her diary—were his anxieties about the future. He'd given up on being a doctor to pursue the theater and was now facing the uncertain life of a dramaturge. Technically, he'd taken only a leave of absence from med school, so he could go back, finish his MD, have a stable life, be the bread-winning husband. This seemed to be the responsible thing to do. But he'd hated med school, loathed it with a part of himself so primal that the very idea of going back drained him of the will to leave his bed. In those classes, he'd felt "like he was dissecting not just bodies but the mysteries of what animated those bodies. What he'd found, he had not liked" (G. McWeeney 25; E. McWeeney 131). And yet graduation was quickly approaching, "heading for him like a freight train" (ibid.). If only he'd gone to war, he thought, he "could have been on the other side of the world by now, killing Germans. He'd be risking—perhaps losing—his life, but at least his life would have a simple goal: survival. Everything else would fall away. None of this dilettante waffling" (G. McWeeney 30; omitted by E. McWeeney).

"What," I asked my English 1 classes a week into the new unit, after they'd gotten a bit more comfortable with the subject matter, "are we to make of this passage?"

"He was tired of being a pussy?" Robert said. He of the squirrely goatee was turning into quite the chatterbox.

"Sure, yes. But what about the timeline here? This ostensibly takes place in January 1941, but when did the United States jump into the War?"

Silence.

"After Pearl Harbor," I said, "nearly a year later! This is clearly a mistake on the novelist's part, an anachronism." (I hated myself for denigrating my father's writing this way, but it was necessary: I had to sacrifice the writer for the man.) "So what does that tell us?"

"That he was a bad writer?" (Robert again.)

"No, no. Not at all, actually. I mean, Shakespeare's oeuvre was filled with anachronisms."

"What's an 'oeuvre'?" a girl in the back asked.

"We can check my anatomy textbook," Robert said.

"Anachronisms do not negate literary merit," I said, straining to be heard over the laughter. "In *Macbeth* people use dollars as currency despite the fact that dollars would not have been around in Macbeth's time." (I felt I saved my dad a bit with that one.) "No, what this tells us is that George's novel cannot be an accurate portrayal of the author's life. The thoughts of the protagonist cannot be the thoughts of the author in 1941 because America was not in the war yet!"

One possibility that did pop into my mind while I was explaining this to my class, but which I did not go into then (I could tell I was losing them a bit with *Macbeth*), was that the unnamed protagonist could have been considering going overseas to independently volunteer the same way Robert Jordon took it upon himself to fight in the Spanish Civil War in *For Whom the Bell Tolls*. That novel is actually referenced reverentially in *Untitled*. It was published in 1940, so those dates do line up.

Regardless, I still have trouble pointing out possible flaws with this war-fantasy passage because I do think it's a transcendent piece of writing. Considering this was the eighth draft of the novel, it's possible my dad kept it in there through all those revisions simply because it was a darling he couldn't bring himself to kill. After all, it's a passage that works at every level: Not only does it anticipate the so-called crisis in masculinity that would beset George's generation when the war ended,

its frantic syntax perfectly captures the inner turmoil of the protagonist and melds it with the equally turbulent New England blizzard that
he is driving through while thinking this. The passage occurs when
he is driving up to Cambridge to see Irene (the character whom Edie
posits is our mother Iris's fictional counterpart). He usually took the
train, but on this particular weekend his old roommate had left town
and let George borrow his blue 1939 Chevy Deluxe. George thought
he'd surprise Iris by picking her up in this "fine looking vehicle" (G.
McWeeney 133).

I've now been looking at those last two sentences for a few minutes. I'm wary of making the same tragic mistake Edie does in con-
flating fact and fiction, in seeing the characters in *Untitled* as reliable
representatives of George McWeeney and Iris Lowell, but I see that I
have let their real names slip in there. I suppose I can be excused since
my mother's diary does confirm that, after a few hours' delay in the
storm, George pulled up to her dormitory in a "eminently handsome
automobile," but this is also the point in Edie's reconstruction that the
George on the page parts ways with the George I recognize as the man
who would become my father. I do not want there to be any confusion
between those two people; indeed, my whole task here is to separate
them. But I am, I must remind myself, dealing with Edie's version here.
So I am forced to refer to this man, this fictional character, as George
also. So be it. I will parse the two Georges in the pages to come.

Either way, the particular scene where these two Georges part
ways occurs shortly after the war-fantasy. George—according to Edie—
had never driven to Cambridge before, had always taken the train,
plus it was blizzarding outside, so he got a little lost and overshot by

about fifteen miles. He was already in Lynn, Massachusetts, when he realized he needed directions and pulled into a gas station and asked a young woman how to get to Cambridge, a young woman who, seeing his fancy wheels, begins flirting with him ruthlessly. I'm referring, of course, to the scene in which he meets the woman whom Edie claims is a fictionalized version of Frances Cochran, Ms. Short's supposed precursor, Annabel Lee to Betty's Lolita. In the novel the young woman is named Fanny and described as having "black hair, a velvet curtain" and "skin whiter than the snow outside," and while it's true that this clearly matches the real Frances Cochran, this does not prove that the real George actually met the real Frances Cochran. As Edie points out, when she went through our father's things she found a scrapbook containing newspaper articles about both Frances Cochran and Betty Short. What Edie admitted to me in real life but makes no mention of in her book is that our father routinely scoured the crime pages for interesting stories that he could use in *Rampart* plots. The only thing this correlation between the character of Fanny in the novel and the real-life Frances Cochran proves is that George clearly drew inspiration from the news. The idea that it reveals anything beyond that is simply ridiculous. But, as I explained to my English 1 classes, we can see actual evidence in the text that proves these scenes were imagined rather than remembered. While the first thirty or so pages of *Untitled* are written with a kind of clarity that suggests they are sourced from memory, from this gas station scene onward the details are blurrier, the lens smeared with a little Vaseline. After page 35, I've noted a fifteen percent decline in tactile descriptions, a ten percent drop in olfactory observations, and a five percent rise in cliché descriptions (sorry, Dad, I'm doing

this for you). The most damning piece of evidence against Edie's claim
that George actually met the real Frances Cochran is that one description of her is actually lifted—though surely accidentally—from George's
source material. On page 39, he describes Fanny as "death on auto
rides," since she would force him to drive dangerously fast, screaming
with orgasmic delight as the Chevy Deluxe reached eighty, ninety, one
hundred. This phrase, "death on auto rides," first appeared in a *Boston
Globe* article from July 20, 1941, in which a friend of Frances's uses
it to describe the then-missing girl. This proves that George's idea of
Frances Cochran was based not on personal experience but entirely
on what the media reported about her. And although this bit of pla-
giarism is just one of the many pieces of evidence that will exonerate
my father, I do feel obligated to point out that there is no proof that
he lifted this phrase intentionally. I'm sure he was simply typing along
when the phrase popped into his brain and, perhaps not remembering that he'd read it in one of the articles he'd clipped and stuck in
his scrapbook, assumed that he'd thought of it himself. It happens all
the time. When I gave Oliver a draft of my first novel, for example, he
pointed out no less than seventeen phrases that, it turns out, I'd accidentally borrowed from Chandler. I made the corrections, no harm
done. Point being, however, that while George clearly based the character of Fanny on the real-life Frances Cochran, it is undoubtedly clear
that he never actually met the woman. During January and February
of 1941, while the protagonist of *Untitled* begins a graphically described
affair with this woman—copulating with her that day in the backseat
of the Deluxe and then continuing to stop off in Lynn for a quickie
with her on his way to visiting Irene in Cambridge—the real George

was surely just sitting in New Haven, pecking out endless revisions of his play and wondering how he'd afford an engagement ring for Iris. This is not to say that I find the chapters describing this affair anything less than vivid ("the brackish bouquet of Fanny's moist fanny" is one of those sentences that really sears itself into your mind and nostrils) and heartbreaking: You can really feel the protagonist's confusion, his frantic guilt. The sex is both erotic and neurotic, the libidinous inseparable from the self-lacerating. He's clearly terrified about his future, terrified about committing to Irene, to adulthood, and is simply acting out. I wisely did not excerpt these scenes for my students, but during one of my pre-class prep-sessions, when I had these pages spread out on my bed, Julia walked in. She'd been in the living room watching pornography for some research she was doing on tropes of female degradation, and said, "You know, there are some fantastically beautiful penises working in the adult industry. But then out of nowhere, there'll be a weird one, like where the head is malformed and pointy. I don't get it. You'd think there would be standards. Anyway. What you got here?" She began perusing the material like a woman at a yard sale, and was soon eyeing the "Fanny Affair" chapters from *Untitled* and tittering like a teenager with a pilfered copy of *Lolita*. "Oh, my, my," she said, "what have we here?" While I continued my work—deciding on the exact order of the readings for my class—she curled up on the bed and read through my dad's racy chapters. "Well," she concluded a few minutes later (the speed at which she reads always unnerves me), "I suppose if you're trying to make the argument that he didn't actually know this woman, all this banging is pretty good evidence."

"What do you mean?"

"It's all just typical male novelist stuff, isn't it? I mean, this Fanny character, or Frances, she's not a real person here. She's just a vehicle for the guy's angst. She's a cipher, a MacGuffin."

"You don't understand. He was writing this in the midsixties— Updike and Roth were now on the scene, *Tropic of Cancer* had just been published in America. Literary sex was going through a radical change, and he's in a dialogue here with his contemporaries."

"Sure, in the way frat brothers are in dialogue with each other. Listen, I don't mean to poo-poo your father's writing. I just mean to point out—and this will help you with your case—that I don't think this woman is a real person on the page here."

"Can I have those chapters back, please?"

"I'm sorry, okay? I didn't mean to upset you. I'm just—"

"I'm not upset. I just need to keep this organized. I have a system here and I don't want my piles disturbed."

"I suppose that's true of all of us, though, right?" She handed back my father's pages. "So I guess it's not really a male thing. I mean, we all look at each other not as fully formed human beings but as reflections and projections of ourselves, right?"

"There's no need to backtrack. You had a valid point, a useful point, and I am grateful for it."

"I'm not backtracking, I'm just thinking aloud. Do we see each other as fully formed people? I dunno. I say I love you and I do, but I'm also aware that you remind me—your hairline, your pale complexion, your thin arms, that weird jaw thing you do when you chew—you remind me of my father. And I also know that my professional ambition is a way, in part, of seeking the approval I never received from my father and a way of proving that I'm better than him. So do I see you—*can* I see you—as a real person? Probably not. I suppose I see all the crazy shit that I project onto you."

That word "projecting," when used in the Freudian sense, always makes me think of cheap special effects in psychedelic films of the sixties, an off-screen movie projector shining wavy pinks and greens onto a character, usually to signify hallucinations, torment, pleasure, anything really.

"But my point," she continued, "is that everyone does that to everyone else, right? There, I'm revising what I said about your father's writing, so you can stop looking at me like that."

I have no idea how I was looking at her, but perhaps—to continue her argument—I wasn't looking at her at all. I cannot be sure. I'm looking at her now, or rather glancing up at her between sentences, watching her as she watches Chris, a sad closed circuit of solipsism. They look like they're enjoying each other, though, smiling and laughing with their projections of each other. They are, at the moment, in the backyard, of which my writing room has an oblique view, barred by some rather Gorey-esque tree branches. Julia—who has now completely moved in—decided to fix up the backyard. She says she has a green thumb. She's repeated that little expression so many times, it's just meaningless phonemes to me now. Green thumb, Greet numb, Greif bum. This was, I know, not only part of the nesting instinct—which extends even to the way a woman will colonize your bathroom with loofahs and shell-shaped soaps: *This space is mine now*—but part and parcel of the need to fix a man. I am a man with a slightly overgrown backyard: I am, therefore, a man with something Julia can fix. A project. I personally enjoy the jungle aesthetic back there. Ever since the weeds first got knee-high, I have enjoyed it as a statement against the Levittown ideology (you know, the idea that the suburbs have tamed nature, contained it to a personal square of greenery, the Eisenhowerian fulfillment of the promise of Genesis), but I do admit that I have begun taking advantage of the now nipple-high weeds for the coverage they offer. When I can't find any storage space for something, I can always put it in the backyard and know that it will disappear among the weeds, which, I admit, is not the wisest strategy. The yard is now filled not just with weeds, but with stationary bikes and real bikes, Ab-Masters and Amway boxes. So when Julia said that she was going to clear it all out, dig it all up and resod the whole mess, I protested, but not too much. (Her teaching load this summer is lighter than mine, so she has more free time to take on this sort of project.) But then she recruited Chris to help her. The poor kid is saddled with work for his summer classes, which he has to take after getting suspended, and now he won't even have time to relax at home because Julia is strong-arming him into a transparently contrived bonding ritual. It's not enough for her to colonize my home, she now must take Chris as well, claim him as hers. I'm overreacting, I know I am. This is good, Chris getting outside. He's pale and fat. He might gain a skill here. That can't be bad. But when they went to the hardware store to pick up some tools for the deforestation project, and I tagged along—despite Julia's casually insistent urge that I stay at home and get some work done, that there was no need for me to come—I could sense, as I walked through the hardware store's overgrown aisles with the two of them, Chris's hesitancy. Sure, when Julia put lawn-aerators into the shopping cart, they joked that it would make it look—Chris here—like there was poop all over the yard but that—Julia here—that would be an improvement over its current condition, and they both laughed, but I caught his sighs, the way he looked at the floor with a knowledge that he was giving up his summer. The floor was cement and lightly saw-dusted like the floor of a kitschy BBQ restaurant, and Chris was dragging his feet through it. While the rest of us were leaving foot-prints, he was leaving two ribbony trails. He needed some cheering up, so on the way to the checkout, as we passed through the electrical aisle, I said, "Hey, Chris," picking a bundled-up extension cord off a hook, "you know what this is?" Both Chris and Julia turned around with matching quizzical stares. "Check it out," I said, "a magic trick." I unsnaked the cord and held up the plug. "This is called the male end, and this," holding up the other end, "is the female end." I plugged the male end into the female end, pushing it through a little resistance, then held it up to Chris like a magician asking an audience member to inspect a rope trick. The spare electrical outlets on the shelf looked on with their shocked, three-pronged expressions, but Chris and Julia weren't nearly as emotive. Had Julia not been there, Chris would have felt more comfortable to give me the laugh I deserved, which would have segued into a casual but bonding talk about sex and—to quote Jack Hale, from the talk he gave me in 1964 after my father died—"the mysteries of the vaginal species." But Chris sensed Julia's disapproval of my cord trick, saw her rolling her eyes, and so when I said, "Get it?" he just grunted, "Yeah," and followed Julia to the checkout. Instead of getting in line with them and listening to their exclusionary banter, I pretended to peruse the wall of Employee of the Month portraits near the door, all those middle-aged men with puffy faces and molester-ish smiles. I wish I could say that I was entirely confident in my attempt to connect with Chris, but I am not above self-doubt. What was Julia's eye-rolling trying to communicate? That she disapproved of my joke? Or perhaps I was being inappropriate? Chris is, after all, a minor, and I do not know at what age it's appropriate to start talking about things like sex. Perhaps he would take the wrong meaning from my little demonstration. Maybe he would think that I was advocating some sort of hermaphroditic autocopulation (the extension cord did, after all, form a perfect ouroboros of sex), or maybe he would think I was saying he should start sticking his pecker in light sockets, driving up my electric bill. I couldn't read anything behind his sphinxian expression, now that I thought about it, so he could have been be thinking anything! He's not even my own kid but I always think of that Philip Larkin poem—or is it Philip Levine?—or Robert Phillips?—the one about how your parents fuck you up—goes something like "Your parents fuck you up." I'm terrified that I'm fucking this poor kid up. Four years ago, when I first took guardianship of him, we returned to my home from the court and sat down on the couch. With nothing really to talk about, I turned on the TV. Apartheid in South Africa had just ended, so I figured I would teach my new ward about this important moment in history and began flipping through the overwhelming number of channels (I'd just gotten cable) to get to the news. I came across one station that made me stop for a moment simply because the image on the screen was at once familiar and abstract, and I had to pause so my brain could make sense of it. After a few seconds I realized what it was: footage of a woman giving birth, the camera staring right into the abyss of an enormously dilated vagina. As soon as I understood what we were looking at, I changed the channel and found a news station—and there they were, the people of South Africa dancing and cheering in the streets, Nelson Mandela clasping his hands together and smiling at a newly free nation—but who knows what Chris's kid-brain had absorbed in that brief moment. That thing on the screen had been absolutely cavernous, like it was opening up to swallow us both, a hungry and angry maw demanding our return to the womb. It was surely Chris's first glimpse of a woman's private parts, and now he was watching Nelson Mandela speechify about the end of government-sanctioned segregation. What had I done to him? Would he forever think, however subconsciously, of women as wormholes to oblivion? And would he forever link, however subconsciously, that terrifying thought to the triumphant end of Apartheid? What had I done?

Yes, parenting is a frightening business—or, as my father wrote in *Untitled*, "To beget another, to be a father, was to be god and mortal at once. You create a life, the life that will supplant your own" (56). In the novel, that line occurs at the end of February 1941, when both George McWeeney and his protagonist found out that their fiancées—Iris and Irene, respectively—were pregnant, and I find it ironic that Edie chooses not to quote this passage since it prefigures how she attempts to "supplant" the real George with the monster she imagines in her book. I should admit, however, that when Edie tries to draw the cor-relation between the protagonist discovering he is going to be a father and our father discovering he is going to be a father, the timelines do match up. Edie was born October 29, 1941, which means around late February of that year, Iris—depending on what Jack Hale once called a woman's "moon schedule"—would have discovered she was pregnant and told George. Our mother's diary ends just before this would have happened. Presumably she suddenly became too overwhelmed at this point to continue documenting her life. It is a tragedy, as she was an effortlessly articulate writer, witty but passionate, and remarkably self-aware. A devoted reader, she understood the value of journaling, but it's as if, with the move into suburban motherhood and wifedom, she willed herself into silence along with the rest of her generation. I mourn the loss of her voice throughout the forties and fifties, not just for her acute insights, both personal and societal, but because her diaries from these years surely could have offered evidence to refute the claims Edie makes about the coming decades. Regardless, when George's protagonist discovers he is going to be a father, it cements his future and slaps him out of his panic-driven affair with Fanny. In the novel, he doesn't so much break it off with Fanny as simply stop going to her. Fanny doesn't have his phone number or know where he lives—he's just been stopping by her home for a quick bang before going to Cambridge—so she has no way to find him. In a way, it's the perfect affair. I'm sure many marriages could have been saved were they all so simple. Edie sees this "misogynistic disregard for Fanny/ Frances's feelings" as proof that both the protagonist and George regard women with a burgeoning sociopathy. This interpretation— shared, unfortunately, by some of my less perceptive students when we analyzed these passages in class—is one hundred percent false, as it completely ignores the fact that the next thirty pages of the novel, describing his fiancée's first trimester and the preparations for their wedding, are filled with passages that show a deep, flowering of love for Irene. For example, "He felt a deep, flowering love for Irene" (49). Not only does Edie completely ignore this evidence of compassion for a woman, but her interpretation is clearly biased by her own feelings of being jilted. Edie writes,

> Imagine, for a moment, nineteen-year-old Frances Cochran (we can drop the "Fanny" pretense), sitting in her parents' home in Lynn, Massachusetts, waiting for George to knock on her door, waiting all night, looking up and down the street, her heart leaping and then falling at the approach of every passerby, waiting all week for anything, a call, a note in the mail, anything that might explain her lover's sudden disappearance. Has she been rejected? she wonders, or has there been some accident? She will never know. Assuming it's rejection—as we women are trained to do—she surely cried herself to sleep, wondering what was wrong with her. Not pretty enough? Not smart enough? Considering the facts of this story, it's impossible for any compassionate and empathetic reader not to imagine this scene. George McWeeney, however, did not imagine this scene. It is noticeably absent. (122)

There is absolutely no evidence in the novel that the character of Fanny invested anything emotional in the affair, so this imagined scene that Edie offers is not only hypothetical, it is at odds with the textual evidence. The scene is absent because it does not exist. Now look at the specificity of what Edie invites us to imagine: the crying, the anxious concerns about being rejected. This is not Fanny or Frances she is talking about here; it's herself. I'm sure years ago some guy left Edie hanging and she apparently never got over it. In my English 1 classes, I tried to use this as an example of how wrong literary interpretation can go when we project our own lives onto the characters, but half the women in the class would hear nothing of it. They were actually siding with Edie!

Either way, Fanny's name doesn't appear in the novel again until page 73, the day before the protagonist's wedding. Again, the correlations Edie draws here, I should admit, are accurate. The protagonist's wedding is on June 20, 1941. George and Iris got married on June 20, 1941. In the novel, the protagonist picks up the June 19 issue of *The Boston Globe* and sees the following headline: *Body of Young Woman Found Slain*. During my research, I did find a microfiche of *The Boston Globe* from June 19. Sure enough, below the fold is the headline *Body of Young Woman Found Slain*. Frances Cochran of Lynn, MA, it says, had been missing for two days, last seen getting into "a black square-backed car." When she was found, her face and breasts had been mutilated, and her body had nearly been cut in half at the waist. In the novel, the protagonist is devastated, sitting in a Cambridge watering hole the day before his wedding:

> His life had seemed to be going perfectly—a newly minted MFA from Yale Drama, a Hollywood job offer, a beautiful fiancée and a child on the way—and now this: The youthful indiscretion he thought he'd put behind him was front-page news, murdered. Her face appeared in his mind, the impossibly green eyes, the button nose, the black, almost Hassidic-looking curls of hair bouncing down around her full cheeks. He held the glass of whiskey. It was

good whiskey. He sipped it. It was sharp, metallic on his tongue, like gun metal. He looked back at the newspaper. He was being punished. He was sure of it. (74)

I love the "Hassidic-looking curls of hair" but I can't help wondering if it clashes tonally with the Hemingway-brand whiskey-as-objective-correlative thing—though perhaps that's the point, the clash between the lyrical and the austere. Anyway, I quote this here because it completely undermines Edie's claim that the protagonist—and by absurd extension George—lacked empathy for Fanny/Frances. He's clearly torn up about this. So torn up, in fact, that the ghost (though not a literal one) of Fanny looms over the rest of the novel, and everything the protagonist does after this is clearly an attempt to put that ghost to rest. What more evidence of compassion could you want?

But of course the real issue here, the real reason why Edie's argument throughout the first half of her book is entirely wrong, is that it's based on a rather blatant logical fallacy. From looking at the basic facts, it's clear that, yes, George McWeeney did draw on his personal life for his novel. It's also clear that he based the character of Fanny on the real Frances Cochran. That much is obvious. Edie then assumes that the affair in the novel was also based on fact.

"To put it another way," I said to my class, "just because *Macbeth* was inspired by the murder of a real Scottish king, does that mean that everything in it is fact? For example, it would be wrong to then conclude that, say, witches are real."

"Yo, witches *are* real, bro," Robert said from a corner desk. "Look, I found one." He pointed to the shy girl in the back whose name I'd forgotten. She had dyed black hair and raccoonish makeup. A handful of people laughed and the girl just stared at her desk.

"It's a logical fallacy," I said. "And if we are supposed to assume then that the affair described in the novel actually happened, then why not assume that everything else in the novel actually happened?"

The point I was trying to make, which no one in that class was listening to anymore, as Robert was off making some other joke, was that Edie apparently has no use for the entire rest of the novel. Just as my George McWeeney diverges from Edie's George McWeeney at that gas station in Lynn, MA, Edie's George McWeeney diverges from this protagonist after the wedding in chapter 7. The next two hundred pages of Dad's novel follow the protagonist as he goes to Hollywood with his new family, writes movies, becomes a big shot, meets celebrities. While this might seem close enough to our father's life, it's nothing of the sort. As much as I love my father, he was no big shot. He spent his life typing away in his home office, occasionally shuffling out in slippers and a cardigan to get some coffee. So how can Edie make the argument that we must take the Fanny affair as fact but then casually discard the rest of the novel? It doesn't add up. It's sloppy, illogical detective work.

This is the point in Edie's manuscript where she jumps forward to 1995, tells us all about returning to Los Angeles (but makes no mention of how I dropped everything to pick her up at a motel in Eagle Rock). This is where Rory Beach enters her story, though she seems careful to keep him hidden, obscured. Notice how she refers to him only as her doctor, never Rory. At most she'll refer to him as Dr. Beach. But no physical description of him exists in her manuscript, no direct quotes. This is odd, considering what an influence he had on everything that follows, including the writing of this book, which I'm sure he, at the very least, co-authored. So why does she take such pains to obscure him, to cover up the strings, as it were? Well, to continue with the string metaphor, or at least tweak it a little, it is because she must know, at some fundamental level, that he is the puppet master here, and if he were more visible in this book, then readers would see those strings. But I've seen this man, seen how he is with my sister; I've witnessed the dynamic between them. And I can say without a doubt that the "personal journey of discovery" that Edie describes in those chapters was entirely constructed by him. Not only did he surely write the script for her "personal journey," but he probably even wrote those chapters. It's not like my sister—the daughter of a professional writer—to pen such nonsense as "the scent of Old Spice recalled old memories—standing beside my father in his bathroom, watching him get ready" (145). Recalled old memories? That's just sloppy writing. My sister is smarter than that. A sentence like that is clearly the work of Rory, mired as he is in the mnemonic abstractions of his profession.

The evidence in the second half of Edie's book is based mostly, though not exclusively, on memories that she claims to have repressed until Rory extracted them last year, but since she does such an admirable job of intertwining these "memories" (yes, I should qualify that word with the condescending claws of quotes) with what might at first glance seem to be empirical evidence, I cannot dismiss it all by undermining the whole theory of memory recovery. It would be simple enough to do that. Just consider the recent court case of Ramona v. Isabella, which has laid the legal precedent to debunk not just my sister's claims but hold Rory Beach culpable: Just a few years ago,

Holly Ramona—a young woman from Napa Valley who was beginning college in Orange County—began seeing a therapist who helped
her "recover" memories of her father, Gary, raping her. She sued
her father, and her father's life began to fall apart. But then Gary
Ramona brought charges against her daughter's therapist, Marche
Isabella, and proved in court that Isabella had implanted these memories in his daughter's head. Gary Ramona won $500,000 in dam-
ages. Although this was the first case of this sort, a legal landmark,
the phenomenon of a woman making up gibberish—whether that gibberish be doctor-implanted or not—and using it as courtroom slander
has a long and storied history, going as a far back as the Salem witch
trials. In court, if our case gets that far—and I assure you, if you go
ahead with this publication, then I will take it that far—it would be
simple enough to dismantle Dr. Beach's methods; all I'd have to do is
say "Ramona v. Isabella" and the judge would be on my side. But, as
I've said, Edie has knotted together these erroneous memories with
facts, and I must unknot the whole tangled mess.

By late 1946, Edie writes, George McWeeney was well established
in Hollywood. He had a beautiful wife, a beautiful five-year-old daughter ("beautiful" is Edie's vague and sentimental adjective, repeated like
a tic; in truth, the photographic record proves she was an unfortunate-
looking girl, like Kafka in culottes). He had just bought a home in the
beautiful San Fernando Valley, was part of the first wave of suburban
settlers. Iris, pregnant with their second child (me), was spending weeks
on end back East to be with her ailing father, so George was left for
long stretches by himself in their new house with little Edie, balancing
the demands of fatherhood with the demands of his career. He had

been writing for *Rampart*'s very popular early radio incarnation for five years now, and he'd developed a close friendship with its creator, Jack Hale. All this is pretty much true. Although I was not yet born to remember this, I am inclined to believe Edie in chapter 16 when she recalls sitting with George and Jack at our kitchen table. The two men were doing men things: drinking scotch, playing cards, relaxing after putting the show to bed. I never saw our father do any of these things, but I suspect that the demands of having two children, and the increased pressure when *Rampart* made the transition to the small screen, curtailed these moments. I am sure he did do these things at one point, all in the service of homosocial bonding with Jack. Consider, for example, the precision of some of Edie's recollections: the "rustle of Dad rubbing his hand against his unshaved chin like the soft white noise on a record," the way they both looked like "hunched giants" sitting beside her, Jack jokingly offering her a nip of scotch, George laughing and propping her up on his lap where she "could smell the iodinic bite on his breath" that she heretofore had "associated with a scraped knee, a parental warning, a quick dab of Bactine," and George and Jack's prurient banter that her kid-brain absorbed only phonetically— "boy hide shirt tie that caboose"—which she was only able to understand years later—"Boy, I'd sure ride that caboose" (156). Scenes like this strike me as genuine—even though Bactine was not yet commercially available in 1946—in part because Edie sticks to a child's understanding of the scene. As more of these "recovered memories" come out, though, the more you can see Edie (or, more likely, Rory) imposing adult consciousness on five-year-old Edie, our only witness. For example, Adult Edie then writes that she recalls a scene shortly after this

where she is riding in the front seat of our dad's black 1939 Ford
Mercury as he drives through "the serpentine roads that wound
through the Hollywood Hills like termite-trails in ancient wood" (160).
Forget for a moment Adult Edie's sin of piling two metaphors onto one
image, forget that those two metaphors are competing not just at the
imagistic level but at the ecosystemic level as well (snakes are predators,
termites prey), and just remember that this is a child's consciousness
we're being asked to enter here. No five-year-old would think this.
Adult Edie is taking control of this scene, contorting it. This becomes
even clearer when George stops to pick up another passenger and Edie
has to sit in the back. The new passenger is "alabaster-skinned, her
curtain of black hair melding into the slinky black silk cocktail dress
she was wearing despite it being the middle of the day" (161). As Adult
Edie steps in, the sentences get sloppier. This particular tongue twister
(just try to say "slinky black silk" with out mashing it into "slilk") seems
to reveal some cattiness that only Adult Edie would intone (the observation about the evening dress in the middle of the day implying this
is a walk of shame for the passenger, something young Edie wouldn't
know or care about). But what is most glaring is the perfectly recalled
dialogue. Gone is the impressionistic wash of meaningless adult-speak,
all sounds, shapes, and colors. It has been replaced with dialogue so
precise it is impossible to believe that it has survived fifty years in Edie's
brain. The sheer specificity of it draws that specificity into question.
This is, in other words, not remembered dialogue, not even recon-
structed dialogue, but purely constructed dialogue. When the mysterious passenger—whose "curtain of black hair" is surely an intentional
echo of Frances Cochran—turns around and starts talking to young

Edie—introducing herself as Betty, saying she's going to be famous one day, saying she's met so many nice people since moving to Hollywood from boring ol' Medford, Mass—doesn't it strike you as unrealistically expository? Yes, of course, this is Elizabeth "Betty" Short's first (live) appearance in Edie's book, but the artifice here is transparent. And it's not just the fact of the exposition that is revealing but the content as well. Edie has her say things to our father like, "I like Jack just fine. I mean, he's a big shot, but not a *big-shot* big shot. I've been with some big shots, honey. Ray Milland. You know him? And Joel McCrea. No, but my biggest big shot you'll never believe—*Mister* Orson Welles. That's right. But I like Jack better than all them. He's nicer, less crazy." Since this scene is fiction, it is particularly interesting that Edie chooses to introduce Betty Short in a way (reeling off all her johns, still dressed in the previous night's cocktail dress) that suggests our father is picking up a *fille de joie*, knowing that readers will carry that connotation, however subconsciously, with them for the rest of the book. (I feel compelled to admit here that I've now paused at my keyboard for a good ten or fifteen minutes staring at that phrase, *fille de joie*. Approximately fifteen minutes ago now I finished typing it, clicked my Wheelwriter back a dozen spaces, and underlined it. The underlining is perhaps what made me stop, drawing such attention to the obscure phrase, but I must defend the underlining, pedantically, on the grounds that as a foreign phrase it must be marked as such—it must be copyeditorially Otherized. What I'm less certain that I can defend is the use of the phrase itself, which is, according to my Webster's, French for a "girl of pleasure, used euphemistically for a prostitute." I know that's the precise definition because I have the dictionary right here. Worse, just behind that, is the thesaurus. That's where I found the phrase. That's right. I was sitting here, knowing I could just use the word "prostitute," but I felt the need to reach for something slightly more obscure. So I got French with it. While I understand that casually dropping a foreign—usually French or Latin—phrase into a sentence adds to its authority, implying that the author has a wealth of cultural knowledge to draw on, even if he chooses to keep the specifics of that knowledge veiled in italicized foreignness, I do not myself know French or Latin, so I have no recourse but the thesaurus, despite the fact that everyone in the writing biz regards thesauri as demonic, warning you that it will turn clear and direct Anglo-Saxon prose into something so Latinate it could have been written by one of my ESL students, who are an enthusiastically thesauric bunch. While I am suspicious of the idea that there are right ways and wrong ways to discover new words, I feel admitting all bias adds more authority than a condescending, faux-polyglottic posture. But of course what I'm really concerned about here is that initial impulse to posture, to impress you with my authoritative voice. Am I still operating under the delusion that you might sense a novelist's voice buried in this cease and desist letter and casually recommend that those literary boys down the hall reconsider my work? No, I must shed myself of those delusions. You are my opponent in this case. I will not undermine the integrity of this project by attempting to ingratiate myself with you, even if it is in a snobby and condescending way. On with it.) Edie's implicit jealousy when describing Betty Short suggests what Rory would probably call an Electra complex, which might shed some light onto the real motives for her claims here. Regardless, in the montage of memories that follows, in which Edie describes being backseat witness to "countless midday pickups" (not quite countless, I counted seven), George always taxiing Betty Short from Jack Hale's house in the Hills to her apartment in Hollywood, we learn—still in suspiciously expository front-seat dialogue—some interesting information, some true, some not (I will do my best to parse the two). First, Betty is carrying on an affair with the very married Jack Hale. George, trying to balance being Jack's underling and best friend, has been roped into helping them conceal it from Mrs. Hale. (I admit that Edie captures George's insecurities here in some nice, cringe-inducing details, particularly in the way he insists that he's Jack's buddy, as if you can hear how desperately he wants to not feel taken advantage of.) There is a surprisingly long explanation from Betty about how she and Jack are coordinating the logistics of this affair, as if Edie anticipates getting sued by the still-kicking Mrs. Hale who would insist that there was no way Jack ever had a lady on the side, but that's none of our concern here. What is of our concern is how Edie drops into this fiction a few facts. Betty mentions that she has a rose tattoo on her hip. This is true. Both Harry Hansen and Aggie Underwood would report this detail the following January. She also mentions that she is saving up for a trip to the dentist because her teeth are getting bad. This is also based in fact. According to testimony from a woman Betty stayed with in San Diego, she had terribly rotten molars and would try to patch up her cavities with wax before heading out on the town. Edie drops these facts into the conversation but they come across as bizarre non sequiturs, revealing how eager Edie is to assert the veracity of her "memories." It reminds me of when I once came home in the middle of a school day to find Chris lounging on the couch with a bag of Funyuns, and when I asked him why he wasn't in school he concocted this long, elaborate lie about his math teacher: "Mrs. Wise, who is from England and collects elephant stuffed animals on her desk, she had a heart attack so they sent everyone home for the day." It was an admirably bold and nonsensical lie, but I was totally suckered by his transparent attempt to anchor the fiction with two truth-nuggets, that quick aside about her nationality (and doesn't the mere mention of Britishness send a bolt of authority through anything?) and her pachyderm fetish (perhaps an atavistic memory of her countrymen's days colonizing the subcontinent?). Chris and I ended up going out to a movie that day, the one about the retarded fellow that got all the awards, and over dinner at Sizzler we got pretty good at doing his voice. (Stumped for the title, I just now found it in *Fleeber's Encyclopedia of Film*, which I have near my desk here. It says *Forrest Gump* came out in 1994. I keep wanting to think that our movie date was recent, six months ago tops. But, if *Fleeber's* is to be trusted, I guess that was about two years ago.)

Chris has been pretty busy working on the yard with Julia, and it looks pretty good. I can't exactly see it at the moment; it's about 3:00 AM and quite dark outside, but during the day you can really see the progress they've made. With the weeds gone you can see all the patches of dead grass where I'd left boxes (these dead patches remind me of the shadows burned onto the ground after Hiroshima, atomic shadows, though perhaps I think that because of a documentary on World War Two Julia was watching the other night on PBS). Every day, Chris and Julia have been out in the yard, digging up the dead lawn. I keep my window open so I can hear the oddly satisfying sound of their tools ripping into the earth, wet and crunchy. They've tossed most of the dead lawn into a pile in the corner of the yard that through my window the other day I heard Chris refer to as Jabba the Hut, which Julia laughed at, despite her once admitting to me that she found *Star Wars* "more interesting for how it reflects techno-anxieties of the post-Watergate era than for its space-opera sock-puppetry."

To get back to the point, though, the only other verifiable fact that Edie slips into these scenes of George giving Betty rides home after her dalliances with Jack is a reference to Betty's roommate, Anne Toth. Edie uses this to point out that later Toth would tell investigators that Betty had been running around with "a guy named George." While it is true that Toth said this, and it appears to add some validity to this portion of Edie's tale, Edie completely omits the rest of Toth's interview where she describes this George as being "swarthy, about 5'9" or 5'10"." Betty Short may have been cavorting with a George, but not our George. We McWeeneys have complexions closer to a breed of subterranean mole rats and have never been accused of possessing anything near swarth. Plus, my father, as much of a giant as he seemed to me when I was young, was only 5'8". But an important question here is why would George actually take Edie along for these rides? True, our mother (and I, gestating inside her) was out of town, and Aunt Paige had not yet moved to California and become the go-to babysitter, but our father, more than anyone else in our family, had a tight-lipped sense of propriety, and having his five-year-old daughter tag along on these sorts of errands is something he simply would not do. Especially when those errands turn blue, the conversations blatantly flirtatious (Betty to George: "I'll bet you're the real brains behind that show") and bluntly suggestive (Betty again:

"I'll bet you got a big ol' brain" . . . I mean really, come on). As we watch Edie watch George and Betty's relationship develop over the course of these car rides, Edie seems to be able to understand what is happening between them, despite being only five. For example, the first time Betty invites our father up to her apartment, Edie is in the backseat and thinks to herself—Adult Edie rather creepily mixing kid-speak with her adult's understanding of the scene—"Daddy stuttered, fumbled with his seat belt, and accepted Betty's offer of herself" (174). I have three points to make about this, which I will list in ascending order of importance. First, did 1939 Ford Mercuries have seat belts? I have not been able to find the answer to this, but I think we can safely say the answer is no. Second, I find it very hard to believe that a small child could really understand what it meant when a woman asks a man to come upstairs. And third, Edie is then left alone in the car while our father goes upstairs to allegedly bonk Ms. Short. Although I understand that paradigms of child-care shift over generations, and George's parenting instincts here (and, I can confirm, in real life as well) are weak, the likelihood of both George and Betty (who acts very maternally toward Edie in other circumstances) simply leaving the little girl in the back of the car for the fifteen-minute duration of their fuck is pretty slim. And that's another thing, Edie says he was upstairs with her for "about fifteen minutes," but how does she know? It's doubtful the car had a clock, doubtful she had a watch, doubtful that she'd be able to tell time anyway. Of course, when this invitation upstairs becomes a regular thing, George and Betty Short no longer leave young Edie in the car, but the question then becomes why would they leave this child sitting on the couch with only a copy of *Photoplay* magazine to entertain herself and only a thin muslin curtain between her and the noisily passionate porking (although, form a purely aesthetic perspective, I do like that detail about Betty having a curtain instead of a bedroom door, the way the afternoon sun hits it so Edie can see "the Turin-like sweat stains of whoever had slept on that sheet before it had been hung up, an oddly private and personal remnant left on this sad flag of privacy" [178]). But the biggest piece of evidence proving the falsity of these scenes (But wait, now that I think about that pretty curtain description: How the fuck would a five-year-old raised in a relatively secular household know what the Shroud of Turin looks like? Bad writing.) The biggest piece of evidence proving the falsity of these scenes arises when we look at the quasi-domestic behavior Edie observes between George and Betty in their postcoital moments. After just a few midday shags, we're treated to this passage:

> I sat on the couch, probing my fingers into its torn upholstery, exploring its foamy wounds with care, and watched my father emerge from the bedroom, casually tucking his shirt back into his pants, strapping his suspenders back onto his shoulders with a self-satisfied snap. He looked down at me, said nothing. Then Betty was there, next to him, freshly sexed. She was holding his tie—brown, knit, square-bottomed—and gently flipped up his collar. She put the tie around my dad's neck, adjusted its length, and made a perfect four-in-hand knot. She patted the knot as if to say, There, tied tight, a secret safely concealed. (182)

To find out how Edie showed her hand in this passage—among others—we have to look back to my father's novel. When the protagonist of *Untitled* is enjoying the early months of marital bliss with his new wife, George writes:

> After afternoon love-making, when he had to get back to the studio, after he'd tucked his shirt back in, snapped his suspenders back on, Irene would always take great care to retie his tie for him. She'd adjust the length just so and make a perfect four-in-hand, always concluding with a little tap-tap on the knot and a reassuring, "Tied tight." (85)

I'm going to withhold comment on the temporally jarring overuse of the preposition "after" in that first sentence, and just say that if Edie remembered the tie-tying scene, she didn't remember it from real life; she remembered it from our father's novel, which he wrote nearly two decades after the point in time she claims Betty Short tied our father's tie. And this is not the only thing Edie "remembers" from our father's fiction. Consider her description of how Betty Short's apartment smells: "a vague citrus bite mixed with a coiled saline funk from the fishmonger downstairs who used lemons to wash away the smell of his work" (173). Now look at my father's novel: "Irene made *trout a la nage* for dinner, and he watched her wash her hands with a sliced lemon" (102). Edie also writes that a neighbor "had the loping gait of a circus clown," and on page 143 of our father's novel appears the phrase "clown-footed." Edie's memories are, in other words, plagiarized memories. Edie contrasts the development of George's illicit relationship with Betty with an increasing and silent tension between George and Jack. Again, despite the fact that Edie wouldn't start first grade for another year and our mother was on the other side of the country, I want to cast doubt on the likelihood that Edie would actually be present for afternoon script meetings between the two, as well as the likelihood that she could recall their conversations in such detail, but more than that, these scenes betray a flawed logic in Edie's narrative. She wants to suggest that the friendship between the two men is growing tense because they are both having affairs with the same woman (George getting "sloppy seconds . . . literally," as one of my students crudely pointed out), but as it becomes clear later on, Jack is completely unaware that George is also sleeping with Betty. So the tension we see during these scenes should, in theory, be one-sided. But it's not. We see Jack becoming just as guarded and defensive toward George as George is toward Jack. Granted, there are some nicely observed moments in these scenes, like when George and Jack are debating the conclusion of one particular *Rampart* episode—just how empathetic should Det. Mike Nolan be toward the woman who murdered her abusive husband?—and, clearly annoyed by Jack pulling rank to get his way (arguing that Nolan should not show any empathy), George just sits there silently, "tapping an unlit cigarette against the tabletop, flipping it upside-down, tapping it again, flipping, tapping" (198). This is a small gesture of quiet anger that Edie and I learned to recognize. While our mother seemed to smoke because she always needed something to keep her hands busy, our father was not a fidgety-fingered man. He was not in the habit of idly tapping things that did not need tapping. He was also not a man given to overt displays of anger. So when something happened that seemed like it should anger him, we became attuned to these little gestures. When our mother told us over the dinner table that she was going back to Africa: silence, tap-tap. When I, at the angry age of thirteen, told him that my friend Bobby's father could beat the tar out of him in a fistfight: silence, tap-tap. But even though I recognize this gesture, and its inclusion in this scene with Jack is like ice water on the back of my neck, I wonder how it reads to those unfamiliar with our father's particular signifiers of impotent emotion. Or did Edie include this patented George-gesture not for her readers but for herself? Or, perhaps, for me? It's hard not to see the conversation she is trying to have with me through her warped narrative. Hey, Paulie? Yeah, Edie? Remember Dad, that thing he did with the cigarettes? Yeah, Edie, I do. The real question is why can she have this conversation only by injecting us into the Black Dahlia story? Here our family stands, superimposed into the middle of a widely recognized story of unsolved murder. We don't fit here: You can see the faint and fuzzy penumbra all around us that signals to the audience shoddy special effects, bad blue screen, the scene rejecting the subject. Can she decide to hate our father only by convincing the world to hate him as well? (I just realized that I never actually told our dad that my friend Bobby's father could beat the tar out of him in a fistfight. I know I thought about telling him that many times, and there is a scene like that in *Rarer Monsters*, and in writing that novel I must have imagined the scene so many times and in such detail that I suppose I imagined it into existence for myself. But I should come clean and revoke it as a memory. Strike it from the record, Your Honor.)

Although I understand that, while a great deal of the counter-evidence I have offered here so far is empirical, verifiable, and substantive, it might seem that the cornerstone of my argument against Edie's recovered "memories" is simple incredulousness (how likely is it that

Edie actually witnessed what she claims to have witnessed?), so I want to defend that stance on the basis that incredulity, while it might seem more like a disaffected attitude than a legally valid defense, is a result of reason, critical thought, and deductive reasoning. It is, in fact, the cornerstone of legal judgment. I bring this up because as my sister's tale becomes less and less credible, as she stretches the reader's capacity for belief, her feet drifting farther and farther from the ground, it is my job to stay firmly planted in the soil. And so my incredulity should hold just as much weight as tangible counterevidence when you are considering my case against hers. For example, I have no physical proof that my then-five-year-old sister did not attend the New Year's Eve party at Jack Hale's Spanish-style home in the Hollywood Hills; I cannot confirm with an outside source that screenwriter Waldo Salt did not play "got your nose" with my sister before giving her a sip of his Manhattan; I have no corroboration to say my sister did not witness Jack taking George aside in the kitchen moments before the jazz trio in the corner of the living room began playing what Lionel Barrymore appraised as "a very Negroid rendition of 'Auld Lang Syne'"; I have no empirical evidence to prove my sister did not overhear Jack tell George that Betty, who was not in attendance, needed to get down to Mexico to "get a scrape" and that George needed to arrange it; I have no substantial way to unsubstantiate these claims—but keep in mind: neither does Edie. She has only her memories to offer here. So we are left to weigh the probability of the whole scene. And let's face it: It's pretty low. Would a drunken Eddie Cantor really interrupt the band's rendition of "A Night in Tunisia" to do an improvised minstrel act? Would so many of the guests really mistake my sister for child actress Margaret O'Brien?

Would our father really react so calmly to the assignment Jack had given him? It's only minutes later, after all, that he calls New York to talk to my mother, wish her well, and say how much he's looking forward to her return. But keep in mind it would have been 3:00 AM in New York, and my mother was staying with her parents who would not have tolerated a telephone ringing at that hour. But that's the way Edie tells it. After this calm, adequately affectionate and spousy phone conversation, our father—fresh with the knowledge that either he or Jack had knocked up poor Ms. Short and that it was now his duty to take care of it—did the rounds at the party, said his polite goodbyes, wished everyone a happy New Year, then took Edie home. Edie ends this chapter with a rather pulpy line about the fact that two weeks later, Betty Short's body would be discovered, lifeless and bisected, in a vacant lot. This cheap suspense tactic highlights one of the problems I've been trying to address with this part of her book: the conflation of the perspectives of Adult Edie and Child Edie. And while this normally wouldn't be too much of a problem, here it confuses what is remembered with what is projected onto the memory, and in doing so it undermines the very nature of those memories. Although, now that I think about it, the impossibility of untangling memory from projection is one of the more resonate lessons of postmodernism, but that still doesn't mean we cannot, or should not, try. I am not sure if that makes as much sense as I want it to. The thought is there in my brain, but when I see it here on the page it seems like an approximate translation of the original thought. I'm feeling incredibly focused right now, but I can't quite nail down this thought. Of course, I haven't really slept at all tonight, so I should give myself a break. It's 6:00 AM, and the sun is finally starting to come up. I can see the backyard now through my window. The soil, which will soon be covered in new sod, is damp and has that freshly plowed looseness, like it's just inviting you to sink your hands into it. I'm feeling incredibly focused right now and practically tumescent when I look at how much work I've been able to get done tonight, but I should really stop for now. I can hear Julia in the kitchen, the sibilant whisper of her slippers against the linoleum, the considerately soft pinging sounds of her morning tea-making ritual. When I go out there she's going to be annoyed with me for staying up all night again to get work done. She thinks I've put this all behind me and am now plugging away on a new novel, so she's going to give me that condescending eyebrow-raise, that look that asks, "Why do you write?" which I never seem able to answer. She won't believe that I stayed up all night unassisted, so I'll have to tell her I fell asleep at my desk, but it will be difficult to pull off a groggy early-morning mien, considering how fucking focused I'm feeling right now. The guy I usually get Ritalin from sold me a gram of blow last week and it's been helping me through these marathon work sessions. It's the first time I've done it in almost twenty years and I'd forgotten about this overwhelming sense of competence and clarity. Back in my twenties, I'd never tried writing on it, but I really should have. It's making my morning classes a little rougher, though. I have a class in three hours and I should grab a catnap before then, but even with a hundred milligrams of Trazodone, I don't think it's in the cards, so I'll have to go the other direction, take a little bump and just power through. Julia is at the kitchen table now. I can hear her mug when she sets it down on the Formica. I will go out there, kiss her on the forehead, say good morning. I like the way her skin smells when she first wakes up, a mix of sweat and lavender.

I just got off the phone with Jack Hale's widow, Clarice. She is eighty-something and has a voice like tissue paper. I asked her if she remembered the New Year's Eve party her husband threw on December 31, 1946. She said she did. I asked her if she could confirm a few details about the party. Jazz trio: check. Notable celebrities in attendance: Eddie Cantor, Lionel Barrymore, Waldo Salt, Margaret O'Brien.

"Margaret O'Brien?" I asked. "The cha-, child actress?"

"Yes," she said, "there was a little girl here, knotty pigtails. I'm pretty sure it must have been Margaret O'Brien—you know, from *Meet Me in St. Louis*. Oh, that was such a delightful film. I think Arthur Freed had a hand in that one. He was a Jew. Tell me, what sort of article are you writing?"

While this might seem to confirm my sister's version of the story, consider what the old lady said next: "There certainly seems to be a lot of interest in that party. I don't know why. Once Jack's show moved to television, we threw some much bigger parties. At an Easter party in 1951, Rock Hudson said my shrimp cocktail was the best he'd ever had."

"Wha-, what do you mean?"

"I use fresh-squeezed orange juice and a bit of lemon verbena. That's the secret."

"No, I mean about the interest in the pa-, party. What other interest?"

"Oh, a while ago a woman came to see me, asked me all sorts of questions about Jack, said she was writing a book. She was particularly interested in this party."

So: Edith's "memory" has been supplemented. She clearly got Clarice Hale's version of the party and tweaked it a bit to fit herself in there.

"Nice woman," Clarice continued, "a sloucher, though. Pretty common among bosomy women who try to hide their bosoms. It's no way to get a husband."

"That's true."

"Well, I'm very observant. I used to work as a continuity girl before I married Jack. Like your stutter. I noticed that. You should really nip that in the bud. Try tongue-strengthening exercises. Like saying the alphabet with marbles in your mouth, or cunnilingus."

It's true: I've been stuttering lately. The lack of sleep, the drugs, the stress, it's bringing out an old tic. It's particularly noticeable when I'm teaching. The other day, after my last all-night work session, I was lecturing my 9:00 AM class about the balance of logos and pathos in Montaigne's "Of Thumbs," and my stutter got so bad (it's an excessively consonantal essay) that one student said I sounded like a remix. It's really getting in the way, and the worst part is that it's all my own doing. I am not a natural stutterer. Growing up in Hollywood, surrounded by people who recited *she sells seashells* every morning in front of the mirror, the city where people shed their regional dialects for a neutral elocution (until, of course, Brando showed up and turned everyone into mush-mouths), I always spoke clearly, free of tics and clicks. In my late teens, I even survived one short season of TV stardom—and the pressure not just of those cameras but of an entire phalanx of writers, producers, and directors ready to step in and tell you that you're dropping your G's again—without developing a nervous speech impediment. It wasn't until I left that all behind and went to Iowa to remake myself as a serious writer that I voluntarily adopted this record-skipping habit, and now, years after

I thought I'd shed my pretentious affectations, it's shown up again, unbidden, unwanted.

See, there was this guy at Iowa, whom I will leave nameless, a fiction writer with the sad, shadowed eyes of a boxer and the fine cheekbones of a girl. He wrote devastatingly beautiful stories about sad men doing sad things, full of clear-eyed lyricism. He had a stutter, and women loved him. When he read those sad stories at MFA readings, the women in attendance always had one hand delicately touching their throats, anticipating a good cry. They would flock to him, want to clutch his head to their bosoms, fellate him. Whether they loved him for his writing or for the vulnerability they saw in his stutter, I could never figure out. I never conversed with the guy personally, but after one of his readings, when I was mingling nearby, hoping to pick up one of the women who couldn't quite get the stutterer's attention—playing cleanup, I suppose—I overheard him tell one freckled young poetess that his stutter contributed to his prose style, as ever since he was a child his speech impediment had forced him to think relentlessly about words, mapping out sentences in his head before he ever spoke. "Plenty of great prose sta-, stylists have stutters," he went on. "Updike, Maugham, Ba-, Ba-, Borges." I went to the library that night—as none of the stutterer's castoffs were interested in going home with me—and confirmed this claim. Stuttering does seem to give people a step-up when it comes to wordsmithing. So I tried it on myself. I had just started teaching freshman composition, and so I used that forum to experiment with a stutter, dialing in different intensities, levels of impediment, different "problem notes" as I thought of them. That first semester my students thought I was simply insane, but by the spring semester I had really found—to put it in MFA-speak—my own voice. It was a nice, subtle stutter, not abrasive at all, just a slight hesitation at every *P* and *M*. I began doing what the stutterer said he did, mapping out sentences in my mind before speaking, and although I usually did it to hit those problem notes rather than avoid them, I really believe that I saw a marked improvement in my sentence-crafting. Of course I never took the stutter outside my own classroom, as my cohort would have known immediately that I was faking, but I knew it was a good stutter when several of my female students began talking to me after class with that same earnest desire to take care of a wounded puppy that I recognized with the real stutterer's female fans. Unfortunately, the only female students who proved susceptible to my new tic were the zaftig ones, so I did not reciprocate their attentions as I suppose I could have. But I did enjoy their reactions to me, and my awareness of this gave me a rather uncomfortable consideration. Had I been jealous of the stutterer's success with writing, or his success with women? Was there a difference? Or were my literary aspirations simply a ploy for pussy? Surely my intentions were purer, surely I had something to say, something that needed to be said, something that needed to come out, not just some desperate squirts of spunk but something real and meaningful. (Actually, I did take one of the huskier girls up on her offer and she proved very understanding when I didn't last as long as I should have.) It's still something that scares me, something I think about whenever Julia poses the "Why do you write?" question. And yet no one seems to question Darin Erskine's intentions. (I said I wasn't going to spill the stutterer's name, but it slipped out and I'm not about to fetch the Wite-Out for him.) Erskine's latest made the *New York*

Times list of Notable Books. Kakutani said that *Son of Chance* "contains some of the most dazzling sentences an American author has put to the page in years, capable of limning an entire life in one heartbreaking turn of phrase." I haven't read it, but the other day I skimmed the acknowledgments page in the back, worried (needlessly as it turned out) that I might find Oliver's name (I recalled them hanging out some in the Iowa days).

After a couple years of using my stutter whenever I felt the need for some extra sympathy, however, it found hold in some crinkle of my cerebral cortex. After a while I realized I no longer had control of it, and in order to free myself of the damn thing I had to buy speech therapy records, spending endless hours repeating those problem notes in front of the mirror, watching my lips make those soft plosives, to train myself right again. It's been dormant for years now, but it's coming back and this time not in the sexily vulnerable way I'd trained it. Now I sound like someone with a spastic neurological disorder, which makes me more nervous, which just makes me stutter more. I really need to get some sleep.

The chapter after the New Year's party contains what might be Edie's biggest leap of imagination. She attempts here to narrate our father's thought process, but of course she has absolutely no access to those thoughts. She says that George did not take Betty Short down to Mexico to get that abortion as Jack had instructed, which I suppose is true. She also has a lot of statistics about just how dangerous abortions were south of the border, which I suppose are accurate. But then, based on that, and what she claims happens next, she imagines an entire inner dialogue that she has *no access to*. She presumes that George researched the safety of Mexican abortions and then silently debated with himself for two weeks about whether it would be worth risking Betty's life, and in turn Jack's reputation in the event a botched Mexican abortion could be traced back to him. Edie really goes out of her way in these passages to lay on the irony. Yes, we get it: Betty probably would have been safer just going to Mexico. As for Edie's claim that George ultimately decided to perform the procedure himself, I've looked into Yale School of Medicine's curriculum in the late 1930s. George completed only the first two years of med school and there is no indication that those first two years would have given him adequate training to perform an abortion. True, no accredited med schools were providing this training in the 1930s, but the point here is that it is highly unlikely that George would have been confident enough in his medical abilities to go forward with this plan. According to the Yale curriculum, he would have had no hands-on surgical experience. Those first two years were most likely spent sifting through theory, not viscera. George surely would have realized that operating on Betty himself was far more dangerous than taking her to Mexico. But no, not according to Edie's version. According to Edie's version, this mild-mannered Hollywood writer decided it would be a good idea to take a shopping trip to a medical supply store, sedate Betty in the bathtub of our pool house, and do the deed himself. Considering how much Edie claims to have witnessed, it's curious that she makes no mention of how Betty herself reacted to this plan. Betty may have been young, naïve, and susceptible to the seductions of older men, but I really doubt a twenty-two-year-old woman would allow a non-doctor to operate on her in the pool house of his suburban home. But Edie claims to have seen the young woman walk into that improvised OR on her own two legs. "By the time she'd leave that pool house," Edie writes, "those legs would no longer be attached to her torso" (210). Yes, Edie, we get it.

As for the procedure itself, which Edie claims to spy through the open window, I will withhold comment, except to say it is a gratuitously detailed scene that reveals Edie's—and your—sensationalist motives. Toward the end of the chapter, she does seem to offer a kind of justification for all this horrific detail, saying that it was

> the extremity of this horror that cast all these memories into the far corners of my consciousness, not to be retrieved for another fifty years. What I saw that night made no sense, could not be rationalized, was such an aberration from the reality I knew, that it had to break off from that reality. (210)

Perhaps, but there's no need to punish your readers with a detailed description of a botched abortion, though I do admire Edie's dedication to the child's perspective here when she limits her figurative language to things in a child's world (but does a womb really resemble a "swollen tomato"?). Of course, the thing Edie's referring to that made no sense was not so much the abortion itself, or even Betty hemorrhaging and eventually, despite our father's panicked ministrations, dying, but rather what he did after that: walking outside, smoking a cigarette, looking at Mom's now-withered geraniums, then going back into the pool house and calmly mutilating Betty Short's body into the condition in which it would be found the following morning. This (seemingly) monstrous act did not make sense to Edie until a half century later when she read about the unfortunate fate of Frances

Cochran. She posits that our father needed to cover up his fatal mistake and the only way he could think to do that was to make it look like Betty had fallen victim to the same fiend that Frances Cochran had years earlier, butchering and dismembering the body in all the same ways. Cochran's killer had never been found—though there hadn't been much of a search—and it's important to note that Edie does not accuse our father of that first murder; she simply accuses him of imitating that killer's MO in a desperate cover-up. This is an important point because Edie's logic is flawed on many levels. First, if our father had really had an affair with Frances Cochran, wouldn't he be concerned that he could now be traced, however tenuously and circumstantially, to both victims? Second, as I've pointed out, Edie goes out of her way to depict our father as having a "sociopathic detachment" from women (122). But according to her version of Betty Short's death, he was acting out of need and a genuine concern for Betty's well-being. And her whole "sociopath" theory is further contradicted when she begins to postulate that the whole incident threw our father into a fit of despair, thinking that these two women were being punished for his unfaithfulness. Doesn't a sense of guilt disqualify someone from sociopathy?

The third issue here is the autopsy report, which supposedly says Betty Short's killer removed her womb. This fact, Edie claims, was used as the "control question" when the LAPD interviewed suspects, the question all those false-confessors got wrong. I can finally say that, yes, the autopsy report Edie is working from does in fact say her womb "had been removed" (like most governmental documents it's rife with the passive voice; grammatically it's as if her killer simply didn't exist).

The real question here is whether or not this document is legit. I have
it here on my desk, and I'm going to give it to Chuck this Sunday
so he can finally confirm my suspicions that it's a fake. Getting my
hands on this thing has been no easy task. Of course Edie had it, but I
didn't want to deal with the unpleasantness of our last meeting, when
I retrieved the copy of my father's manuscript and we got tangled in a
mess of miscommunication, and, just like then, I worried that asking
for the document outright would reveal my plans to officially counter
her argument and cause her to block potential paths of research. But
a few weeks ago, sitting right here at my desk, as I was narrating that
unpleasant scene from February, I found myself describing—and in
doing so, remembering afresh—those red plastic filing boxes on Rory's
kitchen table. I've been thinking about them ever since, imagining my
way into them, flipping through those files, and since Rory's Canoga
Park apartment is actually on my way to Pinz—where I've finally convinced Chuck to relocate our Sunday evening game—it's been unavoid-
able that I've driven down Rory's street enough times to get a general
sense of their weekend schedule. Based the absence of Rory's station
wagon in his assigned parking spot, it seemed that on Sunday evenings,
between 7:00 and 9:00 PM, they are always out. Of course, there was a
chance that Rory was out and Edie was home, so I took the precaution
of phoning a few times—having practiced a good fake voice (a hint of
a Sicilian accent, dulled by an American education), and an even better telemarketing pitch (for something of my own imagining called a
LintDuster)—but no one ever answered during those hours. Though
oddly disappointed that I didn't get a chance to use my telemarketer
character, since I'd put so much time into making him believable in

the event Edie or Rory actually answered the phone, it did seem that the coast would be clear for me to do a little investigating.

So last night I canceled my bowling game with Chuck, claiming, perhaps with Italy still on my mind, that I'd eaten a spoiled cannoli ("Paul, you puke more than a sorority sister," Chuck said), and drove over to Canoga Park. After sitting in my car across the street, staking the place out for a few minutes—noticing that Rory's apartment in the gateless complex faced an unlit alley—I grabbed the green flashlight from my glove box and walked over to his front door. I promptly learned just how much either (a) detective novels, for the sake of narrative momentum or out of authorial ignorance, radically gloss over the difficulties involved in clandestinely and forcibly entering another's residence, or (b) home security has greatly improved since the days of Philip Marlowe. While fidgeting with the window beside Rory's front door, I remembered Marlowe, in an early chapter of *The Lady in the Lake*, slinking into a suspect's house so easily that Chandler writes (something like), "A hard push sprung the window." *Sprung!*—as if the house were a jack-in-the-box waiting for you to open it up. Not quite. I suppose I should take a lesson from the aforementioned "narrative momentum" and not waste too much detail on the problem of entering, but suffice it to say I was out there long enough, and suspiciously enough, to be thankful that Rory lived in a community apparently apathetic to home invasions, as when an old woman pushed a cart of groceries hunchingly past me I quickly offered her the explanation that I lived here and was simply locked out before realizing that she hadn't even bothered to look up, much less give a shit that I was prying my way into a locked window. Regardless, I did eventually—bloodied fingernails and a busted bottle opener later—manage to get inside the apartment. I flipped on the flashlight, shone it around. I knew what I was looking for, but the problem was that no matter how banal an object is—a broken umbrella half opened like a giant spider, an unstrung Spanish guitar, a still-wrapped pack of plastic coat hangers— when framed in a little spotlight surrounded by total darkness, any- thing can look important, like a detail in a scene that the director irises in on to let the audience know it's a clue. So I did get a bit dis- tracted, had to investigate the grocery list magnetted to the fridge. In Edie's still girlishly loopy scrawl, there was listed *Pepsi, Cap'n Crunch, Kraft Singles*, and in what I assume was Rory's handwriting, so sharp it looked like a Richter-scale readout, was *broccoli, black beans, wheat germ, whole-seed mustard*. Below that, Edie had added *Gas-Ex*, which Rory had crossed out and replaced with *ha-ha*, and Edie had written *Gas-Ex* again in insistently blockish letters. In the living room, on the enter- tainment center, there was a half-Stonehenge of VHS tapes. Rory had hand-labeled a few: *Frasier, Civil War doc pt 3, Super Bowl Commercials*. Edie had labeled one *random*. I turned on the TV, turned the volume all the way down, and put *random* in the VCR. The first few minutes were a chaotic collage of the beginnings of everything she'd recorded on this tape, a few hazy seconds of *Kids Say the Darndest Things* deterio- rating into static, then the ghostly image of Barbara Walters forming from the fuzz only for the pixels to reconstitute themselves into an episode of *Friends*. The effect was less like channel surfing, where each jump is a glimpse of a world in medias res, those images continuing on after you look away, and more like witnessing the arbitrary destruction of those images in order to make room for the next, the space being so finite. Similarly, when I start to notice what my own memory has lost, I worry what sort of contemporary detritus I've supplanted it with. What insipid piece of trivia has replaced that thing my mother said to me that one time? How many students' faces did I have to remember before the details of my father's began to deteriorate? And that's when I saw it—or rather, me—in the midst of the snowy transitions on the TV. Having a decades-old image of yourself ambush you, only for it to fade away in a second, it's like déjà vu transmitted by a cattle prod. Moments later, when my brain was able to make sense of what it had seen, I realized Edie had taped an episode of *Loose Cannons*, presumably watched it. Then she'd taped over it.

I got back to work, focused myself to my real task, went over to the red filing boxes on the kitchen table and started flipping through them. I was right: Here, labeled and (occasionally) laminated, were all the supporting documents for Edie's book. Here were copies of some of the same newspaper articles I'd found in my own research. Here were the same crime scene photos. Here, even, was the (so titled) "Profile of a Killer" that James Richardson at the *Examiner* had commissioned from our father. It was typewritten, spelling errors X'd out. Now that I saw it and was able to read it in its entirety, I realized that perhaps it is authentic after all, and that those passages Edie quotes from it—which she claims are so self-revealing (e.g., "The Killer clearly has medical training, but also a flair for the theatrical . . . a curious combination of interests") that they can only be his veiled confession— are obviously, when seen in context, our father having a bit of fun, just as Ben Hecht was doing with his sardonic profile. Edie never did get our father's sense of humor. I kept on looking and eventually found,

laminated in hard plastic, the copy of the autopsy report that Edie pins
so much of her case on. I quickly read the thing over. And while, yes,
it does say the things Edie claims it says, I was looking for the flaws in
its composition that would prove once and for all that it, like so much
of Edie's book, is a work of fiction—until I realized that I was not the
person to do this. To me, it just looked like an old tax form that someone had filled in like a psychotic Mad Lib. (Similar to a favorite game
of Chris's when he was younger, playing Mad Libs "in character," picking words as Darth Vader, or Hannibal Lecter, or Queen Elizabeth,
depending on his mood.) Chuck will have to be the one analyze the
report, to show me the specific methodological anachronisms that
reveal it to be a fake, and I will record those as soon as he does. But
beyond the evidence I recognized from Edie's book, the filing boxes
also contained some primary sources she hadn't made use of. Here was
a postcard, addressed to Edie, dated late September 1961, just after our
mother had returned to Africa. One side showed a touristy painting
of the Egyptian pyramids, and the other side said, *We had a storm last*
week. The rain was so loud on the tin roof of the Quonset hut it sounded like
rat-a-tat-tat! Dori and I sang songs all night long. –Love Mom. Her omission
of the comma after *Love* made it seem less like a sign-off and more like
a command, or a plea. I wondered who Dori was, wondered if they
sang "Alouette." I'd like to think they did, shouting the lyrics to hear
each other over the rain. I put the postcard back in the filing box.

So that was last night, but back in April, when we were discussing
the issue of the autopsy report in my English 1 classes, and the only
thing I had to prove that it was an unreliable source was the fact that
Edie, in her book, fails to offer any reasonable explanation for how

she obtained a still-classified document, my students didn't seem to be bothered by its obvious unreliability. "I mean, it's probably pretty real," said one guy who always hid behind a large backpack on his desk.

"Probably?" I asked. "How do we know? This is a matter of evaluating sources. Is an unsubstantiated rumor as reliable as an encyclopedia? Is an issue of *People* magazine as reliable as an issue of *The Economist*?"

"I suppose, if it's in print . . . " I didn't catch who mumbled this, but people started making assenting noises.

I could feel myself getting angry, so I decided to earmark that debate for another time and change routes: "Remember that this supposed autopsy report is anomalous here. Physical evidence is not a big part of this author's repertoire. What is she basing this all on?"

"Her memories," said a woman in a red Circuit City polo, a pin stuck to her breast that implored people to *Ask Me!*

"Exactly," I said. "The mysterious recovered memories. And how reliable a source is that?"

"I think it's probably pretty reliable," the Circuit City woman said.

"Her memory is completely *un*reliable!" I said. "She has nothing to back it up!"

"But what about the car?" she continued. "That kid said he saw a black Ford where they found her body. It says here that Edith's father had a black Ford."

"It proves nothing! The Ford Mercury was one of the best-selling cars in the 1940s, and black was the most popular color. It would have been strange had George *not* had a black Ford sedan."

"There's also the watch. According to her mom's old diary, her grandfather gave George a . . . " She riffled through the photocopied pages on her desk until she found the watch passage. "A 17-jewel Croton wristwatch. And at the crime scene, the cops found a 17-jewel Croton wristwatch."

"Again," I said, "that was an incredibly popular wristwatch at the time. Every wrist in the country had a 17-jewel Croton strapped to it."

"I've never heard of that brand before," she said.

"But we're getting off topic," I said. "Most of Edith's case is based entirely on memory and that in and of itself throws everything into question."

"But why?" she said. "What's the difference between that and someone testifying in court?" She was talking faster now, leaning forward over her desk. "I mean, I understand that it sounds shady, but memories are all we have. They might be unreliable at times, but if we start distrusting memories simply because they are memories, then we're left with nothing but . . . I don't know what."

She suddenly seemed self-conscious about how worked up she was getting, so she just looked down at her desk and remained silent for the rest of the class while I moved to smaller-picture issues and pointed out some of my sister's more lamentable writerly tics, like slipping into the passive voice and overusing the word "basically."

After class, the woman in the *Ask Me!* pin came up to me as I was packing up my satchel and said, "I'm sorry, Mr. McWeeney. I didn't mean to be contrary." She was small, probably in her thirties, a thin scar dividing her left eyebrow, her fingernails painted hammer-thwapped purple.

"It's okay . . . "

"Yolanda."

"I appreciate your energy, Yolanda."

"So . . . have you, like, talked to your sister about all this?"

"I'm sorry?"

"Your sister. That's Edith, right? I'm sorry. I know you don't want us to know, with the last names blacked out and all. Please don't be mad. I looked you up online and it said your dad was named George and wrote for that cop show, and that's pretty much this guy, so I just figured . . . I'm sorry, please don't be mad at me."

I finished stuffing my stuff into my satchel and then turned to wipe down the whiteboard. COLA had been circulating many passive aggressive memos about making sure to leave each classroom as tidy as you had found it.

"Are you mad?" Yolanda asked. "I'm sorry. I didn't mean to pry. You seem mad. I'm sorry, I'll leave."

The following week, I was happy to leave the issue of memory and get the class back to assessing tangible evidence through textual analysis. A few chapters after Betty Short's death, after Edie describes the deterioration of George and Jack's relationship (though I have to admit that the scene in which Edie eavesdrops on George telling Jack just how wrong things went is chilling, even if it is entirely fictitious), and George's retreat into his work (pointing out that there was a marked increase in *Rampart* episodes that dealt with homicide after it moved to television in 1948, which I suppose is true but the new medium also demands more sensationalism, so what Edie claims is our father "working stuff out" is really just an issue of subject supply and demand), she takes aim at a now little-known book that Jack Hale wrote called *Badge and Gun*, published by Random House in 1952. This was the peak of *Rampart*'s success and the book sought to blur the line between the television show and reality. Jack had, since the show's radio days, worked closely with the LAPD. Officers (including, briefly, Det. Harry Hansen) served as consultants, offering their wisdom, guidance, and even personal experience to help shape the weekly narratives. This seemed to be Jack's territory, rubbing elbows with men he considered real men, while my father was more inclined to sit in his office by himself and fuss with a story until it took shape. Jack understood, perhaps more than anyone, the value of making these working relationships known to the public: If the television audience knew that this show had real police officers' genuine seal of approval, it did more to establish verisimilitude than an airtight plot or a character's sympathetic backstory. In the end credits of each episode, there appeared two brief notes, the first one—*Any Resemblance to Actual Persons is Entirely Coincidental*—at the insistence of the legal department, and the second one—*Thank You to the Fine Men of the Los Angeles Police Department for Your Guidance and Wisdom*—at the insistence of Hale: a formal and suspiciously defensive disavowal followed by a wink-wink, the latter being, in Hale's mind, the most important element of the show. His book *Badge and Gun* is a collection of real-life cases that he had heard about from his LAPD consultants, stories that inspired *Rampart*, but which, due to the constraints of the form, could not be translated directly into episodes. The book, then, according to Hale's introduction, was his attempt to give those stories a voice, as well as, according to my own gloss of the material, an attempt to further connect, in the eyes of the average media-consumer, the fiction of the television show with the reality of policing the mean streets of L.A. Edie points, quite naturally, to chapter 5 of *Badge and Gun*, called "The Black Dahlia." It is the only

unsolved murder that Hale addresses in the book. The rest of the cases
were all solved in hyperbolically heroic fashion. So in such a lapidary
book, why bring up a murder that, five years later, had not been solved?
It's a fair question for Edie to ask, though she and I answer it in different ways. Hale places all the blame on the media, saying that the reporters who arrived first at the crime scene stomped all over crucial
evidence, and that in the months that followed they riled up the public
with the sensational aspects of the case, which led to a glut of false
leads and false suspects. "So many red herrings," Hale writes, "the big
fish got away" (30). Edie's claim here is that Jack is covering for the
LAPD, that his effusiveness and refusal to blame the police for the case
still being open is proof that there must have been some sort of quid
pro quo: They must have been covering for him. From there, she gives
a series of absurd—and rather irritating—rhetorical questions designed
to lead the reader to her outlandish conclusions. I disagree with this
tactic not just as a writing teacher but as the perpetually annoyed
younger sibling: This long string of rhetorical questions, each one
increasing in shrillness, is an old habit of Edie's. I remember the night
our mom left for Africa for the second time, I found Edie sitting in the
living room. She had what I would later be able to identify as red-wine
mouth but at the time I thought was simply the result of a pen leaking
in her mouth—as she was always chewing on pens, pencils, her fingernails—and she was idly playing a few notes on the piano. No one in the
house knew how to play that thing; it had been an investment in bour-
geois refinement and then our parents were too busy to sign us up for
lessons. But here was my sister, walking her fingers down the black and
white sidewalk, each step plunking out a note, so gently I could hear

the soft pad against the wires. I asked her how long she thought Mom would be gone this time. She stopped playing, looked at me, and said, "Do you think she's coming back? Or do you think she's hightailing it out of this family? Do you think, maybe, that she's had enough of this place, had enough of this family, and has finally found her escape? Do you think that maybe," leaning in close to my face, "just maybe," so I could smell her tannic breath, "she knows what's good for her—and we're not it?" Though it was an effective rhetorical move at the time (I could feel the tectonic shifts beneath my feet, suddenly aware that my fears were well founded), here, in her book, it's just baldly manipulative. The series of rhetorical questions she poses to the reader attempts to lead them from the evidence (that Hale adamantly defends the LAPD on their handling of the Black Dahlia case) to the illogical conclusion that they must have been covering for him, that they knew all along that he was involved somehow in the young woman's death (explaining why they never followed through on the supposed evidence connecting both him and George to Betty Short). The problem with this is not just the distance one has to leap from evidence to conclusion—it's a chasm of logic!—but that it completely ignores the much simpler explanation for why Hale brownnoses the LAPD. Not only did Hale have an enormous amount invested in blurring the line between his show and the LAPD, but he had an enormous amount invested in advertising his patriotism. He wrote most of this book in late 1951, just after the House Un-American Activities Committee began holding trials again. The Committee had begun officially Red-baiting the entertainment industry in 1947, most notably with the Hollywood Ten, a group of unfriendly witnesses who stood up to the McCarthyite tactics.

After that, the industry began self-policing for a while, blacklisting many of its own who might appear even the lightest shade of Red. I have no idea how my father managed to escape this firestorm of paranoia in the late forties. He never spoke about it. It's one of the many things I wish I could ask him now. I suspect it had to do with the fact that both he and Hale were pretty small fish in 1947, still only on the radio, but by the time the Committee returned in 1951—asking directors, writers, producers, actors, "Are you now or have you ever been a member of the Communist Party?"—*Rampart* was a hit TV show and suddenly vulnerable. One of the first to get added to the blacklist this time around was Waldo Salt. He was: an up-and-coming screenwriter who'd gotten a lot of attention for the now sadly forgotten Western *Rachel and the Stranger*, a confirmed member of the Communist Party who refused to testify before HUAC, and a rumored guest at Jack Hale's 1946/47 New Year's party. Shortly after getting blacklisted, Salt resumed his writing career under the very comfy nom-de-screen Mel Davenport. Many in the Hollywood community were hip to blacklisted writers using fronts and pseudonyms, and rumors spread about which projects were really the work of suspected Commies. According to *Waldo Salt: A Screenwriter's Journey*—an excellent documentary from 1990 that follows Salt not just through this dark period but also through his late career renaissance when he steps off the blacklist and picks up an Oscar for *Midnight Cowboy*—one of the many projects he was rumored to be involved in was *Rampart*. I really doubt that he had anything to do with *Rampart*—for the simple reason that by this point my father was doing all the writing and was never a very gregarious collaborator—but the rumor was enough to potentially harm Jack Hale.

So it's no coincidence that Hale then churned out a book that sought to not only align himself and his show with the LAPD but with the good ol' US of A as well. Just look at the evidence: In the Black Dahlia chapter, he says that among the hundreds of letters the LAPD received that professed to be from the real killer, Det. Hansen gave particular credence to one typewritten note that said, "I killed her because she came to Hollywood to become a commodity" (32). Hale spends a solid paragraph on the Marxist rhetoric of this one-line note, concluding that Reds are by their very nature sociopathic. The way he tells it, you'd think the LAPD was waging its own McCarthyite war on the streets of Los Angeles. And yet, in my research, I've come across no other reference to this note. Not one, except for those that reference Hale's book. I am not saying that the note did not exist, just that, if it did, Hale is clearly giving it unnecessary importance. Once we see *Badge and Gun* from this perspective, what's more likely? That (a) Hale was attempting to cover for the LAPD in exchange for them covering up his (and my father's) connection to Betty Short? Or that (b) he was attempting to align his show with the LAPD for higher ratings while simultaneously trying to quell suspicions that he was Red-friendly? Since I've already chided my sister for her annoying use of rhetorical questions, I'll just go ahead and answer this one: The correct answer is b.

But I worry that I have presented Jack Hale as chauvinistic and calculating, so I want to be clear that, while those are not unfair assessments of him, he was nothing but kind to me in the years after my father died. In 1964, I was seventeen and newly fatherless. I'd spent the three years since my mother died hating my dad for what I saw as weakness. I thought he'd let her go, driven her away, and remained apathetic

to my sister's and my grieving. From 1961 to 1964, I spent every opportunity I could at the house of any friend whose father seemed to have
a kind of John Wayne–type presence that I felt my life had lacked. But
when an artery clogged with midcentury diet felled my father, I began
skipping school, driving out to Burbank and talking my way onto the
studio lot. At first I'd just wander around, hop on one of those intra-
backlot bicycles, pedal past soundstages, those strangely blank boxes
that open up geode-like to reveal fully imagined, if fragmented, worlds.
I hadn't visited the lot since I was maybe ten or eleven, so now I enjoyed
being old enough to be mistaken for a lackey of some sort, fetching coffee, delivering scripts. But this required that I look like I was heading
somewhere with great importance, so I didn't allow myself the leisure
to stop and peek into the soundstages, as I desperately wanted to, and
I affected a scowl that I thought made me look stressed and therefore
important but that probably made me look like exactly the person I
was: a confused teenager biking furiously around a place I shouldn't
be, trying to transfer all the anger I'd felt toward my father to a new
and frighteningly nebulous subject—my father's death. Where precisely
was I supposed to direct my anger? The backlot bikes, it seemed; I ped-
aled the shit out of those things. Actors, too. Whenever I saw people
who seemed put-together but nervous, I pegged them for actors anxiously making their way to auditions, and I made a point of swerving
around them, shouting to get out of my way, just to make them feel as
out-of-place as I knew I was. While that never stopped being satisfying,
I began to set my sights elsewhere. I found Jack Hale's office, a bungalow out past the important stuff. At first, I would just cruise by, trying
to spot him through a window. My rubbernecking, however, did not

complement the furious pace I'd set for myself on the bicycle, and one day my front tire met a rather steep curb. I'd like to say that I sailed clean over the handlebars like people do in the movies, but instead, when the bike stopped and my body kept going, my groin met the handlebars and I folded over the contraption, quickly crumpling myself into a neat pile of pain on the lawn outside Jack's bungalow office. I used to tell this story so that I looked up and saw Jack standing over me, offering me his hand and quipping, "Your dad couldn't drive for shit either." I told it that way for so long that I now distinctly remember it that way, but Jack was not there; what actually happened was that I dragged my deflated scrotum into his office and begged his secretary to show me the bathroom. She obliged and I spent a few minutes vomiting into his toilet. When I limped out, Jack Hale was standing there, quipless. I'd last seen him at my dad's funeral where he'd delivered a perfectly satisfactory eulogy but hadn't said much to me, and he still seemed unsure what to say. "I need a job," I said.

His secretary said, "You need to look where you're steering that thing, is what you need."

Jack turned around to give her what I hoped was a reproachful look, then turned back to me. "How old are you?"

"Eighteen." It was a lie, though a small one. I'd be eighteen soon enough.

"Go home," he said, and I felt the blood rush from my groin to my face, and I prepared to yell something at him, but then he said, "Come back tomorrow at eight."

I tried to reconfigure my face into something less homicidal and said, "Yes, yes, okay."

"That's AM," he said, "not PM."

I thanked him again, might have called him "sir" a few too many times, and ran out in a rush, somehow thinking that if I promptly followed the first part of his instructions, the "go home" part, then it would show him how promptly I would be back at 8:00 AM.

It was my final year of high school, and I'd been cutting classes to go haunt the backlot, but only a couple days a week. Now that I'd be a regular employee, however, I figured I could just drop the pretense of school altogether. That simple realization, that I would be waking up tomorrow to go to a job rather than a classroom, felt like an initiation into adulthood, like with those words Jack had essentially said to me, "You're a man now." Which is why I spent that evening dipping liberally into the liter of Gordon's gin that Aunt Paige kept in the kitchen cabinet. (She had moved in after Dad died, and was now my legal guardian, though I can't recall where she was that night.) When I showed up to my first day of work the next morning, festeringly hungover, I'm not sure what I was expecting, but I certainly didn't find it. I walked into the bungalow and the secretary said, "Report to Stage Five."

"Where's Jack?"

"Report to Stage Five."

"Is Jack going to be there?"

"Stage Five."

Jack was not in Stage Five. First, a husky and handsome woman, holding pins in her teeth in a way that made me nervous she'd skewer her tongue, hustled me into wardrobe where she told me to take off my clothes (Levi's, white T-shirt) and gave me different clothes (slightly different Levi's, slightly different white T-shirt) to put on. "I think there's a mistake," I said, stepping out from behind the oddly Victorian changing curtain.

"You're Paul McWeeney?" she asked.

"I am."

"No mistake. Says right here on the call sheet," eyeing a clipboard, "that you're playing Wallace."

My heart and stomach tried to trade places. "Who's Wallace?"

She just blinked, tightened her lips in a sphincterly fashion, those pins pointing right at me.

On her advice, I reported to the assistant director, a small man whose too-large flannel suit made it look like he was in the slow process of shrinking. He also held—or rather, brandished—a clipboard, and I began to realize that my transition into adulthood would not be complete until I had a clipboard myself. Where could I get one of these totems of authority?

The A.D. handed me one page of a mimeographed script with the header *Presidio*, which I recognized as the new show Jack had been trying to get off the ground ever since *Rampart* went off the air. (It only now occurs to me that Jack was strangely fixated on wall-themed titles, though I am resisting the urge to offer any armchair psychological insight into this motif.) My dad had been working a little on this new show, though I didn't really know the details. From the shard of a story I had in my hands, however, Jack seemed to be setting up a new cop show, this time with a lady lead (I'd turn out to be correct). There was just a setting (INT. HIGH SCHOOL CLASSROOM—DAY), a few lines from the LINDA character that gave the basic setup (she's saying goodbye to her students, leaving teaching to join the police force), and one line from WALLACE: "But Mrs. Polk, I thought we had a great thing here. If you're looking for criminals, you got me!" To which Linda responds, "Oh, Wallace." This was presumably Wallace's only appearance in the show. After this, the setting would surely be limited to the mean streets and the meaner police station. Wallace was just there for this one scene to establish the kind of stern but loving camaraderie she had with her students, the idea being that she would establish a similar relationship with the lowlifes she'd encounter on the beat. But there was something about that one line of Wallace's, its attitude and humor, that I recognized—or thought I recognized—from my father. I know I'd heard him use that expression before, "I thought we had a great thing here," always ironically, though I couldn't quite place a specific instance of it. He'd surely written this line. I knew how dense and striated the archaeology of teleplays could be, each script a palimpsest of different drafts, different writers, different ideas, but this one line was clearly a relic left behind by George McWeeney, and now it was my job to brush the thing off, hold it up to the light. Things on the set moved a bit too fast for much relic-dusting, though. The A.D. sat me down in a classroom set with a dozen kids of indeterminate age. The actress playing Linda took her place. The lights were painfully bright, like that shock of the bathroom light at 3:00 AM, and my eyes couldn't adjust. Linda started speaking. When I heard my cue, I said my one line, confused and robotically. As I spoke, I heard my own voice the way you do on a recording: detached from the person you think you are, from the way you think you sound, the words like strange, alien phonemes, unmoored from meaning. I'd thought it was just a run-through, but I heard the director—speaking somewhere behind the blinding lights like an adenoidal and annoyed voice from the beyond—say, "All right, moving on." Was that it? Had I just *acted?* While everyone seemed to know where exactly they were "moving on" to, and hustled off accordingly, I was lost and just wandered around the soundstage in a haze, trying not to get in anyone's way but also hoping someone would notice me, tell me I'd done a good job, tell me where to go now. No one did. I eventually found my way back to Jack's office and was relieved to find him there, his door open. He was sitting at his desk, reading what I assumed was a script. He was wearing a suit, the tie tight, not one button undone, no concession for comfort made, and I suddenly realized that he always dressed like this. Without looking up, he asked me how it went.

"I don't know."

"Talk to Maud. She has some paperwork for you."

"Did my dad write that script?"

Jack looked up, though not at me. The venetian blinds we closed, but he stared at them as if looking out on the sunny day. "He did a pass on it, yes."

"Oh."

Jack finally looked at me. I got nervous and left.

The next day, however, I went back, ostensibly to fill out that paperwork. Jack wasn't in but Maud said she was expecting him back any minute. I sat across from her desk and took my sweet time with the paperwork, partly to wait for Jack and partly because I'd never filled out tax forms before and had no clue what my social security number was. When he finally walked in, he nodded to Maud, gave me an unsurprised hello, then walked back to his office. After a minute fussing with the tax form, I walked into his open doorway and asked if I could ask him a few questions. "Certainly," he said. But I wasn't sure what those questions were. All I had was an abstract curiosity. So I sat down and mumbled the aborted beginnings of many questions—what, how, why—thinking the rest of the question would formulate itself once I got there, but it never did. Finally, mercifully, Jack interrupted me and said, "I'll tell you my favorite story about your father. This was a couple years ago. My wife threw a dinner party. She'd been reading this French cookbook and was really excited to try it all out. It was our usual crowd—George, a few producer friends of mine and their wives, but also that actor, um, Albert Finney. I can't remember why he was there, but he was. Well, Clare had seen that movie he was in, the British one, *Tom Jones*, and she was all nervous about the house looking just right, even though she'd met plenty of actors over the years. Guess she really took a shine to this guy, though. And it's all going well and everyone is having a great time, and Mr. Finney and my wife are getting on famously, and the food is full of butter and cream and delicious. But later on in the evening, when we're all in the living room, we, uh, catch a whiff of something. We all do our best to ignore it at first, but eventually that Albert Finney says, 'I do believe it smells like sewage in here.' And he was right. Turned out there were some plumbing issues, and our toilets had begun to back up. So I call a plumber and we all spend the rest of the evening in the backyard to get away from the stench. It's all fine, but of course Clare is mortified, even though we're all still having a great time, enjoying our cocktails by the pool. At the end of the evening, after the guests have left, after the plumber has righted whatever wrong needed to be righted, and while the maid was cleaning up the mess in the bathrooms, I have to go comfort Clare, tell her it's all right, that the night was a success regardless. She starts crying, takes a Klonopin and goes to sleep. I go into the living room to have a nightcap with your father. But of course now I'm stressed because I had to deal with Clare. Anyway, George, he just looks at me and, with that straight face of his, says, 'Jack, maybe if Clare had served more fruits and vegetables, your guests' shit would smell a little better.'"

Jack looked at me for the first time in his monologue, and I could tell from his expression that he was expecting me to laugh at this line, but I had been too busy dissecting every detail of the story (who was Albert Finney? did he know my father? who were the other guests? what was the significance of it being a French cookbook? is bad plumbing a metaphor for my father's clogged artery?) to see any humor.

"Well," Jack continued, "it was a damn funny thing to say, but only he could have said it, and only I could have found it funny, and he knew that."

The next day, I came back to Jack's office, again without much of a plan. Again, it was just Maud there and beneath her show of annoyance I could tell that she was starting to like me, especially when I offered to help with whatever it was she was doing. She put me to work collating scripts. She told me about her family. Her son was in the military and she paid close attention to the developments in South East Asia, fearing he'd be sent over. After collating, I delivered the scripts to production offices elsewhere on the lot. I was back on a bike, though this time at much calmer pace. I kept going back to Jack's office, and Maud kept humoring me and giving me stuff to do. Jack was always in and out, and always made me feel welcome there. As much as I appreciated having a place to go, however, I was growing increasingly anxious about my line on *Presidio*. It was a good line, probably my father's, and I'd screwed it up. One day, I went to Jack and said that I'd like to do some more acting jobs, that I could do better. He smiled, said sure. This time, however, it wasn't as easy as him just plugging me into a role. With *Presidio*, I discovered, I'd stumbled into his office just hours after he'd found out the guy originally cast as Wallace had dropped out. Now, however, I had to do it the normal way. Pictures, auditions, the whole deal. Jack did a lot to help me out, though. He set me up with an agent and an on-set acting coach. And suddenly my life had a focus, a clear trajectory. I was handed a list of things to fill my head with, a list of things to care about: what shows and movies were currently casting, which casting directors were the ones to get in front of. It doesn't matter, I don't believe, that years later I would discover that I did not, in fact, care about these things; at the time it was all I had and so I attacked it with all I was worth. I spent those years hauling myself to auditions all over town, occasionally landing a commercial, which buoyed my hopes and gave me something I could take to Jack, always hoping for his approval, which he always gave. When I landed the role of Donny Cannon on the new pilot *Loose Cannons*, I thought, This is it, the final piece of validation after which I won't need any more. But of course the show was trivial, absurd. The lines were hackneyed and I had to repeat them so many times in rehearsals and take after take that I began to remember my first moment in front of the camera, when I said my father's line and heard nothing but meaningless sounds come out of my mouth. By the time we were filming *Loose Cannons* before a live studio audience, their desperate, rabid laughter just embarrassed me, shamed me even. After that show was canceled and I returned to school, I had what felt like an epiphanic moment—although, sure, in those days epiphanies were frequent and drug-tinged, but no less exhilarating—when someone—a girl addicted to polka dots and opium—played for me—on vinyl, the white noise hissing and popping like grease on a pan—Gertrude Stein reading her poem "If I Told Him," and I listened to the way she explored and repeated words and phrases in endless variations—*Would he like it would Napoleon would Napoleon would would he like it*—until they were just sounds—*If Napoleon if I told him if I told him if Napoleon*—empty of all meaning. It was how I had felt standing on the set of that TV show, but the emptiness had horrified me then, and now it struck me as brilliant, revolutionary. I tried to explain this to the girl in the polka dots, how I'd been an actor and knew exactly what Stein was doing here, but she (the girl, not Stein) was unimpressed with my exegesis and did not let me fuck her.

Nor did my students seem impressed with my exegesis of Edie's manuscript. By the end of the spring semester, over half the students in the four sections of English 1 that I had submitted to this pedagogical experiment had dropped. Perhaps the reading load was too much, perhaps being asked to sharpen their analytical abilities against the stone of a real-life tragedy (as opposed to the usual fluff: gun control, death penalty) proved too overwhelming—either way, I was, I admit, slightly relieved to have significantly fewer essays to grade. Their assignment for the final paper was to offer an analysis of a passage of their choosing from the excerpts I had provided them of Edie's manuscript, explaining how and why Edie's claim is spurious.

They had to support their analysis with at least three other sources, chosen from a list I had provided. Most of the students—that is, those who had stuck with the demands of the course and not fled for the hills—did a pretty good job with this. They zeroed in on relevant passages and, using the analytical framework that I had provided them in class, showed me, with wonderful insight, the errors in Edie's logic that we had discussed in class. The one exception was Yolanda, who deviated slightly from the prompt. In her essay, she focused on one passage that technically appeared in the pages I'd excerpted for them, but only incidentally. I had highlighted a passage that started halfway down page 155, when five-year-old Edie observes George and Jack conversing around the kitchen table. Just above that, however, is a section break preceded by the end of a scene that I had not intended on bringing into the discussion. It's just one paragraph, completely decontextualized, in which Edie describes George letting her tag along to the grocery store. It's not a very exciting scene; it's filler—do we really need another scene of a husband struggling with basic errands while his wife is away?—but in her essay Yolanda focuses on one particular passage in which Edie, walking beside her father in the cereal aisle, sees

a bright red box with a friendly black man smiling back at me. I thought the man on the box looked like Philip, who tended our garden and fiddled with the chemistry of our swimming pool twice a week. I wanted to show the box to my father, wanted him to see it, tell me that it was in fact Philip, congratulate me on my sharp eye. I pulled on his pant leg. He did not respond. I pulled

harder, called, "Daddy." He was looking at the small shopping list
in his hand and did not look down at me. It was overwhelming,
my need for him to look down, to see the box I'd found, to see me.

Yolanda argues that this passage acts as a microcosm of sorts, reveals
a theme of invisibility in Edie's narrative. She then goes through the
rest of the manuscript—or at least the Xeroxed passages I provided—
and pulls out sixteen other instances in which people either do not
make eye contact with Edie or she otherwise feels unseen. Yolanda
then claims that, regardless of whether or not Edie's accusation about
her father is true, this "theme of invisibleness" (*sic!*) gives us insight
into some of the subtler motives behind the accusation: "The need to
be seen," Yolanda wrote, "to be acknowledged, is a powerful one for a
child, for anyone really. Edith is asking us not just to see her father, but
to see her, and I think we should at least try to acknowledge that this
is a woman in great pain."

I gave the paper a C+, wrote a quick note saying she should stick
to the assignment.

To be fair, though, Yolanda's impulse to draw attention to material that I had not technically included in the curriculum was not
an entirely bad one. There were, in fact, some crucial passages from
Edie's manuscript that I had omitted from the unit's course packet.
Specifically, there is a chapter I left out because I myself make a small
appearance in it, and I was nervous that my students would be able to
identify the young Paulie. I'm referring to the tattoo chapter. In 1961,
as I think I mentioned earlier, shortly before our mother returned to
Africa, she pulled Edie into the laundry room to show her (Edie) a

tattoo that she (Mother) had gotten on her hip, something called a sankofa. A month later, when news reached us that our mother had become an innocent victim of the Eritrean War, Edie decided to honor our mother by getting the same tattoo. (I almost typed the word "allegedly" there—perhaps the word is becoming something of a tic—but then I remembered that I do in fact remember these events, so I can attest to their veracity; besides, I bring up these tattoo passages not to doubt them, as with so much of her manuscript, but to draw a correlation that I think will shed light onto the pathology that underlies Edie's book.) Like our mother's tattoo (which I never saw) Edie's tattoo (which I have seen) is small, a knotted little design on the curve of her left hip. The correlation I wish to draw here is one that Edie surprisingly doesn't make herself. Betty Short also had a tattoo on her left hip. Betty's, however, was not some esoteric African doodle—an American commodification, and quaintification, of eastern spiritualism, a conformist claim to individuality through ritualistic scarification—but rather a simple rose tattoo, designed solely for the purpose of seduction: In a *Los Angeles Examiner* story from January 17, 1947, Will Fowler quoted Santa Barbara Juvenile Officer Mary H. Unkefer, who'd arrested Short for underage drinking in 1943, as saying that Short "loved to sit so [the tattoo] would show." Though the impetus that led my mother, my sister, and Betty Short to get their tattoos were all different, the parallel is interesting as it suggests that Edie identifies with Betty more than she would care to admit. This might add some shading and nuance to the bald jealousy that we have seen cropping up in Edie's descriptions of the victim, and it allows us to see Ms. Short as a window into Edie's brain. I'm thinking specifically of Betty's tendency to construct entire narratives out of tragically misunderstood gestures from the men in her life. In his investigation, Fowler uncovered a whole cache of Betty's correspondences in the years leading up to her death. In early 1945, Short received some flirtatious telegrams from Major Matt Gordon, who was stationed overseas. It's clear from these telegrams that the two had had a brief sexual encounter sometime in late 1944. In response to his casual flirtations, Betty wrote a number of letters to him that she never actually mailed, letters overflowing with sentiments of love and devotion. In letters she did mail, however, she told her mother that she and Gordon were engaged and would be getting married as soon as he returned stateside. She had similar wartime "relationships" with Lieutenants Joseph Fickling and Stephen Wolak. The latter even wrote her a letter that very graciously attempted to disabuse her of these romantic delusions, writing, "Infatuation is sometimes mistakenly accepted for true love." This seemed to be something more than infatuation, though, something a bit more pathological. Major Matt Gordon, unfortunately, did not get a chance to disabuse Betty of her marriage fantasy: In November 1945, he died in a plane crash. When Betty read his obituary in the newspaper, she cut it out, carried it around in her purse—the same purse that investigators picked through after her death—and began telling people that she was his widow. The young woman we see emerging in these letters and telegrams is someone whose loneliness and desperate need to belong has begun to eclipse not just her rational judgment, but her view of reality. Edie admits as much when she covers this material in her book, but, just as Nick's description of Gatsby reveals more about Nick than it does Gatsby, I posit that Betty's habit of using the misconstrued actions of men as the basis for an entire fantastical narrative is one my sister shares. To illustrate my point, let's go back to the chapter in which Edie describes getting her tattoo. Edie writes,

My friend Moose [she doesn't mention this gentleman anywhere else in her manuscript, nor do I remember him, so your guess is as good as mine as to how trustworthy a man with this moniker could be] had recommended a tattoo parlor in Venice Beach called the Branded Bull. The only real tattoo advice he'd given me, though, was a caveat emptor: "Buyer beware, baby." A week after Mom's funeral I drove down to the Branded Bull. It was a square brick building with trails from recently removed vines snaking up the walls and an Old West–style awning out front. I parked, and when I put coins in the meter I hesitated: thirty minutes, forty-five, sixty? I remembered how Mom would always pay for the minimum amount of parking on her errands, thinking it would force her to be efficient and not dilly-dally. I paid for just half an hour.

Inside, there was only one guy, the tattoo artist presumably, sitting behind the counter with a dime novel, his arms a jumble of sailor tattoos. On his neck, between his ear and his shoulder, was a bulldog, a simple contour outline that looked like it might have been my high school mascot. I figured this was a good sign and thought to myself, Go Bulldogs! He had a face that was just starting to drop from boyish to jowly, framed by sparse red sideburns.

He asked what I wanted, his voice exasperated in a way that reminded me of Paulie. I told him I wanted a sankofa. A what?

I showed him a picture I'd torn from the encyclopedia. I said I wanted the tattoo "here," pointing to my left hipbone.

The tattoo artist—who was wearing a patch on his shirt that said *Aaron*—led me back into a cubicle-like area with what looked like a dentist's chair. He told me to take off my pants and underwear.

"My underwear?"

"Listen," he said, with his eyes down and one hand up, "I've done these hip tattoos before, and the panties always snap back in my face." Now he looked at me. "You don't want me to screw up, do you?"

He sat on a desk chair and scooted over to the counter to pre-pare the tattoo gun. I removed my shoes and put them side by side next to the chair. I took off my jeans, folded them, and placed them on top of my shoes. I tugged at the bottom of my T-shirt. With the chair between me and Aaron, and his back still to me, I took off my underwear, folded them in half, and placed them on top of my jeans.

Aaron turned to me. He was now wearing thick-rimmed glasses. He told me to take a seat. I did. The chair's vinyl was cloying on my skin. He pulled his chair over to me. He had on latex gloves and was holding the tattoo gun in one hand, raised like a quill in mid-thought. "Just relax," he said, laying one latexed hand on my thigh. He poised the tattoo gun over my crotch. He started the little motor. It was a tense buzzing. While I was waiting for him to ask if I was ready, he began. I could feel the needle, but not with the precision I'd imagined. The sensation was sharp but spread evenly over my skin in a blurred spotlight of pain. It was a pain I learned to anticipate, noticing that there was no fluctuation in it. Relax into it, I told myself. The ceiling tiles were spotted with brown water stains.

Aaron's left hand was holding my inner thigh, keeping a firm grip, while his right hand did the work. Needing something more specific, less painful to focus on, I concentrated on his left hand. My own hands were clenched on to the edge of the seat, its vinyl cushion and metal frame. His thumb seemed to move up. He was surely just trying to steady my body while he worked. I didn't want him to screw up, did I? He probably had no idea how close his thumb was. He was probably too focused on his work to realize. Without looking, it was hard to tell if I was just imagining it, but when I squirmed I felt the dry touch of latex pull some of my pubic hair. It would be dumb to ask him to move his hand back down. Dad always said I was an overreactor. Then his thumb inched over and I felt him push inside me. It hurt, and this pain, unlike the vague territory of the tattoo gun, was precise. The ceiling tiles were spotted with brown water stains. "Steady," he said.

When he was finished, he sat back, wheeled his desk chair over to the counter, and set down the tattoo gun. He sighed and took off his glasses. He returned to me with a warm, wet cloth, and wiped some blood from my skin. Then he pulled off each latex glove with an elastic snap. I looked down to see it for myself: The little design was there on my skin, black and simple, dabbed in blood and glistening like a newborn.

Aaron was in the corner now, washing his hands and telling me how to care for the tattoo, but I couldn't follow what he was saying. He came over and taped a patch of gauze over the sankofa. I stood up, and he offered his hand for a shake. I took it. His grip was surprisingly weak. "It looks great," he said. I got dressed, paid, and left.

On the drive home, the clutch and brake of Dad's Ford felt like they were stuck in tar. I was too weak to pull the heavy steering wheel all the way around and so made some drunkenly wide turns. The other cars gave me the wide berth I needed. Finally back in Van Nuys, I pulled into our driveway and ran into the house, through the living room where Paulie was watching TV, all the way back to Dad's office and pounded on the door. I was crying, and shouting something, though I'm not sure what I was shouting. He did not answer the door and it was locked. He'd barely stepped out of that office all week—all my life, for that matter. I was asking to be let in, and he did not let me in.

I crouched on the floor, my forehead to my knees, my arms tucked against my stomach. My new tattoo burned like hell.

(105–109)

She then claims that our father apparently ignoring her suffering was proof that he'd detached himself from the suffering not just of his daughter but of all women, the residual effects of what he'd done to Betty Short. But, realistically, he probably just wasn't home and so, ipso facto (see? Edie's not the only one who remembers high school Latin!), could not open his office door. Like Betty Short, Edie—not just in this particular passage but in her entire book—has the ability to (mis)read volumes into the smallest and most meaningless details, with tragic results.

Okay, I know I told myself no more sunrises, told myself that I needed to manage my time better, but here I am at the beginning of another day, the end of another all-night session, hunched over my IBM Wheelwriter 1000. I'm clenching my jaw like a lunatic and I know I'm going to have a killer headache later. I'm going to have to tell Julia that I fell asleep at my desk again, though last time I said that she said she'd heard the typewriter going all night. I said that must have been old house sounds, a branch against a windowpane, the pipes rattling. Tonight, however, I've kept the humidifier running, so hopefully its pleasant blanket of white noise has absorbed all my key-clicking. The humidifier is a new purchase, a gift, I suppose, from Julia. She was concerned about all the nosebleeds I've been getting recently, and when I told her that they were probably just from the dry weather, she immediately bought me a humidifier. It's a strange contraption, built in the shape of a penguin. You fill its belly with water and it spews vapor from its beak. She said it was the only kind the store had.

With the sun up now, I can see our brand-new lawn in the backyard. Chris and Julia just finished it, and it looks pretty great. The new sod arrived yesterday. It came on a flatbed truck in patches, as if for a large grass quilt, each square green and healthy. I had just come back from a long day at COLA and watched them for a while before sitting down to get my work done. Julia told Chris that they had to lay the new sod slowly and carefully or the roots wouldn't take. Chris said okay, but they didn't talk much as they worked. The only sound I heard was the damp *thump* when one of them dropped a square of sod on the ground. It didn't take long, and when they were done, they stood back. The sun through the trees spilled coins of light onto the new ground, and Julia pointed out the lines where the squares of grass met each other, the vague grid beneath the new green lawn, the seams of the quilt. The lines would disappear in time, she explained, once the roots took hold. But first, she said, they needed to try it out, take it for a test run, break it in. Julia bent down, untied her laces, and pulled off her dirty sneakers. She peeled off her socks and draped them over her shoes, then started walking around on the new grass. "Come on," she said, looking back at Chris. Chris took off his shoes and socks and began walking around. They both walked slowly, cautiously almost, as if walking out onto a frozen lake, feeling for a certain stability beneath their feet before making any sudden movements. Julia was now in the middle of the yard, and she leaned down to pluck a blade of grass from the ground. "Hey, Chris," she said, "you know this?" She fit the blade of grass between her thumbs and cupped her hands together. She blew through her palms, the blade of grass the delicate reed. A tone came out, a whistle, the sound itself strained but steady. Then she spotted me watching from the window and stopped. She waved and said, "Come check out your new backyard! Feels great between the toes!" Chris turned around to see me. He was smiling and said, "Yeah." I thought of my pale feet, my yellow woodlike toenails, and I declined, waved back, said it looks great but I have so much work to do. Julia cocked her head a bit, out of suspicion or concern I couldn't tell. She shrugged, said okay, then lay down in the new grass.

Maybe I'll go check out the lawn now, with Chris and Julia still asleep. I'll take off my shoes, walk around, feel the dew on my feet.

The grass felt nice, really nice. I was out there a good long time, walking around barefooted, thinking to myself that it felt, somehow, mentholated. This is the prefect way to describe the feeling of dewy grass on your bare feet first thing in the morning: It mentholates you. I then walked inside and found Julia making herself some tea and told her how good the grass felt, that it felt mentholated, but she just looked at me in that way of hers that is both concerned and condescending and said I didn't look well. She started making me some of her chamomile tea and wasn't listening to my further descriptions of the grass. I said I didn't need the tea, that I could just take a Trazodone, but she asked me to stop pacing, sit down, and have the tea. I said fine, humoring her, and I sat down. As I sipped the perfumy but largely flavorless tea, she told me that I would be canceling my classes today so I could stay home and get some much-needed rest. I said there was no need, that I've canceled too many classes this summer as it is, and she looked at me and poked her head forward like a chicken. "How many classes have you canceled?" I told her that my writing was going really well. "Paul," she said, "how many classes have you canceled?" Not that many, I said, really, but, you know, canceling one class in the compressed summer semester is like canceling a whole week in the normal semester. My writing is going really well, I said again, trying to steer the conversation away from my occasional truancy. "Ah, yes," she said with a sigh, "the new novel, right?" She untied and retied the belt of her robe. "Paul, when you were wrapped up in your sister's book, I thought it was great. It was between semesters so it didn't interfere with your teaching. It was a real project, with a real goal, and I know it was good for you. But I was happy when you finished with it. I thought I'd get you back, not just watch you disappear into some made-up story. Listen, I support you, of course I do. But you need to be realistic.

After all these years, you need to realize that your job is teaching, not writing, and your responsibilities are to your students, not a bunch of imaginary people." The tea was affecting me more than I anticipated. I needed to lie down, needed to sleep. I got up, said something to Julia, and walked into the bedroom and fell asleep. Or least my body fell asleep—my brain leapt into hyperconsciousness, frantically listing, on this very machine, all the things I'd missed, all the things I hadn't seen, frantically going back to scenes with the horrifying feeling that it had missed something, just as Ms. Short's killer apparently returned to Leimert Park, hours after dumping her body there, his eyes scanning the dead grass and dry dirt for the wristwatch he'd left behind. I woke in a panic and ran out to my car and tore through my glove box and realized I'd left the green flashlight at Rory's—how long ago was that? Days, weeks? The clock on my dashboard said 7:04, but the dark was disorienting—AM or PM? How long had I slept? I didn't stop to figure it out. I had evidence of a B&E to retrieve. I drove straight to Canoga Park. On my first drive-by of Rory's apartment, I couldn't get a good enough angle to see if any lights were on, so I parked my car down the block and approached on foot, only then realizing that I wasn't wearing any shoes. I could now see a dim light in the small window beside the door, perhaps left on while they're out to discourage burglars. But closer, the rousing sounds of a Spielbergian film score and the soft but prickly smell of curry masala seemed to be emerging from the window, now clearly open a crack. There was a curtain I didn't remember from before, though a diaphanous one, all doily like a cobweb, through which I could see Edie and Rory sitting on the couch, messy dishes before them on the coffee table. Their faces were lit, aquarium-like, from the TV, and she was curled up against his body. The movie's music was building to something, though building to what I couldn't see. I could see, however, Rory and Edie coiling into each other in anticipation. She whispered something to him. He scratched her shoulder. She wiggled her feet. When whatever was happening on the screen finally happened, they gasped, then laughed, and I walked away.

When I got home, I discovered a note from Julia saying she's taken Chris to a movie, which I guess gives me at least an hour or two before they're back, so I have some time to get some work done here while my head still feels clear from the sleep.

So anyway, it was at the very end of this past spring semester, when I'd just finished grading my lightened load of papers and submitted my grades (Yolanda's final grade for the course added up to a B-, but I boosted it to a solid B), when Oliver called me.

I was coming home from the grocery store, walking into the kitchen, my arms laden with plastic bags, the day's mail tucked in my armpit, and Chris walked out of his bedroom holding the cordless phone. As I began unloading the bags, he set the phone on the counter, took a bag of Cool Ranch Doritos—which he loves, forces me to buy, even though I think they smell like feet—and said, "That guy Oliver's on the phone."

Was this it? The call I'd imagined getting for twenty years? The news that Random House, HarperCollins, and Simon & Schuster were now engaged in a bloody, knock-down-drag-out auction for the rights to publish one of my novels?

"Paul," Oliver said when I picked up the phone. "Did you get the package?"

I looked at the mail on the counter. There were two packages, roughly the same size. I grabbed the one on top, but it was addressed to Chris, so I handed it to him as he walked out of the room, and I looked at the second one, a book-shaped box on top of some junk mail. "Yes!" I picked it up. "I'm holding it right now."

"Listen, I'm sorry we couldn't work together on this one."

"What?" With the phone wedged between ear and shoulder, I tore open the box, found the book inside. Before my brain had a chance to process the title and my sister's name—still strange seeing "Edith" instead of "Edie"—I recognized the photo on the cover: Betty Short's 1945 black-and-white headshot, her body angled away from the camera, her head cocked over her shoulder, looking up and camera-left. A man's shadow was superimposed over this. And "My Book" finally had a title. Along the top, the words *The Black Dahlia Dossier: Hollywood's Most Notorious Killer Revealed* were spelled out like a ransom note, each word cut from a different newspaper headline, a stylish choice contrasted by the white band running across the bottom that read in a simple sans serif font, *Advance Reader Copy.* I could feel the blood draining from my head, an elevator descending from my brain to the basement, and I had to sit down.

"I just want to let you know that both Edie and I really did want to bring you in on this. Your perspective would have been invaluable, but they're rushing this to press."

Chris came back into the kitchen holding up a large black T-shirt, a gargoyle screen-printed above the words *Black Sabbath.* "Look what Eddie sent me!"

I looked down at the book. "When did this sell?" I asked Oliver.

Chris walked out of the kitchen.

"You probably heard Paramount is making a movie from that old Cooley novel," Oliver said, "and I guess it's coming out in January, closer to the anniversary of the murder. We were lucky enough to get Cooley's blurb, and we're really hoping for some cross-promotion."

I saw the blurb he was talking about, there on the cover: "*The most convincing case I've yet encountered. Perhaps Elizabeth Short's ghost can finally rest.*" –Thomas Cooley

"The guys at New Wye," Oliver continued, "they want to know that they have your cooperation on this. Edie's going to be doing some publicity. If this gets the kind of attention we're hoping for, people might start contacting you, asking for interviews, seeing what you can confirm."

I covered the book with some flyers for Chinese food.

"Paul? Are you there?"

"Yeah."

"So what do you think?"

Chris was in the backyard now. I could see him through the window. He was wearing his new T-shirt, so large it hung dress-like to his knees. He had his headphones on and was holding a Discman in one hand; in the other hand he was holding a ruler, using it to whack at weeds.

I said, "I think . . . "

I rarely saw Chris out in the sunlight, and I was oddly pleased by how he'd turned even the outdoors into his own solipsistic bubble.

"I was thinking about Chicago," I said.

I heard a static-muffled sigh. "Why?"

"You remember that, right?"

"I remember something you wrote, yeah. You were angry I didn't like it."

I idly shuffled the junk mail on the table; the tritone printing on the grocery store flyer was unaligned, and all those pictures of mangos and soda bottles were shadowed with reds, blues, and yellows.

"Why didn't you like it?" I asked.

"Ummm. How long ago are we talking here?"

"1976."

"You were always good with dates."

"Thanks."

"You're like Rain Man."

I've always hated mangos.

"So why didn't you like it?" Outside, Chris was now staring at his feet as he walked in circles, mouthing the words to whatever song he'd wired directly into his head. "Hello?" I said. "Oliver?"

"Yeah," he said. "I'm here. Jesus, I'm just thinking."

"Thought we'd been disconnected."

I tapped on the window. I'm not sure why, perhaps to get Chris's attention. Though, at such a strange moment, I'm not sure what I would have done with it had he given it to me.

"I guess," Oliver said, "you wrote some shit in there I didn't like, can't remember what."

"But you remember that night in Chicago, right? That guy's apartment? We stayed there all night. We drifted apart after that, and whatever that night was about seemed to have been the beginning of it. I'm not talking about the story—I'm talking about that night."

"I *am* talking about the story," he said. "Your version of me, I remember it being pretty—ruthless. Some phrase stuck with me. 'His sociopathic charm,' or some shit, and 'his mannequin good looks.' Something about being a 'trust-fund fake.' You were always so hostile toward people you thought had it easier than you—people you considered better looking, better educated, more socially adept. It would always come out in these oblique, passive-aggressive ways, but that story was the first time I saw it so clearly."

"You should know better than to think a character in a story is—"

"You called me up, repeatedly asked, What do you think of that character? What do you think of whatever his name was?"

"The character's name was Ron."

"You were so aggressive about it. Like you had this idea that I would see myself in the mirror and break down crying and apologize to you for the fact I got laid more than you did."

"That's bullshit! I'm a fa-, fucking author, a fa-, fucking artist. That character was my creation. I'm not just some hack writing for cheap therapy. Fiction isn't real! This is just the kind of shit Edie does and now you're taking her MO, you're ta-, ta-, taking her side!"

"Paul. Listen to me. The guys at New Wye chose that title. If you've read the book, you know that it's clearly about more than that. Her hypothesizing about that murder is a small part of it, a mere thought experiment, couched in a very moving investigation into memory. I hope you can see that. I'm sorry we couldn't work together on this, but I tried. Edie tried."

"She has no pa-, proof. Memories are nothing. Ramona v. Isabella! Orange ca-, ca-, County, 1994, set the legal pre-, pre-, precedent! Judge threw out the case!"

"Are you back to your fake stutter? Jesus, Paul, that cheap ploy didn't even work on eighteen-year-old Iowans. I thought you'd given that up long ago."

"I ca-, ca-, can't stop!"

I had Chris's attention now.

Since I started writing this letter on June 3, that conversation with Oliver must have taken place on June 2.

It's now been two weeks since I wrote that last sentence, this sheet of paper having been stuck in this machine, waiting for me, the whole time. I had to take a break from this project—the summer semester was wrapping up, and I needed to get things back on track with Julia— though now that I think about it, I haven't really been taking a break. That's one thing Julia got right, I suppose. We just had a fight. She said I'd been lying to her about this. I said I hadn't been, though she's right that I haven't exactly put it out of my mind. But I know what to do now. I know how to end this. Orson Welles. It's all right there in the imagery. Julia and I watched *The Lady from Shanghai* tonight. It was our date night, our end-of-the-semester cooldown: a movie, a box of wine, the unspoken promise of sex. During the mirror scene at the end of the movie, it hit me. All those images of bisected bodies. I wish I had the TV right here so I could take a closer look at that scene but the TV is in the living room and Julia is now back in the living room and Julia is very angry. I can hear her stomping around in there.

I should back up. A couple of weeks ago when I was writing about the phone conversation I had with Oliver—what turned out to be, in a sense, our breakup—I found myself typing Cooley's name a lot, and it occurred to me that in all my research I had been focusing only on the facts and I'd been ignoring completely how the Black Dahlia has shown up in film and fiction. Thomas Cooley's 1983 novel *Dahlia* is certainly the most widely known pop culture artifact featuring a fictionalized Betty Short, and I realized that I had not actually read it, so I ran out to the bookstore and picked up a copy. As Oliver said, they were making a movie of it, coming out in January, and the paperback I got is the movie tie-in version, the cover showing Winona Ryder made up like the Dahlia. Even though the story is an entirely fictional account of Betty Short's murder, it's the version that the layperson thinks of when he or she hears that sobriquet. Just as people assume that the real Richard of Gloucester was a hunchback because of Shakespeare's play (he was actually able-bodied), and that the real William Wallace was a lantern-jawed looker because of *Braveheart* (he was, according to contemporaneous accounts, a chinless man with bug eyes), people usually assume that the real Ms. Short was mixed up with lesbian smut films and gangsters like Mickey Cohen and Bugsy Siegel, because of Cooley's novel. It wasn't until I read the novel that I realized I myself had harbored those assumptions going into this project, and seeing how much a piece of fiction can influence the popular understanding of history underscores how important it is to halt publication of Edie's book, especially since it will, presumably, be shelved as nonfiction.

Cooley's novel was a fun but surreal read. Fun because it reminded me of the pulp fiction I was obsessed with as a young man: a detective story full of double-crosses and double-entendres, dialogue so snappy it makes me feel very unclever. Surreal because, like Edie's book, it tangled the real and the fictive in a way that started to jumble all the facts that I'd been accumulating on the case. More than once I had to stop and wonder if I was thinking about a plot point in Cooley's version, Edie's version, or my version—which is to say, the real version.

I heard the garage door just now. I think Julia is going out. It's nearly eleven at night, where the hell is she going? I think she just wants me to go out there, which I won't do. We've never had a fight this bad and I'm still twitchy with adrenaline from the yelling. We're not real arguers; we generally prefer condescension to catharsis. So I guess it makes sense that when we open the sluices it all comes rushing out.

But the point is that what really struck me about the Cooley novel was how it was structured like many *Rampart* episodes. It starts with the murder, followed by everyone hunting down the seemingly obvious suspect; our detective-protagonist has his doubts about this suspect and begins his own investigation, even though it makes him unpopular in a department where everyone wants to go with the simple answer. He eventually finds the real killer and the initial suspect is let go. What I took away from the novel was not any new evidence, not a new perspective, but rather a realization that the best way to exonerate my father is to find the real killer.

I know I shouldn't worry about where Julia went, I know that she's probably just driving around to de-stress, but it's still really bothering me. She's never just left in the middle of the night like this. She has a pager but she didn't take it with her. I know because I just called it and heard it beep on the coffee table in the living room. The night had been going so well, too! This was our special date night. We'd been planning it all week. Chris is spending the night at a friend's house (yes, he made a friend, a portly Asian boy he met through some Internet chat room where, according to his explanation, people discuss wizardry—personally I think Chris can do better), so I made a curry masala and Julia made a garbanzo bean salad, and we sat together on the couch, our legs inter-twined beneath a blanket that she brought back from a trip to Mexico (she insists the pattern is traditional but I think it looks like a psychedelic game of Space Invaders). I suppose things weren't entirely perfect; there was a little preliminary tension. She'd bought some box wine, which I made the mistake of grumbling about, saying I prefer the bottled stuff. My distaste for box wine has nothing to do with taste. Rather, it has everything to do with the uriney sound the wine makes when it comes shooting from that plastic spout, pressurized from the weight of those three liters of pinot. The sound of wine splashing into your glass should not have that kind of oh-my-god-I-barely-made-it-to-the-bathroom-in-time urgency. Any oenophile would agree. It should be a pleasant glug, a soft trickle, relaxing. I tried explaining this to Julia, but she didn't believe me. She said my resistance to drink from cardboard has to do with reverse class resentment, snobbery as it used to be called. She's wrong. I told her I'd quaff chianti from a penny loafer, so long as its pour didn't sound like I was in the men's room at Dodger Stadium. She said I was just being vulgar and not letting her enjoy the perfectly decent wine.

So there was a little tension at the outset of our evening—some of it, I admit, my fault. Chuck had called me earlier in the day to tell me he'd compared Edie's copy of the autopsy report to others from that era and it looks pretty legit. A little annoyed with Chuck's ignorance on a matter he'd claimed to have some level of expertise in, I was per-haps a bit too short with him. By the evening I was starting to regret some of the words I'd used in ending our conversation, and maybe that frustration is what made me a little too eager to engage Julia in a trivial but passionate debate over wine.

But then we started watching *The Lady from Shanghai* and I brought the levity back in by making fun of Orson Welles's atrocious Irish accent, which sounds like the leprechaun in the Lucky Charms commercials. The movie has a classic noir setup: An average man—Welles's hapless mick—meets a beautiful woman and pretty soon he's being made an offer, which of course will turn deadly. It's amazing to me how many murder plots in the 1940s begin with a simple proposition that will eventually turn a good man bad, as if every man in the country was certain that all it took to become a monster was a sweet-enough deal, that they were all just saps ready to be turned into sociopaths. Welles plays a sap here, for sure, but he plays the role poorly, probably because in real life he was the furthest thing from a sap; he was calculating, megalomaniacal, a perfect auteur—Welles in this role is like Mephistopheles cast as Faust. You can see just how cunning Welles was in the way he staged all his signature set pieces: the extended tracking shot that opens *Touch of Evil*, every scene in *Citizen Kane*, and of course the mirror scene in *The Lady from Shanghai*, in which Welles and Rita Hayworth are hiding in a funhouse hall of mirrors when Welles learns that Hayworth has double-crossed him, and that's when her betrayed husband shows up. Everyone's image is reflected into infinity, distorted, refracted, so when they start shooting each other no one knows if they're shooting the person or the reflection. Glass shatters, everyone's image cracks, breaks, falls apart. All those images of bisected bodies set off alarms in my head. I jumped up from the couch and ran in here and started tearing through the three-volume biography of Orson Welles, titled *Orson*

Welles, which I have here on my shelf. Volume one: In his early days as a magician, Welles specialized in *cutting women in half* and he continued doing so well into his Hollywood career. He was even known to perform the trick with his wife, Rita Hayworth. Here's a photo of a young, pre-*Kane* Welles, mid-trick, his saw poised just above a coffin like box, the poor woman's head and feet popping out each end. Here, in volume two: details about how obsessed he was with getting every image in *Lady*'s mirror scene just right, and here: pictures of Welles on the set, standing next to a lady mannequin, her body torn in two in *just the same way Betty Short's body was*, the mannequin's face mutilated in *just the same way Betty Short's face was*. I knew when I first saw those pictures of Short, when I first began my research so many months ago, that they looked familiar. Here they were, the obsessive's re-creation of the murder victim. Or prefiguration? Dress rehearsal? It says here he was filming in late '46 and early '47. I must have shouted something when I read that because Julia was suddenly standing behind me asking me what was going on. I tried to explain it to her but I must have been talking too fast because she asked me to slow down so I slowed down. I hope my explanations are clearer here in print than they must have been when I was speaking to her because she still wasn't following me. I backed up and took the Dahlia crime scene photos from my desk so Julia could see the similarities, and that's when she freaked out, started yelling at me that I was still working on this, that I'd been hiding it. She got a glimpse of what was in my desk drawer (these pages) and got angry at me that I hadn't sent this off like I'd said I did. I told her that this was just a rough draft, that I had in fact sent off the final draft last month and that I had completely moved on but she was already yelling at me.

She said I was hiding things from her. She asked me what else I'd hidden from her. I said, "Nothing." She asked to see this letter. I said nothing. She moved to reach into the drawer and I blocked her, and she hit my chest with open hands and stormed out of the room. I followed her into the kitchen and said that she was overreacting and she called me a liar and said that lying is habitual. She said her father was a liar and so she knew that where there was one lie there were hundreds, thousands, and she said that if I loved her I would admit three other lies I'd told her right here and now. I have to admit it was exhilarating. I liked her calling me a liar and I kept defending myself because I liked the way it felt when she flung it back in my face. We went back and forth for a little bit and I didn't want it to stop, like on blow when half the exhilaration is the fear that the feeling will leave just as suddenly as it arrived and the knowledge that you just have to keep upping the ante, and so I wondered what would happen if I yielded a little, confessed another lie. So I did. I said that time when we first started dating, before she'd got back on the pill, when the condom broke inside her and I said I hadn't realized it until after I'd come—I admitted that I *had* realized it, that I just didn't want to stop, that I'd come inside her knowing that I was really coming inside her. Her eyes widened, she reset her jaw in a strange and skewed way. I thought this would be it: She'd now admit a lie she'd told me and we would go back and forth, confessing our equivocations, our fabrications and deceptions, and then we'd rip each other's clothes off, buttons flying off like sparks, and I'd hoist her onto the countertop, and she'd bite my lip when we kissed, draw blood, scratch my back with her fingernails, even though she bites her nails and really can't do much scratching with those soft nubbins—but no matter, we'd fuck with brutal abandon. But that did not happen. What happened is that she just turned and ran into the bedroom. When I realized she wasn't coming out, I came back in here, started typing while this Welles revelation was still fresh in my mind. But I should come back to this with a clearer head tomorrow.

Julia finally came home last night after a couple of hours. I'd gone to bed and heard the garage door groan and a few minutes later the bedroom door opened and the light from the hall did a *Cabinet of Dr. Caligari* thing to Julia's shadow against the wall as she crept into the room. She closed the door and I closed my eyes and pretended to be asleep and listened to her change into her nightgown and I felt the equilibrium in the bed shift as she crawled in behind me. She whispered, "Are you awake?" but I didn't answer and with her back to me she rubbed the soles of her feet against my calves. This morning when I woke up she'd already slipped out, leaving a note that she'd gone to the library to get some work done. I've been getting some work done myself. This Welles connection is so clear that I can't believe I didn't pick up on it before. It reconciles so many loose threads in the Black Dahlia story and also makes sense of so much of Welles's behavior documented in his biography. On page 161 of Edie's manuscript, she mentions that before Jack, Betty had been having an affair with Welles. And in the biography, there are countless passages that describe Welles's unstable and even frightening actions. It seems he'd always been unhinged, but this behavior seemed to be escalating around 1946. In 1941, after his production of *Native Son* opened on Broadway, he checked into a sanitarium. There's no information here on the details of this stay— the why, the how long—but the cure clearly didn't take because the following year, after returning from South America, he checked himself into another sanitarium. He'd been in Brazil filming the never-finished documentary *It's All True* where he'd gotten into trouble with the local authorities for countless violent outbursts, throwing dishes, trashing hotel rooms. He grew even more volatile later that year when RKO took control of *The Magnificent Ambersons*—reports of him striking a studio executive in the face are unconfirmed but surely true. He was growing increasingly violent and uncontrollable, this man who'd been raised to believe that he was—to quote Welles himself—"the axis mundi, the center of it all," always, even from childhood, told that he could do anything and everything and that he was a true genius—now this man was finding that Hollywood was not bending to his will, was not bowing before him as obediently as he felt it should, was discovering that movie sets, those small worlds where he could control everything with godlike power, could easily rebel, could easily be taken away, so he began looking for other things that he could control: women. So far I haven't been able to find any evidence that he abused Rita Hayworth during their five-year marriage (1943–1948), but it is common knowledge that Hayworth had been abused by her father growing up and women who experience this sort of thing often seek out abusive men later in life, so for now we can safely assume that Welles abused the shit out of her. I plan on verifying this with some more research at UCLA but Chris borrowed my car so I can't get to the library at the moment, but I will. Hayworth finally pulled away from Welles while they were filming *The Lady from Shanghai*, saying, "I can't take his genius anymore." It would make sense, then, that when he lost one punching bag, he would try to find another. We already know that

Betty Short had been one of his ladies on the side, and the first place every guy goes in this situation is the old Rolodex.

Just got back from UCLA Special Collections. Found out Welles shot most of *Lady* on location in San Francisco. Finished location filming and returned to Los Angeles on or around January 6, 1947—resumed filming on a Columbia Pictures soundstage on January 10, but—this is it!—halted production with no explanation from January 14—the day before Betty Short's body was found in a vacant lot—and resumed filming on January 17 to shoot the mirror scene, that nightmare of bisected bodies.

Julia's home, says she wants to talk. Seems in a better mood.

Welles had a black car! 1944 black Plymouth! Found a new Welles bio today, had to drive all the way to USC's library to get it, but it has a picture of Welles's car. It's not a late-thirties black Ford, like the paperboy saw near the crime scene, but it looks close enough and the paperboy probably didn't know cars very well.

Haven't been able to find any info on whether Welles had a 17-jewel Croton wristwatch with a leather, steel-snapped band, but still checking into it. Really wish book indices were more thorough.

More: a picture of Welles at boarding school in the late twenties, must have been in his early teens, dressed like a circus clown for some sort of theater thing, the red mouth makeup extending slash-like into the cheeks, looking a lot like the Glasgow smile that the killer gave Betty Short. Early obsession with facial mutilation?

The librarians at the library are getting attitudes with me, not being very helpful anymore.

Still looking for confirmation that Welles abused Hayworth.

Today's latest: Found a picture of Welles on set of *Ambersons*, sitting behind the camera, leaning into the viewfinder, wrist plainly visible, clearly wearing a wristwatch, looks like a Croton, can't be sure yet, need more pictures.

Sorry about the stains here—had a nosebleed, dripped on the paper a little.

Found this out: On January 24, the Dahlia investigation heating up, Welles applied for a passport. Eager to fly the coop! I saw his passport photo today at Special Collections. It's a funny picture: He's clearly trying to look his usual suave self—his head cocked slightly, one eyebrow arched into a circumflex—but not even a movie star is spared the unforgiving gaze of the passport-photo camera. The harsh flash and gray backdrop flatten the image out so that it would be no surprise at all to see a rubber stamp from customs smeared across his dimensionless face. But you can imagine him going in to get his photo taken and demanding multiple shots to get just the right one, just as he, as a director, demanded countless takes of countless scenes. When Edie and I were kids—this would have been in the summer of 1956, so I was nine and she was fourteen—Dad took us to get our passport photos taken for a trip to London, and Edie had been poring over French magazines, which (I'm guessing) our mom had given her for the untranslated articles on patriarchy or the sins of the bourgeoisie but which (I know) Edie loved for the photos of androgynously glamorous models. So Edie, excited about the idea of having her photo taken (which was a novelty: Our parents were not ones to document things on film, seemed utterly indifferent to the midcentury miracle of 8 mm Kodachrome, whereas our friends' parents were bent on validating their every waking moment with an endless ticker tape of the stuff, as if to say, "Yes, we were here, we existed, see us playing in the sprinklers, see us unwrapping presents on this or that holiday, see us smiling and waving into the Grand Canyon and failing to appreciate the horror of its yawning abyss because we only saw it through a centimeter-wide viewfinder, see us"), strutted into the post office pretending to be a supermodel, demanded, in an accent she surely thought was French but which sounded more like she was deaf, the consonants rounded into vowels, that the lights be dimmed and—snap, snap—that the boy bring her an express (transl: espresso), and I could see how embarrassed our father was, this man who never liked to draw attention to himself, who because of this aversion was cursed with children who sought that attention from strangers, but I also saw, in a brief flicker of a smile, quick as a camera flash, to the poor civic cog whose job it was to snap our pictures, a glimmer of pride in his stupid children—Yes, that's my daughter, being a big, loud idiot, now take her picture—and the guy did, and for years Edie was blowing a kiss in her passport picture, and I wish I could see that picture again because I remember sneaking into her room and looking through her stuff and seeing that passport and thinking it was the greatest.

The real point I want to make about Welles, though, has less to do with the events leading up to the crime and more to do with the post-mortem: That's the real smoking gun. Just after *Shanghai* wrapped, just as the Dahlia investigation was reaching a fever pitch, Welles dove into his next film: an adaptation of Shakespeare's *Macbeth*. He filmed it in twenty-three days, and though critics often disregard it as a rush job, it's clear to me now that his hasty pace and the end product's so-called imperfections reveal it to be not a rush job but rather a desperately and frantically composed confession. Many people have not seen this film. You can't get it at Blockbuster. The copy I have, the one I screen for my English 2 students every semester when we read the play, is one I taped from TV when it aired on The Movie Channel five years ago, taping over parts of the 1988 summer Olympics, so the film is bracketed by static-fuzzed clips of a small Asian woman doing that ribbon-twirling dance on one end and the women's synchronized swimming finales on the other, and I've fast-forwarded through that goddamn Rascal Senior Scooter commercial so many times that last night I dreamt I was being chased by marauding gangs of nonagenarians on souped-up three-wheelers traveling at terrifying speeds. For the last three days, ever since Julia moved out, having found a two-bedroom in Culver City where she says she'll do some thinking, I've been watching the film repeatedly and am now intimately familiar with every one of its numerous shadows. Welles was clearly using Shakespeare's pitch-dark exploration of murder-induced guilt to admit his own guilt.

First, consider the art direction: Welles filmed it entirely on a Republic Pictures soundstage—the sky, which the signature low-angle shots give you many views of, seems more ceiling-like than sky-like, which creates an unnerving claustrophobia. The o'erhanging firmament offers no escape, which is fitting since the real setting here is not eleventh-century Scotland but rather Orson Welles's feverish mind. Also consider the visual motif of the trinity—not the trinity of Christianity but that of the inverted triangle, the mythic symbol of the female: the staffs that the witches carry throughout the film, those two prongs forming a very vaginal shape; the shields the soldiers carry, the inverted triangle; and all those compositions of three paths converging. Welles is fixated on the image, but it is always at the nexus of violence—which not only hints at murder, the unspeakable violence done to Ms. Short's inverted triangle, but reveals a darker obsession that illuminates why her body was displayed the way it was: her legs splayed in a way so that her whole body formed this shape that clearly haunted Welles.

(That London trip, now that I've been thinking about it, was fun, Edie and I laughing hysterically as we tried to force each other to eat blood sausage, Mom and Dad kissing in Westminster Abbey, touring the Tower of London.)

Welles himself plays the titular Scotsman, the ambitious Thane of Glamis who murders King Duncan and then descends into madness, and it's very telling how Welles chooses to emphasize the passages that inflect "direst cruelty" on women. Ten minutes into the film, Lady Macbeth looks up at that sky and asks the gods to "unsex me here"—just as Betty Short's killer unsexed her—and come to her "women's breasts / And take my milk for gall"—just as one of Short's breasts was mutilated; Lady Macbeth is in effect describing the physical violence done to Short in psychic terms. And in a production that focuses so much on dueling modes of religiosity—Welles playing up the paganism of the witches and even adding a Christian priest to the dramatis personae in order to show them both to be essentially empty, the "Signifying nothing" soliloquy spoken in voiceover while we look out at the same impenetrable sky that Lady Macbeth here is pleading to—then Welles himself, who in a 1972 interview said that the director "is God" on a movie set, becomes the god that Lady Macbeth asks to do violence to her, and is, by extension, the one responsible for its physical, extradiegetic analogue, Ms. Short's murder—a byzantine but startlingly bold revelation on his part. As the film goes on, though, his confession becomes more and more direct, as at the thirty-minute mark when, just after killing Duncan, Macbeth looks at his bloodstained hands and says in soliloquy, "Will all great Neptune's ocean wash this blood / Clean from my hand?"—remember that Short's body was drained of blood and washed before being dumped—"No, this my hand will rather / the multitudinous seas incarnadine, / Making the green one red"—and remember that much was made in the investigation about the bloody (red) shoeprints left on the (green) grass—but most shocking of all is how Welles chooses to frame himself in this scene: We see him from a typically low angle and as he looks at his bloody hand he extends it to the camera, palm up, in effect offering his guilty hand to us. Indeed, Welles's most self-revealing moments are those when he confronts us, the audience, directly, as at the hour mark when, after the witches have revealed to Macbeth prophesies of his fate, and Welles is framed from a high angle, a lonely speck of a man in the middle of darkness, the camera slowly pushing closer until we're bearing down on his panic-stricken face, he looks directly into the camera and says, "What, is this so?" and the disembodied voice of one of the witches responds, "Ay, sir, all this is so," and suddenly, still staring intently into the camera, Welles cracks a dagger-carved smile just as the screen fades to black. Let me repeat that: He looks directly at the audience, the only time in the film he does this, and admits, through the voice of the witch, that "this"—the murder, the obsession, the guilt—"is so"—and then he smiles—the smile being that of the trickster whose pleasure in offering a coded confession (toying with us just as those notes the killer sent to the LAPD toyed with the cops, teasing them with clues) momentarily transcends his overwhelming sense of guilt. But not all Welles's confessional moments are this obvious. The scene that I've had to watch more times than any other, in order to ensure that I wasn't just hearing things, doesn't actually have Welles in it at all—or at least not corporeally. About fifteen minutes after the "this is so" scene, we see Macduff—played by Dan O'Herlihy, who was surely cast because he looks remarkably like Welles, the similarities in makeup and facial hair—eyebrows like Groucho's mustache—further emphasizing the fact that we are to see him as Macbeth/Welles's doppelganger—talking to Malcolm and Ross and say, "Cut short all intermission. Front to front." Now listen closely to the audio track. Just before this line, you hear a slight suture in the white noise, a small, barely perceptible edit, and then O'Herlihy's mouth does not quite move to the shape of the sounds. It's true that Welles pre-recorded much of the dialogue, so the film is filthy with awkward lip-synching, but the question here is: Whose voice do we hear in this line? The timbre and texture of the sound are different from O'Herlihy's, a bit more baritoney, and when I first heard it, I immediately thought of that mouse in that cartoon, the one Chris used to watch, the one whose voice was clearly meant to sound like Welles, and I wanted to consult Chris, to show him this clip, ask him if he heard the similarity too, but he'd left the day before, saying he wanted to stay with Julia for a while, which is fine: I have the house to myself, have plenty of time and space and to get my work done. Point being, though, for this line of Macduff's, Welles dubbed in *his own voice*—and to say what? Listen: "Cut short . . . Front to front"! "Cut [Betty] Short"! I've been rewinding and playing those few seconds of tape all day and have now listened to Welles himself say "Cut Short" so many times that there is no doubt in my mind that this is his confession.

It's all right there, the ocular and audible proof, indisputable and irrefutable, that identifies Welles—not my father—as the real killer!

I have to water the lawn.

When she moved out, Julia left Chris instructions to water the new lawn, and when Chris moved out he left the instructions for me. Simple enough instructions, but I've been forgetting about it until just now, so I ran out and cranked on the water, just watched it for a while, the sprinkler screwed to the end of the hose, waving its lazy curtain of water back and forth, the midday sun making rainbows in the mist, and I walked over and lowered my head and let the water splash over my face, starting at the top of my head, moving down to my chest, then moving back up my face, gurgling into my nostrils, and it felt good. I'm dripping water on the keyboard, should get a towel before I short-circuit my Wheelwriter.

Just got off the phone with Dean Hockney at COLA. By "just," I mean about an hour ago. Been doing a lot of pacing since then. Since last sitting down at this typewriter been in a bit of a panic. The fall semester starts in a week and still haven't received my fall teaching schedule. Usually get it midsummer, should have gotten it a while ago, but been too busy with this to notice. Yesterday, was toweling off my head and saw the light on the answering machine blinking and pushed play, heard Rory saying he found the flashlight and was glad to have it back but that if I came around their home again without being invited they were going to call the police. Next message was Julia awkwardly asking what my teaching schedule for the fall would be, asking that we keep things nice and professional if we bump into each other in the halls. Thought about calling her back—I now have an answer to her "why" question—but I got distracted, realized I didn't have my teaching schedule for the fall. So I called Dean Hockney, but he was already gone for the day, had to wait until this morning to call him back. His receptionist tried to block me with excuses, said he was out, but she's a terrible liar—I could actually hear the sound of her looking into Hockney's windowed office, seeing him sitting there with his Hush Puppies resting up on his metal desk, and formulating that lie—and I was persuasive enough that she eventually, after a few callbacks, patched me through. Asked Hockney where my teaching schedule was, hadn't received it yet. Hockney said he needed to talk with me. I said we are talking. He said over half my English 1 students dropped in the spring semester. I explained they couldn't handle the new workload, that I was shifting pedagogical paradigms. He said look. At what? He said listen. I said I am. He said if a business lost half its customers, that business would not be in business anymore. He said if a worker lost half his clients, that worker should not be working anymore. He asked if I agreed. I asked him who he was talking about. Listen, he said. I am, I said. "In this economic environment, COLA cannot tolerate a fifty percent customer attrition rate. I cannot offer you any classes for the fall semester. I'm sorry, Paul."

Was standing in the middle of the living room, the phone still at my ear, listening to the growl of Hockney's post-hang-up dial tone for so long I no longer heard it. The TV was on, didn't remember turning it on. Had been watching something the night before, a painting show hosted by a man with a soothing voice, had thought it might help me fall asleep (woke up on the couch this morning, guess it worked), so it's possible the TV had been on all night. Now one of those morning shows was on, maniacally cheery hosts wearing pastels and bleachy smiles, sipping from coffee mugs, saying *good morning* so frequently and insistently that it was unclear if it was a greeting, a command, or they were simply and insanely repeating the name of the show, some sort of existential reassurance: I am here, this is the show I am on, this is the world in which I am existing. The orange-faced host introduced a movie clip featuring Winona Ryder. I wondered why I was having trouble hearing the dialogue, realized I was still listening to the dial tone, hung up the phone, massaged my ear, and watched the rest of the clip: Ryder in a glossy black wig and a glossy black dress, her skin so white you half expect to see a network of blue veins beneath it, sitting at the counter of what must be Schwab's Pharmacy, flirting with a fat, gangsterish man. The clip was suddenly over and the host was in the studio, sitting on plush but unforgiving-looking chairs with a man definitely not from the *good morning* universe: no pastels, no smile visible beneath his Stalinesque moustache, just beady eyes behind round black-rimmed glasses, wearing a rumpled gray suit and a fedora. A ribbon rolled across the bottom of the screen, introducing me to "Thomas Cooley, author of *Dahlia*." Host gave some incongruently cheery-sounding exposition to the camera about Cooley's long and illustrious career writing novels that "expose the dark underbelly of the Los Angeles underworld," comparing him to a latter-day Chandler or Hammett, and that his first and most popular novel *Dahlia* was now a major motion picture, itself a fictionalized re-creation of the famous Black Dahlia murder. Cooley didn't blink. What was it like watching your novel hitting the silver screen? the host wanted to know. I was expecting Cooley to just mumble monosyllabically and continue to stare murderously at the host. Instead, he took a breath and launched into: "They call it the silver screen, sir, because supposedly—silver thread once laced the screen so as to better reflect the lily-light faces of Mansfield and Monroe—a glowing light, a pure light." He spoke in a quavering voice, pausing Shatner-like several times in a single sentence. "But Mansfield lost her head, and Monroe—her heart. The silver web in that screen—catches even the wiliest waifs—and doesn't let them go. Such is the tale—of Miss Short. Caught in the silver-spooled gossamer— of Hollywood, only to find herself bitten—by a sinister spider." Elmore Leonard adapted the novel for the screen, the host continued, and the two of you are seen as contemporaries. What was it like to work with him? "The Dahlia has haunted me since—I was a boy," Cooley contin- ued, in a voice that seemed to be providing its own reverberation. "Just as her killer—fed on her soul, I too—have stolen a part of her. Just as her killer—turned her into his plaything, I too—have turned her into mine, by writing—my masterpiece, *Dahlia*." The host then asked if Cooley thought the popularity of the film might cause the police to relaunch the investigation. "No one," Cooley said, "can know the Dahlia, but— no one knows her better—than I." The host then recapped the details about the movie and threw to a lady at a desk who began talking about how I might spruce up my house with some fun fall colors. I turned off the TV, but perhaps I should have kept it on and listened to the deco- rating advice. My living room is not looking very seasonal these days.

stripped the east wall of all its clutter—mostly framed black-and-white photos of French bistros that I'd bought because I thought they looked authentic, but also a few family photos, me and Chris—and replaced it with a Black Dahlia timeline: a fifteen-foot-long strip of electrical tape, the start of which I labeled *1941*, the end *1965*, and in between I've tacked every photo I've found, every bit of evidence scrawled on an index card, a length of yarn connecting it to its precise moment on the timeline. The 1947 part of the timeline is so crowded, all the evidence branching out like a sunrise on the horizon, that I've had to devote the opposite wall to a 1947 inset. Julia was right: Getting organized has really helped. And I now know what I need to do with all this evidence. Cooley said it himself: No one knows the case better than him. Sure, he was a little nervous in the interview, perhaps, and had prewritten all his answers, which didn't always align with the questions, but he was out of his element. His real element isn't TV—it's this case. He clearly cares more about it than any cop or true crime publisher. And with that fucking blurb he gave his seal of approval to Edie's book, endorsing my father as the real killer. He's the real judge and jury, he's the one the public will believe. I need to find him. He needs to see the evidence on Welles.

Having trouble finding him.

Not in the phone book, of course. Not sure where else to look. Never went looking for anyone before.

Talked to a neighbor today, the one whose drained pool is starting to fill up with pine needles. She asked where Chris is these days. I asked her how you go about finding someone you can't find. She looked worried, said if Chris has gone missing, I should call the police.

No, no, not Chris, a famous person, or moderately famous person, moderately famous in certain circles, I need to find a person who is moderately famous in certain circles. She suggested the Internet. Of course—Chris helped me find Oliver like that. But Julia took her computer with her. Chris took his computer with him. No computers in the house. Heading to the library.

Back from the library. Success. Or partial success. Searched for Cooley online, found nothing but press stuff for the books and movies. Looked at some interviews, skimmed them till I realized he would probably not mention his address or personal phone number as an aside while expounding on the fate of the crime genre. Tried searching his name plus the word "address," only found a picture of him delivering the keynote address at the Mystery Writers Guild's 1989 conference in St. Paul, Minn. Wearing the same fedora I saw on TV. Tried searching for his literary agent. No dice. Somewhere in all that searching, I found myself reading a review of his latest novel, about a retired private eye who finds himself framed for murder. The idea of reviewing got me distracted, and I made a brief detour to Grade-a-Prof.com to see if there were any more positive reviews of me. None, but I did scroll back to that one kind review—*he's nice i liked the class*—dated two years ago, wondered again about the shy waif who'd posted it. Realized I needed to get back on track, clicked the back button till I was at the review of Cooley's new book again, saw the words "private eye" sprinkled across the page. Of course. I'm going to get a private eye to find Cooley for me. That's their job. I found dozens of private eyes online, wrote down their phone numbers, have the list here, going to call.

Just got off the phone. First number didn't answer. Second number said only does cheating cases, motel work. Said he just invested in an infrared camera. Third guy said he'd find Cooley, hundred bucks a day plus expenses.

Met with my PI today. Wasn't what I was expecting. Kind of fat but in that womanly way, very hip-heavy. Smelled like Starbursts. Lots of paperwork around his office, said he was also a CPA. I paid him, he handed me an envelope, said all Cooley's info was inside. Said if I did any harm to Cooley, he wouldn't take any personal responsibility. I said I wasn't going to hurt Cooley. He said if I wanted to, he could put me in touch with a guy. He also told me to keep him in mind come tax season.

Got Cooley's info here on my desk, address and phone number handwritten on a four-by-five card. Going tomorrow, spending tonight organizing my thoughts. Need to go in there ready to make a clear and concise pitch. Must have all the evidence clearly laid out, all the movie clips ready to cue up, all the photos and passages ready for him to see. My one chance, can't fuck it up. I think it's Thursday. Have to water the lawn again.

Was wrong. It's Wednesday. Had already watered the lawn when I realized it is Wednesday. Saw some sick-looking patches near the back. Brownish grass creeping in along the seams in the sod, like linoleum tiles curling at the edges. Gonna just water the fuck out of it. Maybe pick up grass food tomorrow when I see Cooley.

I didn't pick up any grass food. I completely forgot about it until just now when I sat down and saw that last sentence there. I think I had it in mind that after seeing Cooley I'd swing by the store (though by "the" I'm not really sure which, as I have no idea where one might find grass food—a crematorium?), but by the time I left his house today I felt pretty unsettled and wasn't thinking that well. I wound up driving to Pinz and playing a few frames to clear my head. I hoped Chuck might be there, but I couldn't find him. Haven't seen him in a while. He'd be happy to see that I'm improving. Four strikes today. There's really nothing like the satisfying sound of the ball connecting with the one pin, the initial crack melding with the crash of the other pins, a perfect chain reaction, a perfectly controlled violence, a rudimentary chaos you create only to see it swept away into darkness, the pleasure of destruction meeting the pleasure of tidiness, order restored. In reducing the sport to a simple math of movement you can convince yourself that you're not really thinking anymore, that you're not really here. It wasn't working as well today though. I couldn't disappear my thoughts quite as easily. I'd gone over to Cooley's house with a clear plan, all my material ready for the pitch, the Welles evidence all laid out, but I never even got to exhibit A.

He lives off Benedict Canyon, up one of those winding streets with no sidewalks, just ancient houses whose protective phalanx of flora you can no longer distinguish from the houses themselves, where Joe Gillis might have met his end. Finding the actual house was difficult, as addresses were more often than not obscured, but after parking my car at a little overlook—the view from which you could imagine being impressive at night, when Hollywood is just a jewelry display case of glittering lights below, but at eleven in the morning the smog was so dense it turned the whole panorama sepia tone—I walked from house to house, pushing aside bougainvilleas to find addresses stenciled on walls, and finally found Cooley's. A wall of hedges surrounded the house. I pushed open the gate and on my way to his front door passed a menagerie of what might have been unkempt topiary sculptures or simply bushes that had grown into strange Rorschach shapes: Is that a bunny rabbit, or is that my own projection of my mother's genitalia, or is that just a nice myrtle bush?

I rang the doorbell and was surprised by its obviously digital chime. It had been so long since I'd stood on the doorstep of a stranger, rung the bell, waited nervously for them to answer, almost hoping they wouldn't just so I'd have a guilt-free excuse to retreat. I remembered collecting for my paper route when I was a kid, and something about this experience made me feel that same childlike sense of vulnerability: I was on someone else's property, anxiously invading someone else's space, hoping they would accept me. By the time Cooley answered the door, I was feeling so sheepish about my mission that my slouch must have taken two inches off my height. This was exacerbated when I saw just how absurdly tall Cooley really is. I hadn't noticed it on TV, but he's well over six feet. Instead of feeling intimidated, though, I felt an indignation that made me stand up straight, suddenly combative. Writing fiction, I've always felt, should be a short man's game. It's something for the underdogs, those of us who know that the world was not made for us. And yet I am consistently shocked by the number of novelists I encounter who are Cooley's height or taller. These lumbering giants bump into things, have no sense of their own body's cruel imposition on the world around them. This is all backward. It is the fiction writer's job to be acutely aware of how little space he does take up, of the cruel imposition the world makes on him. Making art is something one should turn to only after serial failure with the opposite sex, and this is simply not something tall men are familiar with. I have thought about this a great deal and was willing to explain it all to Cooley right there on his doorstep, but when he glared at me, his eyebrows flaring like two animals bristling to fight, and bellowed, "What are you soliciting, sir? Something salacious, I hope?" it snapped me back to my mission.

"Mr. Cooley," I said. "I have something very important I need discuss with you. It's about the Black Dahlia. I have new evidence." I held up my satchel. "May I come in?"

He relaxed his brow and lowered his head toward me. "The Dahlia? My dark damsel. Yes, come in, sir."

He stepped aside to let me into his living room and that's when I realized that he was wearing his fedora, the same one I'd seen on TV, even though he'd surely just been lounging around his home. He was also wearing a pinstriped suit, so wrinkled that the pinstripes were squiggles, his whole body a crumpled-up piece of lined paper.

His living room looked like it smelled, like the underside of a rock. Sofas that looked like large game animals—shot, dead, deflated—cluttered the room, but each one was covered in so many old newspapers and file boxes that they were no longer functional as sitting furniture. Cooley closed the door behind me and the room went dim.

"How did you find me, amateur shamus?" Cooley was suddenly in front of me, standing too close, though his tone was inquisitive and eager now, not threatening. "Unless you are no amateur? Do you have an affiliation? A badge?"

"Um. No."

"Wonderful. Institutions of law enforcement have become lack-adaisical, laconic—no, sorry, I mean lugubrious. It is time that real power be placed in the hands of the individuals. When the night is dark, the dumb will wait for sunrise, but the enlightened man will strike a match. Who said that?"

"I don't know."

"Good. It's probably original, then. I'm going to write it down. I should probably change 'enlightened' to something else, though. Might seem like a cheap pun. Puns are the lowest form of wit."

"Right. Samuel Johnson."

"No," he said, suddenly angry. "Thomas Cooley." He leaned in close to me and I could smell—or rather feel—a warm, chemical halito-sis, and he said, "How did you find me?"

I hesitated. But he didn't seem paranoid. He seemed excited. "A private investigator," I said.

There was a little smile, quickly concealed. "Really. Fascinating." He idly smoothed the front of his suit. "Follow me."

I followed him down a hallway, its walls covered in framed copies of his reviews, some of which, I noticed as I passed, were not positive.

I needed to focus, needed to turn my thoughts back to Welles, those production stills from *The Lady from Shanghai*, all those passages from his bios that confirmed his emotional instability, his violence, all those clips from *Macbeth*. My opening remarks would set the course for my entire case—they needed to be good.

He opened a door and led me into a dark room. He flipped on a light, but the light didn't stay still. There was a single bulb on a ceiling-hung cord, and as it swung back and forth it stretched our shadows all over the walls, elastic and alive, creatures separate from us. That's when I saw what was covering the walls: He'd painted a single horizontal black stripe around all four walls of the windowless room. Pictures, note cards, and newspaper clippings were tacked to the wall above and below this line, each item connected to a specific point, along with a date. As far as I could tell, his timeline started just to the right of the door at 1924 ("Elizabeth Short is born," read one note), continued around the room to the other side of the door, where it ended at 1983 (*"Dahlia* is published"). In between, I saw the usual crime scene photos of Short, the usual mug shots, but his timeline was more elaborate and detailed than mine—I felt a sharp pang of inadequacy—and became a dizzying web of connections when I saw that he'd taken string to connect points on one side of the room to the other, easily a hundred separate pieces of string connecting disparate points on his timeline, different parts of the room, more note cards dangling like ornaments from seemingly random points on the string. Standing in the middle of the room, in the middle of the web, I felt like we were caught in a cat's cradle.

"I've been investigating this case for nearly three decades," Cooley said, "and I'm always so excited to find another Blackhead."

"A what?" I squinted at the pores in his nose.

"A Blackhead, a Dahlia Devotee, the bearers of her torch. There are more and more coming out of the woodwork these days—it's marvelous. Tell me: Even though born and raised in Massachusetts, Elizabeth Short is buried in what city?"

"Oakland, California," I said, thrilled and relieved to know the answer.

"Correct! In the 1975 made-for-TV movie *Who Is the Black Dahlia?* . . . who played James Richardson?"

I panicked. I'd seen the film. I knew who played Betty Short, it was Lucie Arnaz, daughter of Lucille Ball and Desi Arnaz, but James Richardson? I could see the actor's face, his amiable smile contrasted by his demonic eyebrows. But his name? I must have glanced around the room without realizing it, because suddenly Cooley grabbed my face with both hands and shouted, "Don't cheat! Don't look at the timeline!"

His hands were surprisingly soft. "I don't know," I said.

He gave a quick and curt exhale, a kind of respirative punctuation, and his moustache hairs quivered. "One more," he said, not letting go of my face. "Best two out of three." He gave a long blink, and said, "As a child, Elizabeth Short had what condition?"

I thought I knew this one, but wasn't sure. He seemed to have worded the question in an intentionally ambiguous way. I took a breath. "Asthma?"

He let go of my face. The hand-sweat he'd left on my cheeks felt cooled by the air.

"Correct," he said. He took a step back but didn't take his eyes off me. "You say you have some new evidence. I've been contemplating some new developments as well. Here!" He tried to walk to the corner of the room, but got tangled in his own web of strings, so he had to take a moment to untangle himself and duck under the string in order to point to one spot on the timeline: 1952, where a dense batch of evidence was clustered, crime scene photos I didn't recognize. "Rachel Cooley," he said. "My mother, my Dahlia before I even knew who the Dahlia was. Murdered one nihilistic night by some pernicious predator. Her killer was never found. Look!" He was studying the grainy crime scene photo tacked to the wall, his nose an inch from the black-and-white glossy.

"The arrangement of the legs! Just like the Dahlia. Look!" He was point-ing so emphatically at the photo, he seemed to be trying to push through it, to enter it. "The lacerations on the breasts. Just like the Dahlia. The vile villain's vicious violation has yet to be avenged!"

I recognized that phrase, or at least part of it. Vile villain, or some-thing like that, had appeared in the climax of *Dahlia*. But it was not just his absurd phrasings that seemed hacked from his own work—the fedora, the crumpled pinstriped suit: They were from that novel too, worn by his detective-hero. I looked around the room, looked around the inside of this man's brain, while he continued his occa-sionally redundant alliterations (I'm pretty sure he actually said "fiend-ish fiend" at one point), and I felt the need to escape. Perhaps this man had succeeded in pushing himself into that picture, succeeded in becoming two-dimensional, black-and-white, one of his own improb-able characters, stranded in another time. But that still didn't change the fact that I had to make my case, didn't change the fact that his judgment on the matter would be crucial. My evidence-filled satchel was in my hands. My spine was straight. Cooley was getting louder. There was a dog barking somewhere, a man yelling at a dog. I began to hear a ringing in my ears. I closed my eyes, saw dim, bruise-colored phosphenes marble and gel beneath my eyelids. I tried to think of my opening comments, but the only words in my head were *If I told him would he like it. Would he like it if I told him*. "The hellacious horror!" Cooley was shouting. "The harlequin and the harlot!" *Would he like it would Napoleon would Napoleon would would he like it*. "We are the avengers! We are not the memory keepers—we are the memory mak-ers!" I opened my eyes. The old man had gotten tangled in the strings and was yanking them violently from the walls. The pictures, the note cards, the newspaper clippings, which had been clipped to the strings, were flying into the air, spinning back down. He crumpled one scrap of paper, threw it to the ground, a crash-landed dove. *If Napoleon if I told him if I told him if Napoleon.*

Later, after I had left Cooley's house and headed for Pinz, having not said a word about Welles or my father, having just slipped out while Cooley had run off to another room to find one of Betty Short's shoes that he'd recently bought from a collector, I was just trying to concentrate on the seven-ten split I'd made for myself, when someone said, "Mr. McWeeney?" At first, I didn't realize it was a human voice. I thought my brain was simply taking the chaotic din of the bowling ally—the relentless crashes of balls and pins, the hundred shouted, beer-impassioned conversations, the pings and alarms from the arcade—and trying, as it often does, to find a pattern, a familiar sound, in this case the sound of a student with her hand raised. But then I heard it again, louder: "Mr. McWeeney, is that you?" I turned, ball in hand, and saw a large woman in overalls, middle-aged, holding the hand of a little boy in a conical party hat. "Yeah," she said, "I thought it was you. It's Darlene Hendricks. I took your English class at COLA—oh, must have been a few years ago now."

"Darlene Hendricks," I said, my tone as flat as a roll call.

"You don't remember me, do you?" She didn't seem saddened, just oddly excited by the opportunity to tell me who she was. "I was having trouble with a paper for my history class and I brought it to you and you helped me with it even though it wasn't for your class."

She raised her eyebrows, as if to tell me it was my cue to speak, my line. But I had nothing.

She continued: "I was stuck trying to make sense of these two different interpretations of the Great Depression, and I remember something you said to me."

I tried to smile in a way that would suggest I remembered this without actually committing myself. I looked down at the boy at her side and realized two things: First, judging from his flat and affectless smile, he was probably mentally retarded.

"You said that history isn't so much about facts as it is a battle for authorship."

And second, I realized I was probably smiling the exact same way.

"I got an A on that paper," Darlene said. "I wanted to go back and tell you and thank you, but I didn't get the paper back until the semester was over and I wasn't around anymore because I had to drop my classes after that 'cause Dominic here needed me around."

I was so desperate to remember this woman that I began forcibly inserting her into random classroom memories, grafting her face onto other students' bodies. What did she want me to say here? I'm not accustomed to students coming up to me like this, am unclear on the protocol.

"I've been wanting to go back for a long time now, finish my associate's. Grant's going to—Grant's my husband—he's going to be working from home more now, so I might be able to take a class or two. I'll be sure to look for your name on the schedule!"

As I struggled to think of something to say, I remembered Cooley tangled in those strings.

"Mr. McWeeney? Are you okay?"

The bowling ball suddenly felt impossibly heavy. I bent down and put it in my bag, then said, "Yes. I'm well, thank you. It's great to see you, Darlene."

She seemed to take that as a concluding statement. Her smile became a little pursed. She wished me well, then said, "C'mon, Dom," and scooted her child back to the arcade.

Dear New Wye Press, True Crime Division, I lied to the very kind Darlene Hendricks. I am not well. I need rest. I need a lot of rest. I have little pinprick pains in my chest and tremors in my hands. The penguin-shaped humidifier isn't helping my nosebleeds. I want to be rid of this. I have these two hundred plus pages on my desk, stacked beside my IBM Wheelwriter 1000, and when I mail it off to you, when it is finally out of my hands, when I've done everything I can do, then I'll be able to sleep. I set out, three months ago, to prove, beyond a shadow of a doubt, that my father did not kill Betty Short as my sister claims he did, though I am no longer certain that I have provided that proof. Perhaps all I can offer is myself as a character witness. Perhaps all I can really say is that my father was not the monster my sister remembers. I think I have done that. I hope I have done that. I will forever remember him as the man who watered Mom's geraniums while wearing a suit, so worried over the instructions he couldn't even see he wasn't following them. Certainly my memory of our father is more human, more believable, than Edie's. Just look—more proof. Here. Page 97. I mention him being distraught at the news of Mom's death. He's locked in his office, being distraught. See? Human emotions. There's more. On page 204: I remember him saying that funny thing at the dinner party. Humor: humanity. More. Page 214. A week after Mom's death, locked in his office. Page 235. He smiles when we got our passport photos. A smile: human. And there's more. Because he's in here somewhere, he has to be, my version of him, because I knew him, I did, I knew him, I knew him. He's all over this thing, he's everywhere. See him.

Sure, I suppose that thing on page 214 is also Edie's memory, but I can remember it too—I was there, she says I was, down the hall, watching TV, so I can remember it too. I can't, however, provide any cross-memory confirmation of the last hundred or so pages of Edie's book, the part that covers her early adult years—the addictions, the endless string of abusive men, that part about searching for the child she gave up for adoption—I wasn't there for any of that, and it's of no real concern here. But there is just one small part toward the end I find myself going back to. It's in the second-to-last chapter when she is offering a kind of memory collage of our mother, interwoven with scene-snippets of how she coped in the months following our mother's death. A couple weeks after getting that tattoo, she was desperate to get out of the house and stayed on a friend's couch down in Long Beach until she could find an apartment of her own. She briefly mentions one night that she took me down there to hang out with her and her friend and got me drunk for the first time at the age of fourteen and at the end of the night she slept on the couch and

> Paulie slept on the loveseat. He was short enough that it wasn't cramped for him, but when I woke up in the morning he was sleeping next to me on the couch, curled around my back, like we were about to tandem-jump from an airplane, his arms wrapped desperately around me. (312)

I just want to tell her that I remember that night. And I've been trying to tell her that. I've been calling her—I think she's still staying at
Rory's—but no one answers. There used to be an answering machine,
but now the phone just rings and rings and rings, little sonar blips
sent out into the universe, bumping into nothing, refusing to echo
anything back. I've been calling for hours now. Nothing. If she could
just answer, I'd tell her that I remember that night. I'd say, I remember you picking me up at our house in Van Nuys, saying it was an
early Christmas gift, one free night, and I remember the drive down
to Long Beach, seeing that strangely beautiful wash of coppery lights
in the expanse of industry just south of L.A. I remember your friend's
apartment, the plywood-and-cinderblock bookshelves and mismatched
furniture, the realization that life could be improvised in such a way. I
remember sitting there while the two of you smoked a lot of cigarettes,
drank a lot of beers, and you kept handing me beers, and they made
me feel good, and I loved you for letting me drink them. I remember at
the end of the night, when your friend went to bed, we lay awake for a
little while longer, you on the couch and me on the loveseat, and like
a lullaby you started humming the tune to "Alouette" and I was apparently drunk enough to start singing along in a whisper: "Alouette, jump
into the water. Alouette, jump into the rain." You stopped humming,
looked over at me with a teasing smile, and made me repeat the lyrics.
I did, and you laughed. "I didn't realize Mom's French was *that* bad,"
you said. "You've misheard it all these years. It's not about water or
rain or whatever you thought. Listen. *Alouette, gentile alouette. Alouette,
je te plumerai.* It's about a kid, singing a nice little song to a bird," you
said, as if narrating a bedtime story. "And he says to the bird, 'Pretty

bird, I'm going to pluck out your feathers. And I'm going to pluck off your head. And I'm going to break your beak. And I'm going to break your neck. And lastly, pretty bird, I'm going to break your wings.'" You rolled over, your back to me, and said, "Still a pretty song, though," and you hummed the tune for a few more bars, the melody skipping lazily through your voice. At the end of the song, you said, "Now go to sleep," and I did.

I remember waking up in the baby-blue light of dawn, cramped and thirsty, and getting up to get a glass of water. When I came back into the living room, I thought I could no longer feel the beers. You had some room beside you on the couch. Your frizzy brown hair had been pushed straight back, as if blowing behind you in some dream of running you were having, finally exposing your ears, delicate seashells of skin, and the Braille of moles on your neck. I sat down next to you and listened to the distant surf of your steady breathing. I'd never really slept in the same bed with anyone, and I often thought how strange that must feel. How could you ever get to sleep with another body right there beside to you, uncomfortably close? So I lay down next to you and stared up at the cottage-cheese ceiling. I could feel the warmth of your skin and closed my eyes and imagined you glowing with Technicolor body heat, blurry and bright. You stirred a little, a dreamy twitch of the arms, the movements dimmed through layers of consciousness, then suddenly you turned your body toward me, moving your arm under mine, your head onto my chest, instinctively taking the body next to you to be someone else, someone who could protect you. I reciprocated, with the same lazy ease you had, moving my arm over your shoulders and back, exposed by your tank top. Still asleep, you reacted, nuzzling my neck, the anonymous comfort of another body. I was just going to stay like that for another couple of minutes, then get up and go back to the loveseat. But the next thing I knew, it was late morning and the sun's rays coming through the window were sharp and painful. I let my eyes adjust. You were no longer there.

I have to water the lawn now. When Chris and Julia come back, I want it to look nice for them.

Love,

Paulie

Author's Note

This is a work of fiction—filled, as many works of fiction are, with (perhaps ethically dubious) appropriations of just about anything its author has encountered over the years, including anecdotes both personal and journalistic. In appropriating—or should I say commandeering?—any given "fact," I have, more often than not, dressed it up, slapped a wig on it, told it to do a funny dance. To still call that poor little fact a fact after such a performance is questionable. In other words, any resemblance to actual anything is not so much coincidental as it is incidental.

That being said, all information, no matter how inconsequential, has its source, and even though a novelist's sources are always, at least to a certain extent, unwitting, I should still name a few of them. The following books provided both initial inspiration for some of Paul's troubles as well as specific "facts" (see above) with which to populate them. Most obviously, there was *Black Dahlia Avenger: A Genius for Murder* by Steve Hodel (revised edition, Harper, 2006) and *Daddy was the Black Dahlia Killer* by Janice Knowlton with Michael Newton (Pocket Books, 1995), but also *Childhood Shadows: The Hidden Story of the Black Dahlia Murder* by Mary Pacios (AuthorHouse, 2007), and *The Black Dahlia Files: The Mob, the Mogul, and the Murder that Transfixed Los Angeles* by Donald H. Wolfe (Regan, 2005).

Although Paul cites many sources, he is not the best researcher, and he is often inaccurate, or at least his sources differ from mine. For example, when he cites *Hollywood Citizen News* about the "17-jewel Croton [wristwatch] with a leather bound, steel snap band," he might or might not be correct, but I got that from Hodel, page 266, and Wolfe, page 15. When he quotes William Fowler's memoir as the source of the quote, "[James Richardson] shared William Randolph Hearst's penchant for sensational news and . . . could be inhuman," he's probably correct, but I found it in Wolfe, page 31. Paul claims Ben Hecht's diagnosis of the killer as "a dyke lesbian with a hyperthyroid problem" originally appeared in *The Herald-Examiner*, but I doubt that's accurate; I found it in Hodel, page 182. When Paul cites *The Boston Globe* as the source of the quote "death on auto rides" (vis-à-vis Frances Cochran), he is, once again, probably wrong; for my part, I found that in Knowlton, page 86. Paul does not cite his source for the quote from Stephen Wolak's letter, "Infatuation is sometimes mistakenly accepted for true love," but I can: Hodel, page 387, Wolfe, page 88, and Knowlton, page 98. And, finally, while Paul might be correct in citing *The Examiner* as the source for Mary H. Unkefer saying that Short "loved to sit so [the tattoo] would show," I found that in Wolfe, page 41.

There are also a few passages in which Paul quotes, perhaps unintentionally, me. A handful of small moments during his adventure in the Los Angeles County Morgue first found articulation in my short story "Kamikaze June," published in *River Styx*, 35th Anniversary double issue #81/82.

Finally, I am absurdly grateful to: Nathaniel Jacks at InkWell Management; Jack Shoemaker and everyone at Counterpoint; early readers Memory Peebles Risinger and Hilary Zaid; Diana Thow, and my parents.

Thank you for reading.